THE DESICCANT KEEPERS

A Novel by Jesse Maas

ISBN: 978-0-578-70448-7

Library of Congress Control Number: 2020909910

To my wonderful husband and family:

Joshua Maas
Steve Sheridan
Julie Sheridan
Molly Sheridan

Thank you for all of your love and support!

CONTENTS

CHAPTER ONE

Blue eyes fixed dead ahead on the white, brick wall, just as they'd been for the past year. The sound of crashing waves served as the only white noise for the thoughts of the lonely prisoner, Riley Mines.

His mind racing, as it always was, back to thoughts of his younger days and the constant replaying of his worst memories, the ones that placed him in prison.

His hair was a coffee-colored brown, longer on the top than it was on the sides, and a length too long for his clean-cut liking. His face had grown scruffy, as he was close to his weekly, disposable razor delivery, but the dark scruff nicely complimented his naturally sun-kissed skin. He glowed in the sunlight from his ever-present layer of sweat, thanks to the island humidity. Although he could shower as often as he liked, the water was cold and the pressure was low, making it difficult to feel clean in the salty, sticky air.

He felt chills across his body, not due to his cold cell but because of the body fat he'd lost. He rubbed the orange sleeves of his prison jumpsuit in an attempt to generate some heat, but it was a hopeless effort.

He was still a healthy weight at about one-hundred and sixty-five pounds, but his six-foot, one-inch frame made his ribs more visible with each passing day. The prison fed him well, but he never felt like eating. His appetite was often interrupted by the shrill scream he so vividly remembered.

He got up to pace around the cell and just as he did, the guard came stomping down the hall.

"Room service! Get it while it's hot," he called, chuckling to himself.

The joke had gotten old around day three of Riley's five-year sentence. He was housed at Nadirehs Island Prison, a penitentiary located just off the coast of North Carolina. The mountainous island could be seen on only the clearest days from Masada Pier. The prison once served as a beautiful resort for the richest of the rich but after a devastating hurricane in the late 70's, the island was nearly forgotten until it was rehabbed as a penitentiary in the early 90's.

Due to its resort nature, the cells were large, and the facilities were more than acceptable. In fact, only the wealthiest criminals were placed at Nadirehs, in order to make them feel more at home. A twisted concept that had been debated by public officials for years but in an only-the-rich-get-richer-economy, it had stayed that way.

His cell was roughly five-hundred square feet and included a private sink, toilet and bath, as well as a twin-sized cot. Though the space and the facilities were nice, it wasn't hard to see the reminders that the island was still home to what had become the most inescapable prison in the world. The white, brick walls, the double-barred, once picturesque windows and the view of the barbed-wire fences were constant reminders of the place Riley had come to call home over the past year.

On the back wall of Riley's room was a large window with metal bars striped through it. It faced west and overlooked the water toward the North Carolina shore.

Nadirehs aimed to make its prisoners as lonely as possible and no visitors were allowed. In fact, only once a month did anyone go in or out.

The island was surrounded by electrical poles and wires designed to send shockwaves through the water. If anyone escaped the building, they couldn't get off of the island without feeling four-hundred volts of electricity pulsing through their body. It was just enough to cause the prisoners serious pain but not enough to kill them.

Only once had Riley seen anyone attempt to escape. It was a dark night in the middle of September, and he'd been staring out of his cell window when he saw a man sprinting toward the shore. As he hit the water, his body shook violently and with a jolt he hit the ground. It wasn't long until a group of armed guards rushed out. There wasn't any need to use force, as the man was defenseless and weak. In no time at all, he was locked back up again.

Unamused by the guard's poor attempt at a joke, Riley grabbed the covered metal tray through the bars.

"Thanks, Aus," he smiled.

Although his past haunted him, Riley felt no reason to be cruel. He minded his own business on the island, making friends when he needed to and always avoiding making enemies. The prison had many opportunities to participate in physical activities like lifting weights and playing basketball, but Riley never felt like going. He felt abandoned and lonely and had no desire to change things.

Austin Andrews was the head prison guard and was not friendly to many inmates, but he took a special liking to Riley. Due to the nature of the island, Aus didn't have access to many resources above what the prisoners did. His living space used to be a private hut that guests could rent on the island. It had a nice living area with a green floral couch, wooden coffee table and a small television. The separate bedroom allowed him space for a queen-sized bed and a large dresser. It was difficult to get things on and off the island, so his furniture was old and needed updating but he didn't seem to mind. He had a small kitchen with simple white appliances, including a refrigerator, stove and oven. He virtually never used the kitchen to cook because he always ate for free in the prison cafeteria.

Unlike the prisoners, Aus always had access to fresh razors and toothpaste, so his hygiene didn't suffer. However, his shower still offered cold water and little pressure, so it was tough to get clean.

He was an ex-marine, but the only giveaway was his chiseled body. Other than that, Aus looked like he could have stepped straight out of the Flower Power era with his dark brown shoulder length hair and the rounded sunglasses he often wore. He was about the same height as Riley but easily had thirty more pounds on him.

Aus had proudly taken on responsibility as head guard of the island and expressed his love for the relaxed vibe with his clothing. He had multiple, custom uniform tops designed with Hawaiian-like prints ranging from floral blue to yellow with flamingos. His shirts looked like something he could have picked up at any Caribbean souvenir shop. His tops were always paired with navy blue pants and black shoes, regardless of the shirt color.

Despite his deceiving appearance, every prisoner knew better than to mess with him. His reputation preceded him and although the rumors were mostly far-fetched and impossible, like the one that he'd once killed a cheetah with his bare hands on a hunting safari in Africa, no inmate wanted to be the first to test him.

Riley took his tray of food and walked to sit down on the cold, metal chair in the corner of the room. He slowly uncovered his lunch in dejected anticipation.

It was the thirty-first day of August, which meant the food was as bad as ever. On the first of each month, a large sailboat made its way from Pepplepointe Marina out to the island to deliver a months' worth of food and supplies, along with the occasional new prisoner. Being that it was the end of the month, Riley was not surprised when he uncovered a plate of mashed potatoes, undetectable meat and four green beans.

"Lovely," he thought. "Four green beans will fill me right up."

Although a couple years of Riley's life were tough, for the most part, it had been pretty easy. Having grown up on the Southern California coast, just forty minutes south of Los Angeles, he spent most of his childhood days riding the Pacific Ocean waves and soaking up the California sun.

His father, Warren Riley Mines, was a professional chef and menu designer for TL Studios in Hollywood, where he prepared meals for some of the world's most famous movie stars. Food was his father's passion and Riley had many vivid memories of his family hosting extravagant parties with global delicacies and world-famous celebrities.

Riley could handle the cold room, uncomfortable bed and white, brick walls, but when it came to the food, he couldn't stomach it.

After staring at his food a while longer, and deciding not to take a bite, Riley got up and went to look out the barred window. He grabbed a rod and leaned his face on another as he felt the warm ocean air blow in. The day was clear and if squinted, he could almost make out the coastline.

He looked at the wall to his left where he'd been keeping a tally of his days.

"371 down, 1,456 to go," he thought.

CHAPTER TWO

It was a perfect morning in the summer of 2009. Riley could feel the sand between his toes as he ran across the coastline of his favorite beach, Salan Shores, with his dad right by his side.

Nearing the end of their run, his dad started to tease him, picking up the pace just slightly, Riley sped up, then his dad, then Riley again, until they were both at an all-out sprint toward the finish line.

Riley was built much like his dad, and his dad was built like a runner. Not overly tall or strong but clearly toned and athletic with legs a mile long. Warren ran cross country in college at the University of Washington and Riley was planning to do the same. It was early June and he was enrolled to start the first week of September. He couldn't wait to follow in his dad's footsteps and make him proud.

Riley had always been the favorite son over his younger brother, Kyle. Although Warren dearly loved them both, Riley and he had a special, unexplainable bond and all of Riley's life he'd strived to impress him. Wearing purple and running on the same track as his dad seemed like the only path worth heading down, in Riley's opinion.

Riley's earliest memory of Salan Shores came from his seventh birthday. Warren started every morning with a run along the beach before heading to LA for work and for months, Riley had been begging to join him.

Warren woke Riley up early in the morning on October 19th, 1997 and told him he had a birthday surprise. When the two of them hopped in the family's "special car" as they called it, a 1966 baby blue Ford Mustang convertible, Riley knew it was going to be a good day. They drove toward the coastline and Riley's anticipation grew by the second. The sun was starting to rise as they pulled up and parked the car.

Warren smiled back at Riley in the backseat and asked, "Would you like to join me on my morning run?"

Riley's eyes lit up with excitement and he nodded enthusiastically, unable to express his answer in words.

The two ran along the beach at Riley's pace, taking many walking breaks to enjoy the feeling of cool water touching their toes. During one of their walks, Warren declared, "Alright, this one's for all of the marbles. That palm tree up ahead, the one with the crooked trunk, that's our finish line."

Riley nodded.

"Ready, set, go!" Said Warren.

They took off toward the tree about 50-yards ahead and although his dad was much faster, he made the race close until the end when he stepped ahead to win. His dad always said he would never let his kids win so that someday when they actually did, they would know it really meant something.

Riley's mind replayed this childhood memory as he sprinted to the palm tree, they'd deemed the official finish line years earlier. He stuck out his chest in a dramatic effort to win the race, a race he now consistently won.

He looked back over his left shoulder to begin his usual trash talking to his dad, when to his surprise, he saw him bent over ten yards back, trying to catch his breath. It was the first time he'd seen him weak.

Riley's mother, Jane Mines, had been begging Warren for weeks to go to the doctor but he'd refused. He had always been hardheaded and tough but more than that, he was in denial. He knew something wasn't right, but he wanted nothing less than to know what was wrong.

Riley ran back to his dad and slowly helped him to stand. As their eyes met, Riley could see the deep fear his father had once held back creeping into his eyes. Without saying a word, Riley carefully assisted him up and to the car and drove him straight to the hospital.

Once there, Warren was quickly escorted back for a barrage of tests and samples. Riley immediately called his Mom and Kyle to fill them in. Soon, the three of them sat worried together in the cold, white brick walled hospital waiting room.

After five hours, a nurse came out and called, "Family of Warren Mines."

"Yes, yes, that's us," Jane said as she jumped up and ran toward the nurse. Her brown, graying hair was thrown up in a low ponytail and her face was lightly covered with makeup. She was wearing loose fitting jeans and a baggy, black V-neck, an outfit she'd never leave the house in, unless of course, it was a desperate situation.

"Come with me," she responded as she started walking toward the doors Warren had entered earlier that day. When she passed the familiar doors and continued walking, Riley's stomach dropped.

"Where are we going? Wasn't he back there? What's wrong?" He wondered to himself.

She kept walking down a long, white hallway with bright florescent lights until up ahead, Riley could see a sign that read, "Intensive Care Unit."

He couldn't swallow the large knot in his throat and his eyes began to well.

After what felt like an eternity, they reached Warren's room. They found him hooked up to what seemed like a million machines, with his blue eyes fixed dead ahead on the white brick wall.

"The doctor will be in with you shortly," the nurse said as she closed the door and left the four of them in the room alone.

Jane walked to the far side of Warren's bed, tears welling in her eyes. She grabbed his hand and leaned down to kiss him on the cheek. "Everything will be okay," she assured him.

Riley stood at the foot of the bed, staring down at the floor, unable to handle seeing his dad weak. Kyle, as he often did, followed Riley's lead.

The door opened, unveiling a woman no more than thirty years old with light brunette hair and green eyes. She appeared particularly small and petite in her white coat and looked as though she could have graduated from high school only yesterday. Her face was stone cold and the only feature giving away her age were the crow's feet already forming around her eyes.

She reached out her hand to greet Jane and introduced herself, "Good Afternoon, I'm Dr. Scotten," leaving no room for response, she continued, "It appears Mr. Mines has been struggling for quite some time and to be honest, it's a miracle he's made it this long. I can't possibly understand why you wouldn't have taken him to the doctor sooner, as now he barely stands a chance."

Immense fear and overcame Jane's face. She defensively thought, "How dare this woman come in here and tell me I don't know how to care for my husband? Who does she think she is?"

The doctor continued, "His heart is weak, and we have to operate immediately. The bypass surgery is extremely dangerous and for a patient whose heart is as weak as Warren's, the odds of survival aren't high." She paused before asking, "May I be blunt with you?"

"Geez, has she not been blunt already?" Riley thought.

Jane nodded.

Dr. Scotten continued, "His chances of coming out are slim at best and even if he does, things will never be the same," she paused. "The nurse should be in in about 15 minutes for prep. I'll give you a moment."

The room fell silent as she exited the room and the door quietly shut.

Through tears Warren cried, "I'm sorry."

Jane had always been strong, and she'd experience many trials in her forty-two years. She held back the tears welling in her eyes and in the most convincing tone she could muster she said, "Warren, you can do this. You are strong and you are courageous. Look at those handsome boys," she paused and gestured to Riley and Kyle standing at the foot of the bed. "Those boys need you." She paused again, "And I need you. You're going to make it through."

The rest was a blur for Riley.

CHAPTER THREE

"JAMES!!" A harsh voice yelled from down the hall.

"Uh oh..." James Wilde mumbled to himself. James stood six foot two inches tall with dark brown hair that tended to flip up at the ends. He was fairly fit but even he couldn't deny the years of free cop donuts had started to hit his waistband a little more than he would have liked.

His blue uniform was flattering on him and fit well even though it was a hand-me-down the station had given him.

The Wotila County Police Office in Macadia, Florida did not bode well as a place to hide. The all glass windows and open concept design made it easy to see and hear anything happening around the office, especially when it was happening at such loud volumes.

James closed his eyes in agonizing anticipation as Hillsteg barged into the room at the end of the hall where three officers had previously been working peacefully. One of the officers gave James an empathetic look on her way out while the other obnoxiously stuck out his tongue.

James shook his head and rolled his eyes at them as they left the room.

Chief of Police Walter Hillsteg was a gruff man weighing in at an easy three-hundred pounds. He was fifty-two years old with no kids and a wife who didn't much care for him. His thirty years in the police department and his lack of love came off in a red-faced anger that was intimidating to even the toughest officer. His white button-down shirt was so tight on his figure that the middle button always looked ready to pop. His shirt was bulging out at the waist on the front right side and the left side of his mouth still had some leftover strawberry jelly and powdered sugar residue from the donut he'd eaten earlier that morning.

"James," he started again, "How many times do I have to tell you not to go digging up old cases? If a case is closed, then it's closed. Zip, zap, zoobezoobezoo, closed."

"Yes, Sir" James respectfully responded.

"Do I need to say it again? It. Is. Closed." He yelled. "I saw your computer history today and I don't know why you're out there on the interwebs researching the Mines case. That case was as straight forward as a case can get and it's over a year old. It's c-l-o-s-e-d. Closed!"

"I understand, sir, but I really think there is something different about this one" he argued.

"James, I don't give a dimwit's redneck's last cup of homemade blackberry jam if you think this case is different," Hillsteg replied. He was notorious for making up his own sayings that absolutely no one could decipher. He continued, "I don't care if you think you're super man and want to be the hero. Until you can successfully solve a current, simple case, you need to stop digging up old cases!"

"Yes, Sir" James nodded as he dropped his head down.

"Very well. Have a nice day, Clark Bent" Hillsteg said with a sly smirk as he walked out the door.

"It's Clark Kent, you idiot," James corrected him under his breath and turned back to his computer. Defeated, he rested his head on his hand.

After a few minutes, the other officers came back into the room.

"What did you do this time?" Luke Conway teased.

Conway stood five foot, nine inches tall on a good day; his short black hair complimented his dark skin, and his chiseled physique revealed he spent too much time at the gym because he had no one to go home to at night.

"You know what I did, Conway. You were listening around the corner," James replied irritated.

"I know but I'd just looove to hear you tell me," sang Conway mockingly.

"Give him a break!" Rebecca Good said.

"Ohhh, the lovebird speaks again. How sweet!" Conway made kissing noises.

Rebecca rolled her eyes.

"You don't need to be so rude all of the time, Conway. Some of us are actually interested in our jobs and making the world a better place."

James let out a small chuckle and Conway rolled his eyes as he took a seat at his computer across the room.

"You know I love this job," Conway mumbled.

Rebecca sat down at her desk adjacent to James' and smiled.

"Soo, what's the case this time?"

James' eyes lit up as he looked at Rebecca and replied, "Do you remember the Mines case last year? The one where the New York millionaire was arrested in the Miami airport?"

Rebecca replied, "You mean the one where the guy had some homemade jerry-rigged version of a bomb hidden in the bottom of his shoe?"

With a grin, James said, "Yeah, that's the one," he paused. "I don't think he did it."

Rebecca shook her head.

"James, sometimes I don't know about you. I followed that case on the news like crazy and I've never seen a more straightforward case in my life. I heard the jury took no more than five minutes to come to the unanimous conclusion that he was guilty."

"Have you ever heard of fake news?" James replied accusingly. "I know I sound crazy, but I am telling you there is something strange about it."

"Like what, James?" Rebecca said, her brown eyes now undoubtedly questioning him.

James grinned, admiring Rebecca's doubts as she pushed her long brown hair out of her face and behind her ears. Rebecca was slender and embodied a shy beauty about her. Her flattering figure was often hidden by her size too big uniform.

"The pieces just don't connect. Why would a guy who's had everything handed to him his entire life, with a gorgeous wife and a sweet daughter, walk into the airport one day with bomb hidden in his shoe?" James questioned.

Rebecca's dramatically blinked her eyes and started moving her body with dramatic hand gestures. With a valley girl accent she answered, "Probably because he was like bored and had like nothing better to do with his life. Or maybe, he was like on a suicide mission because he'd like cheated on his wife and he knew that she knew. Or maybe, this like one time he was at the Miami airport and someone burned the espresso in his like $7 soy, vanilla, no whip latte-"

"Rebecca, quit," James interrupted. "You don't always have to be so cynical," he paused. "I think he was framed."

"You're full of it, Wilde," Rebecca laughed and went back to working on her computer.

CHAPTER FOUR

It was a cold December day in the heart of a New York winter, a balmy twenty degrees with a soft snow falling down.

The Christmas tree was still up in the corner of the Mines' living room and Riley and Lila sat on the floor by the fire. The room was beautiful with nine-foot windows covering the North wall and vintage décor that mirrored the classic 1920's era. The room was dark with only the glow coming from the white lights on the Christmas tree and the multicolored lights that lined the fireplace mantel.

Lila sat with her head resting on Riley's shoulder, while admiring their daughter, Chandler, across the room.

Chandler was quietly playing with one of the new dolls she'd received for Christmas only a week earlier.

Chandler was four years old and looked like she should be on the cover of a magazine. She had long, blonde curly hair that reached the middle of her back and bright blues eyes like her father's. Her eyes were complemented by her mother's fair skin tone and button nose.

Riley thought back to the day seven years earlier that had changed his life forever.

He and his business partner decided to take a few customers to the Broadway show *Mamma Mia*. Like any 23-year-old male on the prowl for their future mate, the curtain opened, and it was love at first site for the lead character, Sophie. Riley watched her sing, dance and act and by the end of the show, he knew he would marry her.

During the final song, Riley tapped his partner on the shoulder and said he wasn't feeling well so he needed to head out early.

He quickly went to the back of the theatre where he knew the actors and actresses would leave. He waited patiently outside until the slender actress with dirty blonde hair finally emerged from the backstage door. The weather was unseasonably warm for the winter and she donned blue jeans, a black sweater and a red scarf she'd wrapped once around her neck.

She was looking down and minding her own business when Riley called out, "Hey, Sophie!"

She looked around, not knowing where the voice had come from when.

Riley shouted, "Over here!"

She turned to her left to see an unfamiliar face and without hesitation she asked, "May I help you?"

"Are you hungry?" He replied.

"Not hungry enough to eat with a stranger standing in a dark alley," she retorted.

Riley took a step into the streetlight, allowing his perfectly tailored, black suit to be visible.

"I'm Riley Mines," he said reaching out his hand. "No longer a stranger, and no longer in the dark. Are you hungry?"

She smiled and reached out to shake his hand, "I'm –"

"Lila Ridge," Riley interrupted.

"And you're a know-it-all," she finished, pulling her hand back.

"I read it in the playbill," he grinned. "Come on! I'm sure you're hungry after that incredible performance. I know a great little place around the corner." He wiggled his fingers, insisting she grab his hand.

She rolled her eyes and reached out.

"Come on," Riley smiled.

They walked a couple of blocks and entered a small pizza shop.

"Wow," Lila teased. "New York City pizza... How original."

"You've got a lot of criticism for a girl who just walked out of a dark alley with a stranger," Riley countered.

Lila chuckled.

"I'll take a slice of veggie," she said turning to the overweight Italian man behind the counter.

"I'll have the same," added Riley.

The two grabbed a small table in the back and sat for four hours giggling and sharing stories about their lives. Lila grew up in Los Angeles and moved to New York with her mother when she was thirteen years old. Her parents had gone through a nasty divorce and her mom intended to move as far away from her father as she could, literally. Lila spent the summers in California at acting camps and the school years back in NYC, working on her craft. She had always dreamed of starring on Broadway, but her humble nature still had her in awe that she'd landed a leading role at only twenty-two years old.

Riley snapped out of his daydreaming when Lila tapped him on the arm and said, "Should we head out?"

He looked outside and saw the black town car waiting for them. In a poor southern accent, he replied, "I guess we'd better hit the road, Jack. You reckon you're ready for vacation?" He asked, lovingly throwing Lila over his shoulder.

"Let me down!" She pleaded, barely able to get the words out through her laughter.

Chandler, now more interested in her parents than her doll, got up and ran toward them.

"Let her down, daddy! Let her down!" She cried.

Riley set Lila down and they laughed as they put on their coats, grabbed their suitcases and headed out the door.

CHAPTER FIVE

"Alexa!" James exclaimed, startling Rebecca and Conway.

The speaker in the corner responded with a beep, beep and James was annoyed.

"Not you, Alexa!"

The recorded woman's voice said, "Sorry, to disturb you," and beeped off.

"What?" Rebecca asked.

"Alexa Monarch," James replied.

"The actress?" Rebecca questioned. "What about her?"

"She's one of my mom's best friends," James explained. "Growing up, we'd often go to parties with her and her family. It just dawned on me that one of those parties was at the Mines' house!"

Rebecca squinted her eyes and stared back, waiting for James to expand.

"The Mines' case," James replied, irritated Rebecca wasn't following. "The one with the airport shoe bomb. His parents hosted the party!"

Rebecca, still unamused, replied, "You've really lost me with this one."

"I know of the family and everything they've been through," commented James.

Rebecca questioned, "What do you me-"

Conway interrupted, "Can you two lovebirds stop talking for five seconds so I can actually get some work done over here?"

"We're not love birds," James countered.

Rebecca rolled her eyes and focused her attention back on James.

"You've never heard of Warren Mines?" James asked surprised. "He was the most famous chef in all of Hollywood for probably fifteen years. He was asked to be the head chef for all of the biggest events," James continued. "Then, at only forty-four, he died suddenly from an unknown heart condition. They tried to operate but it didn't work." James widened his eyes, seeing that Rebecca still wasn't following. "It was only the biggest funeral of the year. The guy was a legend in the industry and adored by all. His funeral literally could have been the same guest list as last year's MET Gala." James explained with exaggerated hand motions.

Before Rebecca could respond, James jumped out of his chair and yelled, "Gotta go! See you tomorrow!

CHAPTER SIX

Riley was lying on his back in his bed, blue eyes staring straight up at the white ceiling. There was an old, metal blue light hanging down, one that would have fit in well in a sleek and expensive 70's hotel. It was rounded at the top and deep enough to fit one small lightbulb in the center. The warm air would often blow the fixture just enough to rock it back and forth and create a slow squeak, squeak pattern that Riley had come to find soothing.

As Riley was about to fall asleep, a voice yelled from down the hall, "Afternoon delivery," awakening him from his daze.

Riley had lost track of the time and groggily walked to the cell door.

He could see Aus down the hall walking at his normal, quick pace.

"He always looks like he's on a mission," Riley thought.

Aus stopped at Riley's door for a split second longer than usual, he made eye contact with Riley, looked down once at the package in his hands, then up at Riley, then down at the package once more and handed it to him through the bars.

Riley was expecting the package, he had received it every week he'd been there. It was a hygiene kit that included a toothbrush, toothpaste and disposable razor.

"That was odd," Riley thought as Aus continued down the hall.

He opened the brown paper sack and dumped the contents

out on his bed, the normal toothbrush, toothpaste and razor fell out, followed by a small, white packet of silica gel that looked like it came from a box of new shoes.

Riley picked it up.

"Weird…" he thought. "It must have come from the packaging. He tossed it on the ground next to the empty metal tray from his morning meal.

The days felt long but the weeks felt short to Riley. He tried to kill time by writing in his journal, but he'd never been much of a writer. The prison had a nice weight room, but Riley just didn't feel like working out. He didn't feel like doing anything except replaying the memories that got him into prison. He felt lonely and isolated, but he knew that's what they wanted. After all, Nadirehs would hardly be a prison at all if it weren't for the immense seclusion.

Another week passed and Aus came down the hall singing, "Afternoon delivery!"

"Has it really been a week already?" Riley whispered quietly to himself.

"Yes, yes it has!" Aus replied as he stopped at Riley's door.

"How did he even hear me?" Riley thought.

Once again, he paused an extra second at Riley's door, looked down at the package, up at Riley and down at the package again before handing it to him.

Riley set the kit on the corner chair and walked back to the bed. He laid down and focused on the soothing squeak, squeak as he fell asleep.

He woke up to a very dark room and figured it was about eleven o'clock. Not that time was relevant when he never had anything to do but he still liked to know.

He decided it was as good a time as any to shave so he grabbed the hygiene kit and poured its contents out on the chair: a toothbrush, toothpaste, disposable razor and another silica gel.

"What in the world?" Riley thought, "I've been here over a year and never once did a packet come in my delivery and now two weeks in a row. How odd."

This time, he decided to further examine the packet, being careful not to open it because he remembered his mom always warning him that they were toxic.

He remembered her words and frantic hand motions anytime he opened a new box of shoes and spy the packet.

"Warren Riley Mines," she'd call. "Throw that away this instant. Those packages are disgusting and dangerous."

Riley had always thought she was a little hypersensitive to the stuff.

On the white packet, the black letters read,

"SILICA GEL – DO NOT EAT – THROW AWAY."

Riley had always chalked the packets up to being one of those things no one really understands. He didn't know the gels purpose in shoe boxes or new bags, but he knew he wasn't supposed to open it.

Riley had a wild imagination and he'd often played out potential scenarios. In one instance, his skin would break out in hives, in another, he wouldn't be able to breathe or maybe the package would just explode in his hands, leaving him charred and black.

He looked at the package and flipped it over in his hand a few times, as he continued to turn it, he felt the package getting hot and all of his childhood fears came rushing in.

He went to quickly throw it on his meal tray when he noticed it started changing color. The once white packet began getting darker and darker until it was completely black. As it changed, white letters began to appear on the black background.

Startled, Riley set the packet on the bed and continued to

watch in anxious awe.

After a few seconds, he could make out what it said, "HOLD FOR 5 SECONDS."

Hesitantly, Riley picked up the packet again and turned it over. The other side also read, "HOLD FOR 5 SECONDS."

He threw it back on the bed, afraid it was going to explode.

He began to pace back and forth, his mind racing.

"I'm losing it… I'm really losing it," he thought. "A color changing packet with words that magically appeared… my mind is playing tricks on me! What would possibly happen if I held it five seconds? What would happen?!" He nervously questioned.

He picked up the packet again and held it in his right hand, he squeezed tight and counted, "One, two… ahh," he tossed the packet on the bed again, too scared to make it all the way to five.

"What's the worst that could happen?" he continued the debate in his head.

After pacing around, grabbing the packet, throwing it back on the bed and repeating the cycle again and again for a few minutes, he finally stopped and stared at the black packet in the center of the bed.

His confidence and curiosity finally met at common ground, and he grabbed the packet. He stood in the center of his cell, closed his eyes and pictured his beautiful Lila and Chandler, in a moment of serenity, not knowing what would happen next.

He counted slowly to himself.

"One, two, three, four –"

CHAPTER SEVEN

The sun was setting, filling the sky with orange and pink shades for miles across the Atlantic Ocean.

Riley, Lila, Chandler, Jane and Kyle sat on a large deck around a wooden table. The table was next to an infinity pool that overlooked the vast, blue ocean.

Riley raised his glass of red wine and offered a toast.

"Cheers! To a wonderful Christmas vacation spent on an incredible island. Thanks for planning this, Mom!"

They raised their wine glasses, and Chandler her cup of milk, and clinked them together.

"How did you even find this place, Jane? It's amazing," Lila asked.

Jane shot a confused look at Riley.

"Oh, sorry… I assumed Riley told you?" She continued, "The Monarch family owns it. We used to vacation here all of the time with them when the kids were growing up and we've obviously both had our fair share of tough times. I saw her at book club a while back and she insisted that I take everyone out here to get away. And as you can see, this is a tough place to say no to."

To get to the island, the Mines' family flew into the Miami Airport and took a small yacht from Clearbrook Marina. The island had a full-time private staff, including a boat captain to take them to and from the grounds as needed. The trip was about forty minutes one-way to the private, thirty-five-acre island that donned a ten-bedroom, twelve bath mansion. The perfectly groomed grounds included amenities fit for a king, with two tennis courts, a basketball court, four golf holes, a two-thousand square foot fitness center, four pools and a one-mile track that weaved throughout the island.

"I can't believe this is our last night," Lila commented.

"Mommy, I don't want to go home," Chandler whined.

"I know. Me either, sweetheart," she replied.

"Want to take one final swim with Grandma?!" Jane asked enthusiastically in an effort to cheer Chandler up.

"Yes!" Chandler shouted as she tried to take off her cover-up. With Lila's assistance, she was soon running to the pool as Riley called, "Slow down, Chan! Be careful."

"It's hopeless, she's her father's child," Lila laughed, rolling her eyes.

Riley, Lila and Kyle were left at the table.

"How are you doing?" Riley asked, looking at Kyle.

"I'm alright," Kyle replied.

"I know it's been a tough year for you. Are you sure you're okay?" prodded Riley.

"Things have been pretty tough," Kyle started. "Plus, it's pretty weird being here. Mom's never been the same and it's almost been twelve years since Dad died. Obviously, my life has personally been terrible this year but what can you do?" He asked hypothetically. "I don't know. Just, it's been tough, he said. Kyle had never been one to openly express his feelings.

After Warren passed away, Riley stuck around for six months before moving to New York City, but Kyle never left. He had two years of high school remaining and after he finished up, he decided to stay home and take care of his mom. He claimed he wanted to stay and help her around the house, but they had plenty of hired staff to do that without him.

The mansion was far too big for the two of them, but Jane refused to sell it. It reminded her too much of the life she'd built with Warren and she felt like selling their home would mean truly letting go of him – a thought she couldn't bear.

"Have you thought at all about your future? Or trying to meet someone?" Lila asked.

Kyle replied, "I don't know if I really can. I don't think I'm ready."

"I didn't necessarily mean right now," Lila clarified. "But, sometime in the future?"

"I think it's still too soon for me to even think about my future," Kyle replied. "I'm still just trying to survive each day."

Kyle and Riley looked nothing alike, although both were very handsome in their own right. Kyle was fair skinned with green eyes and shaggy, brownish-blonde hair. He was tall at six foot two inches and had a healthy amount of weight on him.

"That's understandable. But just know, any girl would be lucky to have you," Lila kindly encouraged.

"Thanks," Kyle responded. "Right now, I'm content wasting my days away competing with myself to see how much greener I can make the grass. This past year I think we really made the move from shamrock to emerald. Best lawn in the neighborhood three years running," Kyle said with a grin, patting himself on the shoulder.

The three of them laughed.

"Okay, Kyle. We'll stop grilling you if you promise to let us know if you ever need our help." Riley said, "We love New York but you know we'd move back to California the second you said you needed us to."

"I know, I know," Kyle said as he pulled off his shirt, revealing his slightly chiseled abs and took off toward the pool, in an attempt to escape any real emotional conversation per usual.

"Cannonbaaallll," he shouted, as he jumped in and sent a roaring wave crashing over Chandler.

"What are we going to do with him?" Lila questioned, shaking her head.

"I don't know, maybe we shouldn't be so hard on him," Riley replied. "He's had a tough year."

"More like a tough twelve years," Lila agreed.

"True," said Riley, nodding his head. "I might not know what to do with him… but I do know one thing," he smirked.

"What's that?" Lila asked.

"That I lovvve you," Riley said as he leaned in for a kiss.

Just as Lila smiled and began to lean in, Riley leaned back and pulled off his shirt.

"And, last one in's a rotten egg!" He teased as he took off running toward the pool.

"Oh, that's cruel! You are so cruel!" Lila called as she tried her best to catch up to Riley who was already jumping in the water.

CHAPTER EIGHT

James sat in a red, leather booth staring down at his cup of black coffee. His eyes shooting toward the restaurant door every time he heard the bell ring, signaling its opening. His right foot started to tap in nervous anticipation.

He looked down at his watch.

"7:05," he thought. "I'll give it another ten minutes."

Just then, he heard the bell and looked up to see a slender, perfectly tanned women walk through the door. She donned a fitted blue dress with a string of white pearls that complimented her shoulder length black hair nicely.

James lifted up his hand slightly to get her attention. She walked over gracefully, keeping her posture nearly perfect. As she approached the table, she asked with a slight southern drawl, "Aren't you going to stand and greet your mother, boy?"

"Yes, momma," James responded as he stood and held his arms out for a hug.

Before accepting the embrace, she looked James up and down and said, "Still haven't found someone to take care of you, huh? Your hair looks a mess and what's that? About ten extra pounds you've put on?" She gestured to James' stomach.

"I've been working hard, mom," James replied, the southern accent he'd worked to hide coming out slightly as he spoke to his mother. "It's hard to find a girl these days without scouring the internet and I don't want to do that," he explained.

"Well, your father says you'll never find a woman and I try to tell him you will but I'm gonna need you to prove me right one of these days. I'm starting to get a little worried," she admitted.

"Okay, momma. I'll try my best," James shook his head. Although he always expected them, he couldn't help but be surprised by his mother's brash comments.

"You better try your best," she replied as she sat down in the booth opposite James.

"I'm hungry," James commented.

"I'm sure you are," she replied. She looked around, analyzing the small café and James tensed up, knowing more criticism was coming.

"Boy, where'd you make your mother come today? This place looks like a dump," she commented.

"Scoop's Diner. They have the best brunch in town. I thought you'd like it," James replied.

She nodded, acknowledging he'd put some thought into his decision.

"Alright," she said, "Cut to the chase."

"What do you mean?" James asked as the skinny, brown-haired waitress approached the table.

"What can I get for y'all today?" She asked.

"Scrambled egg whites, turkey bacon and wheat toast for the both of us, please," his mom answered as she grabbed James' menu and handed them both to the waitress.

Before James could argued, the waitress replied, "I'll get that order right in for you. She turned back toward the kitchen.

"I was going to get biscuits and gravy," James said annoyed.

"You don't need that," she replied, once again looking at James' pudgy stomach.

Knowing he needed answers, James tried to shift the

conversation.

"How have you been, mom?" he asked.

"Well, let's see… My only son hasn't called me in three weeks and suddenly, he's asked me to brunch. So, I'm a little on edge and I'd like to know what's wrong. Are you in trouble, honey? Do you need money?" She asked.

"Geez," he replied. "Can't a son ask his mother to brunch without being interrogated?"

"Some sons can," she paused. "You? Not so much."

James hesitated and looked her in the eyes.

"Alright, mom," he said shaking his head. "I'm not in trouble and I don't need money but…" he paused. "I do have a favor to ask you."

"I knew it!" she said. "What do you need?"

"Have you talked to Alexa lately?" He asked.

"Of course, I have. She's only my best friend," she answered.

"Good," he replied. "Because I have a theory."

CHAPTER NINE

"Five," Riley finished his count as he squeezed the silica gel in his right hand. In fear, he had closed his eyes and when he opened them again, he was standing in the middle of a street.

"Get out of the way," an old driver yelled out of the window of a yellow taxicab as he laid on his horn and swerved to avoid hitting Riley.

Startled and confused, Riley stumbled backwards until his heels hit the curb and he fell on the ground. He closed his eyes and shook his head as if he was trying to wake up from a bad dream. When he looked up again, he couldn't believe his eyes. He was sitting across the street from his beautiful New York City townhome.

It was a red-brick house situated between two white townhouses that all spanned three stories tall. Ten cement steps led up to a large, dark brown wooden door. The steps were lined with potted plants that were now overgrown because it had been Riley's job to keep them trimmed. He didn't have to keep them trimmed, he could have easily paid someone, but he chose to because he found pleasure in his little piece of nature hidden in the big city.

Riley closed his eyes tight, shook his head and opened them again.

"This is the weirdest dream," he thought as he stared at his old house.

Just then, a gust of cold air blew through. Riley shivered and his teeth began to chatter. He looked down and realized that he was only wearing black, boxer shorts.

"Ahh," he screamed jumping to his feet.

He bolted across the street and up the steps toward the front door. He tried the handle, but it was locked. The house was completely dark, except for a soft glow coming from a second story window.

Riley started banging on the door and yelled, "Lila! Lila! Lilaaaaa!"

He fell to his knees and stared up hopelessly at the sky. A figure appeared in the upstairs window.

The silhouette was dark in the backlit room, but Riley knew it was Lila.

"It's me," he longingly called, "Riley!"

The figure quickly moved away from the window and a few seconds later, the front door opened.

"Riley?" Lila trembled. "What are you doing here?" She asked in shock.

Riley jumped up from his knees, put both hands on Lila's face and leaned in to give her a kiss. He pulled back and grabbed her arms, squeezing them with admiration. "My beautiful wife, I've missed you. How are you?"

Lila pulled back, trying to break free from Riley's grip.

"How am I?" She asked, the shock of her surprise visitor wearing off. "How am... *I*?" She said, her tone condescending.

Riley let go and looked at her with concerned eyes like a sad puppy dog. It was only now in the light that he could see the bags underneath her tired eyes and never-ending stress of life displayed in her unbrushed hair.

"What do you mean 'How am *I*?'" She continued, "You've been in prison for a year and you just show up one night at what? Almost midnight?" She threw her hands up. "And you just casually ask 'How I am?' What the hell are you doing?"

Riley knew Lila was tired. She almost never swore, unless she was drinking or sleep-deprived… and she hadn't been drinking. He felt a knot welling in his stomach, unable to breathe.

"I don't know, Riley. How are *you*?" She continued sarcastically, "This seems like such a wonderful time to get casually caught up. How has prison been? Is it nice there? Do you spend all day thinking about how you're finally free of your family? Does it ever even cross your mind how you ruined our lives?"

"Lila, I didn't do anything!" Riley interrupted her rant.

"I'm sorry…" Lila stared at Riley with accusing eyes. "You showed up at Miami Airport with a bomb on your shoe and you expect me to believe you didn't do anything?! I mean what the hell, Riley? Where do you get an absurd idea like that from anyway?"

Riley was getting angrier every second she continued. He hated when she cursed.

"Yeah, let's just lay by the beach and have the time of our lives. Here I am thinking we're enjoying the perfect family vacation. Oh, but meanwhile, my husband is building a bomb and I don't know… and boom… my life explodes like a metaphorical bomb. How ironic! Thanks, Riley. Thanks for ruining my life," she went to slam the door.

Riley reached his hand and kept it open.

"LILA! Stop it! Do you hear yourself right now? Does that possibly sound like something I would do? I didn't do anything," he argued. "It was the perfect vacation. You're the best thing that ever happened to me. You changed me and my life and nothing mattered until I met you. Don't you know I'd never do anything to hurt you?" He stared back at Lila as tears began welling in his eyes.

Lila softened her stare as she looked back at Riley's bright blue eyes.

"I would never hurt you," he paused. "Lila, you're acting hysterical. I get it. It's been a year of reliving the terrible day, but it wasn't me." He took a deep breath, "I think I was framed. I don't know how or by who or why. I have absolutely no leads, but I didn't do it and you have to believe me," he begged. "I need you right now and I need your help. Without you, I have no one and no way of getting out."

"What do you mean? You're obviously out right now." Lila said.

"No! I'm not," he replied. "I mean, I am... but I'm not... I don't know." Riley tried to explain. "I don't know how I'm here and I don't know if this is a dream or real life or what, but I know that you're here and I need you."

Lila looked back at Riley, unsure of her willingness to believe him.

"Waaahhh," the sharp cry of an infant filled the silence.

Riley's eyes got wide, knowing it wasn't Chandler's cry.

"Who... is that?" He asked timidly.

Lila looked blankly back at him.

"Lila, who is that?" Riley asked again.

She stared a moment longer, deciding whether or not she'd let Riley back into her life.

"Your son," she finally answered.

Riley ran through the doorway, pushing Lila out of the way as he followed the wailing sound. He trekked up the stairs and into the master bedroom where he found a white bassinet next to the bed.

He slowly approached the bassinet until he peered over the edge and saw the baby boy. He stood in disbelief.

Lila stood in the doorway. Riley now understood her immense exhaustion and tangled hair. She was living the life of a single mother and coping with the depression of an unreachable, imprisoned husband.

"I had no idea," Riley said.

"Of course, you didn't," Lila replied. "It happened our last night in Florida. I came back and assumed I was extra emotional from the eruption of everything," she hesitated. "It wasn't until I was late that I realized."

Riley looked down at the boy and up again at Lila, "What's his name?" He asked.

"Warren Riley Mines III," she replied.

Riley smiled, "You still gave him the family name?"

"I had to," Lila said. She walked across the room and put her arm around Riley. "It's late and we're both delusional. Why don't you lie down and we'll try to comprehend everything in the morning?"

Riley agreed and Lila walked him to the bed. His head hit the pillow and he was out like a light.

CHAPTER TEN

James stormed through the office door startling Conway and Rebecca.

"Geez, James," Conway whined. "What is your problem?"

"No one will listen to me," James complained. "I know I'm right."

"Oh, here we go again with your Riley Mines theory," Conway rolled his eyes. "The guy was a New York made millionaire with a hot wife and nothing better to do. He was bored and tried to spice things up at airport security. Now, he's in 'jail'," he gestured with air quotes. "At Nadirehs and no one cares."

"You're a cop, Conway, and you don't even care if a man was wrongfully put in prison? Why are you even in this business?" James asked.

"What now?" Conway sighed.

Rebecca now interested in the conversation turned her chair to face them.

"Remember how I told you my mom is friends with Alexa Monarch?" James asked.

They nodded.

"Well, the Mines' family was vacationing on Alexa's private island. That's why they were flying in and out of Miami. So, I had my mom ask her about them because obviously they're pretty good friends if they're using her island and Alexa said they're the best family. Remember how I mentioned that? The crazy famous celebrity chef?" James rambled on. "She said since then, Riley had just put his nose down and worked hard. He never let anything get in the way of his goals and never broke the rules growing up."

"Great, another irrelevant character witness," Conway groaned.

"But… I had my mom dig deeper and ask about the staff on the island. Alexa kept things pretty short, but she said the same family had been running the property for about forty years. Alexa said she treats them like an extension of her own family and that they're lovely people," explained James.

"Where are you going with this?" Rebecca asked becoming slightly irritated.

James paused, "I went to the island."

"You what?!" Conway and Rebecca yelled simultaneously.

"Yeah, I went over the weekend and decided to do a little investigating for myself," said James.

"You can't just do that!" Conway replied.

"You mean, I can't just go on vacation to a beautiful private island in my free time?" James asked. "Uhh, I think I can."

"Well, now I'm actually interested," admitted Rebecca. "How did you get on it?"

"I'm telling you; my mom and Alexa are best friends. It was easy," James replied.

"What did you find?" Rebecca asked.

Ignoring her question, James continued, "I wanted to get a feel for the staff. I wanted to see if they really seemed like the so-called 'lovely people' Alexa referred to them as."

"And did they?" Conway asked.

"Yes," James admitted. "They really did."

He liked the fact that Conway and Rebecca were on the edge of their seats and he wanted to keep them there as long as possible.

"Stop talking now or get to the point," Conway demanded.

"Well, during my long, tough weekend of laying by the pool and sipping pina coladas," James paused and soaked in their anticipation for one last second. "I did manage to find time to search a few places on the property and interestingly enough, the treehouse held some clues."

He held up his phone with a picture for Rebecca and Conway to see.

"WHAT?!" They exclaimed with dropped jaws.

CHAPTER ELEVEN

Squeak, squeak.

The familiar, soothing sound woke Riley. His eyes slowly opened to stare at the blue light fixture hanging above.

"Ahhh!" Riley screamed and rubbed his eyes hard. He opened them again and jumped up from the bed gripping the orange jumpsuit, he found himself in once again.

Riley heard keys jangling at his cell door and saw Aus unlocking it.

"Welcome home, laddie," Aus teased in a terrible Irish accent as he walked into Riley's cell.

"What do you mean?" Riley asked.

"I know you had a nice, little trip out last night and I wanted you to know that I know and that I'm watching you," Aus replied.

Riley tensed up, a ball knotting in his throat. "I don't know what you're talking about," he replied.

"Sure, you do," said Aus. He moved quickly toward Riley and grabbed him by the throat. He shoved him up against the wall by his bed. "And don't ever do it again," Aus threatened through gritted teeth.

Riley gasped for air.

Aus let go and busted out with laughter.

Riley's eyes were wide as he looked around the room with panic.

"That was a good one!" Aus complimented himself with a

pat on the back. "I am funny!" He sang.

Seeing the panicked look on Riley's face, Aus reached out his hand and offered, "Truce?"

Riley didn't know what to think.

"I guess I just don't understand what's happening here," Riley replied rubbing his neck, red from Aus' grip.

"I'm messing with ya! For leaving last night," he replied, waving his hand to show it was no big deal.

Riley stared blankly back at him.

Sensing the confusion, Aus continued, "Of course, I know you left last night," he said as if it was as obvious as the grass being green. "I'm the one that got you out of here."

Riley hesitated, "That wasn't a dream?"

"Course not! That was some good ole' fashioned silica gel magic!" Aus responded with glee.

"I'm going to need a lot more of an explanation than that," Riley insisted. Slightly annoyed with Aus' carefree attitude but working to stay calm and on Aus' good side.

"Yeah, that's probably true. Sorry, I should have planned this out a little better." Aus said, "Let me start at the beginning."

Riley took a deep breath, finally pleased with the direction the conversation was headed.

"That would be great," he agreed.

Aus started, "Silica gel was around as early as the 1640's but remained a scientific curiosity until its use in World War I, when it was discovered to absorb vapors and gases in gas mask canisters. And I'll skip all of the science behind it because that's pretty boring stuff but fast forward to Washington D.C. in the summer of 1992. A young and," he paused, searching for the right words, "And good-looking man is strolling the streets, trying to find a purpose for his life when he sees a sporting goods store. He walks in and finds a handsome pair of sneakers."

To Riley's surprise, despite Aus' odd looks and military background, when he told this story, he sounded like a Princeton professor who'd been teaching for forty years. His words flowed like a peaceful stream and his knowledge seemed infinite, he talked in a way that begged Riley to listen.

"And I mean they were just a really nice pair," he continued. "He was feeling kind of down, so he tried them on and decided he deserved something to cheer him up. He bought the sneakers and headed home. The next day, he went to wear the sneakers and when he took the first shoe out, a packet of silica gel fell out and he picked it up to look at it. The man couldn't help but smile, thinking about his mother who had recently passed and the way she used to obsessively throw the packets away in fear of their poison."

Aus looked up at the ceiling and smiled at the memory, then continued. "Much like I'm sure you experienced, the packet got hot and started to change color. It suddenly revealed instructions and..." Aus was suddenly agitated. "Have you figured out that I'm the man in the story yet?"

"Uh, yeah, I got that," Riley laughed.

"Okay, then let me continue in a less dramatic fashion," decided Aus.

He continued, intensity rising with every word, "So, I read the instructions and had nothing to lose so I closed my eyes, counted to five and when I opened them again, I was back in Colorado, standing outside of my childhood home. I didn't know what to think and I was scared and confused but before I could process anything, my sister spotted me and came running outside. I enjoyed the rest of the day with my family and everything seemed normal. It wasn't until I woke up the next morning, back in my apartment in D.C. that I realized something strange had happened. I was sitting in my apartment, trying to process the strange dream, when I heard the phone ring. I let it go to voicemail and then, I heard my sister going off about why I had left without saying goodbye and telling me to call her with an explanation as soon as I made it back to D.C."

Suddenly, yelling erupted down the hall and Aus quickly got up, "I'm sorry, Riley, there's so much more I have to tell you, but I've got to go. The biggest thing you need to know right now is that the magic of silica gel only works for those who need it." With a wink, Aus left the room.

CHAPTER TWELVE

"Are we sure we have to leave?" Lila asked as she helped Chandler onto the boat set to take them off of the island.

"I'm afraid so," Riley replied as he kissed her on the forehead and joined them.

The three of them made their way back to a table filled with breakfast pastries and sat around picking at some of the breads and croissants.

"I don't want to leave," Chandler whined as she stuffed a powdered donut into her mouth.

"I know, Chan," Riley comforted. "But, just think, we'll be back in New York soon and all of your Christmas presents are waiting for you! I don't have to go back to work for a few more days so we can test them all out together."

Chandler immediately perked up and smiled until she became distracted again with another donut.

"You're such a good dad," Lila smiled at Riley.

"Maybe, that's true," he replied. "But I'm only the second-best parent she has."

Lila rolled her eyes and shook her head. She'd never been good at accepting Riley's compliments.

"Did your mom and Kyle even make it on the boat?" Lila asked, sensing they'd started to move. Just then, the two came around the corner and Riley pointed, answering her question.

"Let's hope security isn't too bad at the airport," said Jane. "I can't stand having to take my shoes off and fly commercial.

If your dad had lived a few more years, we probably would have bought our own jet. We always talked about doing that," she trailed off.

"Mom, come on," Riley said. "You know I don't like it when you say things like that."

"Agreed," said Kyle. "Flying first class is hardly an inconvenience. Plus, you could buy a private jet if you wanted."

"I know. It just wouldn't be the same" Jane sighed. "So, what's for breakfast?" she asked, changing the subject as she admired the table full of food.

When they arrived at Clearbrook marina, there was a black Escalade waiting for them and without much hassle, to Jane's liking, they made it to the Miami airport with ample time to spare.

The group was waiting in line for security when Riley realized he had a full bottle of water in his backpack.

"Shoot, I've got to throw this away," he said to Lila as he scanned for the nearest trashcan. After spotting one about twenty feet away, he handed his backpack to Lila and ducked under the stanchions to go throw it away.

When he got back in line, the little boy who'd been standing behind him shouted, "No cutsies!"

Startled, Riley calmly turned around and looked down at him.

"Sorry, buddy! I was in line with my family here and just stepped out to throw my bottle away," he explained.

"Hey! Don't you dare talk to my kid like that," the kid's dad pointed, with his Bahamas shirt, vacation-boosted confidence and extra ten pounds from the family cruise. "We've all been standing in line for a while and I don't like it any more than he does when some jerk comes in and cuts us. Back of the line," he shoved Riley.

"Hey!" Kyle shouted, now getting involved. "Don't push

him, he's been with us the whole time!"

Riley never liked to see Kyle upset so he took a step back and worked to calm down the situation. "Hey, no worries," he put his hand on Kyle's chest. "The line isn't that long. I'll just head to the back and meet you all on the other side of security."

Annoyed but knowing better than to fight his brother, Kyle agreed.

Riley walked to the back of the security line as the fat man obnoxiously waved goodbye.

"Some people are crazy," Riley thought to himself as he stood at the back of the line. "I mean really, what am I? A whole ten people further back?" He shook his head and tried to laugh off the situation.

Lila had taken Riley's backpack through, so all he had on him was his ticket and wallet when he approached the security checkpoint. He put his wallet in the small bin and sent it through the x-ray machine before walking into the scanner.

He stepped out and paused to wait for the "all clear" from the security man.

A small red dot lit up Riley's right foot on the screen and the security officer asked to scan him. He took his radar wand across Riley's arms and chest before scanning down his legs. The wand beeped loudly as it ran over his right shoe.

"Sir, could you please take off your shoe for me?" He asked.

"Sure," Riley answered. He could see his family waiting just passed the edge of the security tables and he shrugged, trying to make them laugh.

He watched as the security guard began investigating his shoe. The officer called another officer over, then another and another, until the entire security line had come to a complete halt and all of the guards were surrounding his shoe.

Riley heard the officers whispering but couldn't make out

what they were saying. Suddenly, a group of officers rushed toward him, threw him on the ground and handcuffed his hands behind his back.

He heard Chandler's shrill scream as she watched in a panic.

"Sir, remain calm, sir!" The officer said as he pulled out his gun.

"Remain calm?" Riley thought confused. "I didn't think I was anything but calm."

"Can you tell me what kind of bomb is on your shoe?" Another officer asked.

"Bomb?!" Riley exclaimed, "What are you talking about!?"

"Sir, there is a bomb on the sole of your shoe," the officer replied sternly.

"No, there's not!! I don't know what you're talking about!" Riley argued.

"I'm going to need you to keep calm, sir," the officer replied.

"I can't keep calm!! You're accusing me of putting a bomb on my shoe and I have no idea what you're talking about! This is ridiculous!" Riley jerked his body around on the ground trying to get free.

One of the officers holding Riley down pulled out his Taser and pressed it to Riley's back.

"Riley!" He heard Lila scream before he was knocked out.

CHAPTER THIRTEEN

Riley was stuck obsessively meditating over the conversation he'd had earlier in the week with Aus. He couldn't make sense of the mysterious power of silica gel and he had absolutely no idea how it worked.

He anxiously waited to see Aus again to ask him more questions, but day in and day out, his food was delivered and Aus was nowhere to be found.

Aus was missing in action and Riley didn't understand. His mind raced constantly with thoughts of his visit home and his unknown son and his beautiful wife and his precious daughter and he wanted nothing more than to get back there.

Riley had felt lonely his entire stay in prison, but it wasn't until after his mysterious visit home that he truly felt the isolation that Nadirehs was famous for.

A couple of days had gone by without seeing Aus and Riley was lying hopelessly on his bed, his mind racing as usual, when he heard familiar footsteps down the hall.

He quickly sat up in hopeful anticipation as he heard the voice call out, "Afternoon delivery!"

Riley jumped to his feet and walked toward the cell door. He smiled an eager smile and gave a small waive as Aus approached, hygiene kit in hand. Aus walked with his head down and didn't make eye contact with Riley. He was silent as he passed the package through the bars.

Riley noticed that Aus' arms were cut and bruised. It wasn't abnormal for him to have some scrapes here and there from rowdy prisoners, but Riley hadn't seen anything like this before.

"Hey Aus," Riley said, trying to spark the conversation he'd been so anxiously awaiting.

"Hi," Aus said. He barely looked up, but Riley caught a glimpse of his swollen left eye with black and blue highlights to match.

"Aus! What happened?" Riley exclaimed.

"Keep quiet," Aus whispered as he nodded his head toward the package. With a wink, he continued on his delivery route.

Riley swiftly walked to his bed to dump out the contents. He flipped the brown paper sack over and per usual, a toothbrush, toothpaste and disposable razor fell out. He shook the bag, looking for more.

"Really?" He thought, "After all of that, no silica gel? What a tease!"

Riley shook the bag in anger, crumpled it and threw it across the room.

"UGH!" He screamed.

His mind raced with rage, replaying the interactions of his last few days. He began to pace the room and lifted his right arm in preparation to punch the white brick wall.

Riley tended to stay calm with very little spouts of anger. Over his time in prison, he'd only gotten angry one other time. He though back to the sad day last February, the one-month anniversary of his sentence.

His dinner had arrived and to his surprise, the tray had a small, white sack sitting on top of the vegetables that read, "From your loved ones." He opened it up to find an oatmeal raisin cookie.

"That's not from my loved ones!" He exclaimed, "They

know I hate raisins!"

He threw the cookie as hard as he could against the brick wall, and it broke into pieces that landed all across the room.

He paced back and forth with rage until he punched the brick wall.

"Ahh!!" He screamed in anguish. He shook his hand, already swelling from the impact and began to weep as he sat down on the bed. He was broken.

Riley shuddered at the memory and lowered his arm. He felt the need to physically release his anger and he looked around the room for anything he could use. The white, tile floor was bare, expect for the brown paper sack he'd thrown a few moments ago.

He swept it up off of the floor and began to tear it apart.

His anger had gotten the best of him and like a toddler throwing a temper tantrum in the grocery store, he soon sat down on the bed, exhausted and defeated, tears streaming down his face.

He put his elbows on his knees and his head in his hands as he tried to gather himself. He looked up, wiped his face and glanced at the mess he'd made.

He noticed a black mark on one of the pieces of paper and got up to examine it.

He couldn't tell exactly what it was, so he picked up another piece, then another. He realized the pieces of paper had letters written on them.

With haste, he began to pick up all of the pieces of the brown paper sack and put it on the bed. As quickly as his mind could move, he pieced them together like a puzzle.

After what felt like an eternity, the brown paper revealed a note that read:

The game is dangerous, but the reward is great.
If played correctly, you'll change your fate.
Trust only those who come to you and above all else, whatever you
do,
Don't share your secret or abuse your power, after all you only have
sleepless hours.
With only five trips to clean your slate, you don't have any time to
wait.
Think smart, not hard and with every flight, always come back to
the hanging blue light.

He read the paper and re-read the paper, trying to process the poem.

"Five trips?" He thought. His mind raced, "I don't have any supplies. Where is Aus? Is this just a dream? It can't be. I didn't do it. I deserve to be free and maybe this is really my way out? But, where to start? Even my own wife doesn't believe me...."

His thoughts were interrupted by the sound of quiet footsteps whose culprit clearly wanted to be kept a secret.

Riley sat on the corner of his bed, not wanting to disturb the hallway guest or cause any suspicion of his own. He sat silently, unmoving, until he no longer heard footsteps.

He stood up and walked quietly to the cell door.

To his pleasant surprise, he found one packet of silica gel sitting on the ground. He picked it up, smiled and laughed a soft laugh that perfectly encompassed his fear, disbelief and excitement.

CHAPTER FOURTEEN

James, Rebecca and Conway paced in their office.

"What are we supposed to do with that information?!" Rebecca exclaimed.

"I don't know but I don't want to be involved," said Conway.

"Oh, stop it, Conway! You're already in on it and you better stay in on it or keep your mouth shut," James threatened.

"Alright, alright," said Conway. "It's too interesting to not be involved anyway."

"Good," replied Rebecca. "Then, let's focus on what to do next."

"I think the next logical step is to talk to Riley's family," James suggested. "I mean right now we're going off of very little. In fact, we basically know nothing. We need to look into possible motives."

"How are we going to do that?" Conway asked doubtfully. "Hillsteg would never approve!"

James laughed, "Are you crazy? I wasn't planning on asking Hillsteg. The guy can't stand me anyway. I've got a few vacation days to blow and flights to New York don't run too high this time of year. We could leave tomorrow, have three days in the city and come back on Sunday."

Rebecca sat down at her computer.

"Let me check out options!" She said.

She typed quickly while Conway continued to pace.

"Alright, there's a flight tomorrow afternoon," she announced. "Thursday, January sixth out of Miami at 1 p.m... lands in New York at 4:40. Then we could fly back on Sunday, the ninth and be home by 7:30 p.m. for two-hundred dollars each."

"Perfect!" Exclaimed James. "Book it."

"I don't know," Conway shook his head.

"Come on!" Rebecca shouted, now fully invested. "Conway, you know this case is different. What do you have to lose?"

"Two-hundred dollars for this dumb flight," he retorted.

"Alright," James cut in. "Even though you're an ass most of the time, I think you can help us. I'll make you a deal. I'll buy your flight and if we solve the case, you pay me back. If we don't, it's on me."

Conway shook his head and looked at Rebecca.

"What time did you say we take off again?"

CHAPTER FIFTEEN

"Are you ready?" Riley asked as he tossed the car keys across the kitchen to his brother.

"I don't think I can do it," Kyle nervously replied.

"Of course, you can," Riley encouraged. "Every sixteen-year-old dreams of this day and your time has finally come. Let's go!"

"It just doesn't mean as much anymore..." said Kyle. "Nothing means as much."

It was only two months after Warren's passing and the family was nowhere close to finding a new normal. Jane spent her days lying on the couch, crying and staring at a blank television screen; only eating when Riley forced her to have something. She hadn't worked in years thanks to Warren's successful career, but she'd always been very involved with the local community and her son's activities. Now that Warren was gone, she felt no reason to participate in anything.

Riley had gotten into New York University and was planning to leave in January, but he worried about his mother and Kyle. He didn't want to leave them, but he couldn't go on like this. Losing his father was tragic but he still wanted to make something of himself. He knew that's what his father would have wanted.

"Of course, it does," Riley replied. "Dad would want us to go on living our best lives, Kyle. Mom is struggling and we know that but that doesn't mean we have to."

"Are you really going to leave me with her?" Kyle asked.

"Kyle, I have to go," Riley replied. "I'm sorry."

"I know," he said, "But what am I supposed to do?"

"Well, for starters, you're going to need to get your license so you can have the ability to actually do anything," said Riley. He'd always had a way with getting a conversation to go the way he wanted.

"You're always so literal," Kyle replied.

"Come on! It's all going to be okay. You know I'm here for you if you need anything," Riley said as he lovingly put his arm around Kyle's neck, rubbed his hair and started pulling him toward the door.

Riley pulled into the DMV where Kyle was scheduled to take his test. He helped him get checked in and then they sat in the waiting room for the next available instructor to call his name.

They saw an elderly man, who looked like he could barely drive a vehicle himself, come out of the back room and they smiled at each other, knowing Kyle would surely ace the test if he was the instructor.

"Monarch," the man called.

"Monarch?" Kyle asked, scanning the room. "Is Keagan here?"

They looked around the busy DMV until they saw a girl stand up across the room. Her long blonde hair was up in a messy ponytail and her tight black leggings accentuated her long legs. Her greenish-blue eyes were highlighted by the army green anorak jacket she was wearing atop a gray tee.

"I guess she is," Kyle answered his own question.

"Are you going to say something?" Riley asked.

Kyle's face flushed red at the thought.

"Oh, come on, Kyle! You know she's into you," said Riley. "Hey, Keagan!" He called.

"Riley, what are you doing," Kyle whispered in a panic.

Keagan looked around confused until she saw Riley waving across the room. Her face lit up and she waved back. She made her way toward them.

"She's always been into you. Since you were like four, I swear," Riley said.

"It's different now. We're –" Kyle started but couldn't finish his though before Keagan approached.

"Hi, guys!" Keagan exclaimed, "What are you doing here?"

"Same as you, I'm guessing," Kyle replied. "Trying to get my license."

"Yep, that's what I'm doing," said Keagan. "I am so nervous."

"I think you'll be alright," Riley chimed in. "I'm not sure your instructor knows a car from a plane at this point," he laughed.

The three of them looked over at the elderly man who seemed to be lost staring blankly down at his clipboard.

"In fact, I think he forgot he even called your name," added Kyle.

"Maybe, you're right," Keagan laughed.

"Monarch," the elderly man called again.

"Or, maybe not," said Riley.

"Well, I guess I should probably get going," Keagan said. "Good luck, Kyle," she smiled as she walked away.

"Thanks, Keagan! You too," He replied eagerly.

They sat down again, and Riley looked at Kyle with a cheesy grin. "Oh, she is so into you, bro," he said.

"There's no way," Kyle replied, "She's totally out of my league."

Just then, a large, gruff woman came out of the back room. "Uh oh, I hope she's not –" Riley started.

"Mines," the woman called.

"Good luck," Riley tried to sound confident.

"Thanks a lot," Kyle said as he rolled his eyes and stood up to head toward the woman.

Riley sat and waited anxiously for his brother's return. He wanted nothing more than for him to pass his test the first time and for something to go his way. It had been a tough couple of months.

The DMV door opened, and Keagan walked in, her eyes red and wet, holding back tears.

"Oh no," Riley thought, "That does not look hopeful."

Keagan walked to the counter and spoke with a lady for a few minutes. Then, she walked over to Riley with her head hanging down.

"I didn't pass," she said. "Stupid parallel parking."

Before Riley could respond, she rambled on.

"And now, I have to call my mom because she dropped me off and had her driver pick her up so that I could have a car here to drive myself home and I thought it would be so fun but now it's not fun and I'm so embarrassed and my life is ruined. This is the worst thing I could possibly imagine," she cried.

"Things could probably be worse," Riley responded, not meaning to sound so cynical.

"Oh, Riley! I am so sorry. Of course, things could be so much worse and I'm so stupid for not thinking about what you're going through. How are you?" She asked.

"It's okay, Keagan. We don't have to talk about it. I'm sorry you failed your test. We can give you a ride home if you'd like?" Riley offered.

"That would be so great," she said. "I rescheduled my test for tomorrow and honestly, I could probably find a way to get here and retake it without my parents ever knowing. I really don't like to disappoint them."

"It's not a problem at all," Riley said.

The front door of the DMV opened once again, and Kyle came in smiling ear to ear.

"That looks hopeful," Riley said to Keagan.

"Yes, it does," she agreed, looking across the room at Kyle with soft eyes.

Kyle went to the counter, took his picture and signed a couple of forms. He came back to Riley and Keagan, holding up his new paper license with pride.

"Congratulations, buddy!" Riley said, patting him on the back.

"Congrats," Keagan said.

"Thanks!" Kyle replied, "How'd it go for you?" He asked.

Riley answered so Keagan didn't have to. "Not so hot," he said. "But no worries because you're going to drive her home."

Kyle's face turned beet red.

"Oh, I don't know about that Riley! I'm still pretty nervous."

"Nah, you're a licensed man now. You can do it!" He said, tossing Kyle the keys. "Let's get out of here."

CHAPTER SIXTEEN

"One, two, three, four, five," Riley closed his eyes and clenched the silica gel packet in his right fist.

When he opened his eyes, he was once again standing outside of his New York home. It was around six o'clock and traffic was pretty heavy but this time, he'd managed to land on the sidewalk instead of the middle of the road.

"This is insane," he mumbled as he looked down at his bare body wearing only black boxer shorts.

He slowly walked up to the door and knocked softly.

Lila answered, holding baby Warren in her arms.

"What do you want?" She rolled her eyes.

"Daddy!" Chandler exclaimed as she came running around the corner. She sprinted to the door and jumped into Riley's arms.

"Hi, Chan! I've missed you," Riley smiled.

"Oh, this is just a disaster waiting to happen," Lila mumbled.

"Hey, Chandler, can you please go play with your dolls upstairs?" Riley asked.

"No," Chandler sassily replied. "But I'll play with my stuffed animals," she continued as she took off toward the stairs.

"Wow," said Riley. "Lotta attitude."

"Probably not the best time for a joke, Riley," Lila said sternly.

"I know, I know. Lila, I'm sorry," Riley replied.

"You have two minutes to explain or get out. The past year has already been hard enough, and I don't know what kind of shady activities you're involved in, but I don't want any part of them and —"

"Lila," Riley interrupted, "Please stop talking and let me show you something." He opened up his left fist unveiling the scraps of brown paper.

Unamused, Lila motioned for him to go on.

He walked inside and made his way to the dining room. He began to place the pieces on the large, wooden table and aligned them for Lila to read.

"Let me put him down and grab you some clothes while you do that. You must be freezing," Lila said as she made her way to the living room to set Warren down in his rocker and then headed up the stairs.

She came back down with sweatpants and a long sleeve shirt for Riley.

"You grabbed my favorite?" Riley asked in disbelief as she tossed him a maroon shirt that read "Forest Trails High School Track and Field." It was the shirt he was wearing the day his dad passed away.

"Of course," Lila said as she began to study the puzzle Riley had laid out on the table.

Lila had always been very independent and strong-willed but over the years, Riley had changed her. She greatly lacked trust because of her parent's divorce but Riley was different. She whole-heartedly believed everything he said and wanted nothing more than to trust him.

"Is this real, Riley?" Lila asked. "I need to know that this is real," she insisted.

"Lila, I barely know what this is, but I do know that it's real and I know more than anything that I need your help to figure it out," Riley replied.

"Riley, look me in the eyes," she demanded. "What are you doing here? Did you escape from prison?"

"No… Well, I guess, yes," He stuttered. "I don't know, Lila. I traveled here somehow using silica gel."

"What is silica gel?" She asked annoyed.

"You know those weird little packets you get inside shoe boxes and things? The white ones that you shouldn't open. That's silica gel," he explained.

"You're telling me that you really traveled here using one of those little packets?" She asked, "You honestly want me to believe that?"

"Yes, Lila," he replied. "I don't know much about how this works, but I am learning and the guard at Nadirehs is helping me. All I know is I hold it and I come here and when I fall asleep, I wake up back in prison. Other than that, this poem and you are all I have, and I need you. Lila, I need you to save me and save our family," Riley begged.

"Riley, I need you to look me in the eyes," she said.

Riley stared deep into her ever-changing eyes. They were always shifting colors based on the clothing she was wearing, and her hunter green shirt made them a sparkling green.

"Did you do it?" She asked.

"Lila, I swear to you, I didn't do it," he said. "I didn't do it and I don't know who did."

Before he could blink Lila flung her arms around him and squeezed him tight. Riley lifted his arms and held her close.

"I've missed you so much," Lila cried.

"I've missed you, too," Riley responded. "So, so, so much. It's been the worst year of my life, Lila. I just don't know what to do. I've felt so defeated and now this magic, I mean what is this? Can I really be set free?"

"If it's at all possible, Riley, we'll make it happen," Lila said as she pulled away from his hug and looked him in the eyes.

"You're still so handsome," she said smiling.

"And you're still the most beautiful girl in the world," Riley replied.

"Well, you probably haven't seen much competition lately," Lila said with a wink. "But enough chit chat, let's get you home for good," she grabbed Riley's hand and led him to the couch in the living room.

"Okay, Riley Mines, let me hear your theories. You've been in prison for a while now with nothing to do, so I know you have a lot of them."

"Where do I even begin?" Riley asked. "Let's see, I guess I'll just start at the beginning and try to talk this through," he rambled on. "Okay, well, in all honesty the airport is a total blur. After they tased me I was so lost and I slightly remember them taking me to a room to be questioned but I don't remember what they asked me and all I ever said was 'I had no idea what they were talking about' and I swear, next thing I knew I was on the island with no way to contact anyone or explain myself."

Lila asked, "Did they show you the bomb or anything on your shoe? How did you not know it was there?"

"I think they did briefly, but I couldn't even tell. It was so small, and I didn't know what they were talking about," Riley said. "I also never wore those shoes… the only reason I even brought them on the trip was for Kyle."

CHAPTER SEVENTEEN

"Conway, come on! We're going to miss the flight," James shouted as he ran through the Miami Airport.

"We'll be fine," Conway over-confidently shouted back as he ran behind him.

"Rebecca is gonna kill us," James rumbled, not loud enough for Conway to hear.

The two of them ran until they finally reached their departure gate, J15, to find Rebecca calmly sitting with her legs crossed, sipping an iced vanilla latte and flipping through a magazine.

Hearing James' huffing, she looked up and gave them a disappointed look. She pointed to the watch on her left wrist and said, "You're late."

James' looked around, confused because no one was boarding.

"Is it delayed?" He asked.

"No," she replied.

"What time is the flight?" James asked.

"1:45," she replied.

"You told us it was one!" Conway complained.

"And look at the time…" Rebecca looked down and tapped her watch. "1:05… did you really think I was going to trust you two idiots to make it on time?"

"This is stupid," Conway muttered as he turned to walk away. "I'm going to get some food."

James laughed.

"It wasn't me! He was thirty minutes late picking me up."

"Suuure," teased Rebecca.

"Are you excited?" asked James.

"Yeah, I think so. I just have no idea what we're going to find. What are you expecting?" She replied.

"I really don't know," James continued. "From everything I've uncovered so far, there are a couple of top suspects on my radar."

"Do share," prompted Rebecca.

"My number two prospect is Benjie Mendoza. The Mendoza family runs the island and they have for nearly forty years. They essentially came with the island when Alexa purchased it. I really have no reason to believe he did it, except for the fact that something felt off about him when I was there. You know how you sometimes get weird feelings about people?"

"Yeah, I know what you mean, but what would be his motive?" Rebecca questioned.

"I've wondered that, and I don't think anything toward Riley. I think he would have had to have been bribed by someone else," James said.

"Like who?" pried Rebecca.

"I have no clue, hence the reason we're going to New York to find out more," said James.

Rebecca nodded, "Fair enough," she said, "So who's your number one prospect?"

"Alright, so this is where it gets interesting," James paused. "I think it could have been his brother."

"His brother?!" Conway exclaimed as he returned from his lunch trip with a soft pretzel in hand.

"Conway, can you ever be a little quiet?" Rebecca asked irritated. "Go on," she encouraged James.

"Well, we know he was on the island vacationing with them the whole time and he obviously had easy access to Riley's belongings. So, I did a little digging and when you look at their pasts, he definitely could have had motives. Shortly after their dad's death, Riley up and moved across the country and left Kyle alone with his mom. Kyle graduated high school but never left California and has lived with his mom ever since. Of course, he takes care of her and the property but when a twenty-eight-year-old man still lives alone with his mother, it's something you have to wonder about and take into consideration."

"Does he have any sort of record or past marks?" Rebecca asked.

"He was involved in a drunk driving car accident a few years back but other than that... nothing," responded James.

"Hmm, very interesting," said Rebecca. "I bet it's the island guy."

"I bet it was actually Riley and we're all wasting our time," added Conway.

The intercom interrupted, "We're going to start the boarding process for flight 3522 to JFK. Now boarding group one."

"What group are we?" Conway asked.

"Three," replied Rebecca.

"Ugh," Conway rolled his eyes. "You couldn't have gotten us priority, James?"

James rolled his eyes.

The three of them waited until their group was called and boarded the plane. Conway slept almost the entire the flight while Rebecca read a novel and James researched more about the case on his computer.

They arrived in New York without a hiccup and soon found themselves standing outside of a red-brick townhome.

James looked at his notes and proclaimed, "502 E Polk Ave. This is it."

"Perfect, so, what do we do now?" Asked Conway.

"We knock on the door and see who's there, I guess," said James.

"You guess?" Asked Conway. "We flew all the way to New York, and you didn't think about this part?"

Ignoring the comment, James began walking up the steps, with Rebecca and Conway behind. He rang the doorbell and gave the door a couple of knocks.

"Who the heck is that?" Asked Lila, terrified.

"I don't have a clue," said Riley.

"Answer it," she said.

"I'm sorry. You want the convict who's currently a prison escapee to answer the door?" He replied rhetorically.

Lila's heart felt like it was beating out of her chest, she gulped and replied, "Okay."

She got up and starting walking toward the door. On her way, James knocked again and said, "It's the police, open up!"

"Oh my gosh," Lila whispered in panic as she turned back to Riley for support, but he was nowhere to be seen.

"What are you doing?" Asked Conway, "You're playing the police card already?"

"How else would they let us in?" Rebecca said.

Lila opened the door and suppressed her nerves.

"Hi, officers," she said with a smile, "How can I help you?"

"Hi, there. We're with the Wotila County Police Department and we came here today to ask you a few questions about your husband, Riley Mines."

"I'm not sure that I can really be of any help to you officers. He's been in jail for over a year now and there's not much I know besides that," Lila explained.

"Well… do you mind if we come in and see if you have

any information that could be useful?" James asked. "We came all the way from Florida this morning and we'd greatly appreciate it."

"Umm, sure. Come in," Lila opened the door further and showed the three of them to the living room. "Would you like anything to drink? Coffee? Tea?"

"I would love a water," said Rebecca.

"Coffee would be great," said Conway.

"Same for me, please," added James.

"I'll be right back," Lila turned to walk to the kitchen.

She turned on the espresso machine and grabbed a glass from the cabinet. She closed the door, turned and dropped the glass. It shattered as it hit the floor.

"Everything all right in there?" James called.

"Yes, everything is fine. Thanks," Lila called back. "Geez, Riley. You shouldn't scare me like that," she whispered.

"Sorry, babe. I've got to get out of here and I wanted to say goodbye," he said.

"I don't know what to do, Riley. I'm so nervous," she replied.

"It's going to be alright. Just tell them what you know. Maybe they can help us?" He stated.

"Or maybe they know you're out of prison," she retorted.

"Don't overthink it," he pleaded. "Do we have any melatonin? I've got to go to sleep fast. I don't know when I'll be back but please know I will be."

"It's in the middle drawer between our sinks in the master bath. Purple bottle. You can't miss it," she said.

Riley grabbed her arms and pulled her in for a hug. He rubbed her hair and whispered, "I love you, Lila."

"I love you, too," she replied.

He kissed her on the forehead and left.

Lila cleaned up the glass and prepared the drinks. She made

her way back to the kitchen and apologized, "Sorry, about that commotion. I'm such a klutz sometimes and I dropped a glass."

She sat down on the rustic, brown leather chair and half laid the fuzzy white blanket on her lap. She held her coffee cup with both her hands to soothe her.

The officers sat across the room, spread out on the large white sectional.

"Sorry to barge in on you like this today, Mrs. Mines," James said. "But we have reason to believe there's been suspicious activity when it comes to Mr. Mines' case."

Lila nervously swallowed, thinking of Riley's escapes from Nadirehs.

"This is it," she thought. "I'm now an accomplice and our lives are over. What am I going to do with the kids? I've ruined them. This is horrible. How could I be such a terrible moth-"

"Mrs. Mines, are you alright?" James asked.

Lila didn't realize she'd zoned out.

"Yes, sorry. I'm fine." She managed to get out the words, "What do you mean suspicious activity?"

Her heart was pounding, and she could barely breathe as images of Chandler and Warren flashed through her mind.

"You see, we're not entirely convinced that Riley," James paused. "Well, that Riley knowingly committed the crime."

CHAPTER EIGHTEEN

Riley opened his eyes to the hanging blue light with thoughts immediately flooding his mind.

"Is Lila okay? What about Warren and Chandler? Why were the police there? They couldn't possibly know I'd escaped, and even if they did, they couldn't have tracked me there that quickly. I've got to get back to Lila," he thought.

Riley got up and made his way to the wall where he'd been keeping the running tally of his prison days. He looked out the window and figured it was about 7 a.m., based on the sunrise. He added a tally for the previous day and walked to wall across the room.

"One," he whispered to himself as he drew a black tally on a new wall to keep track of the five trips he'd been given. Riley's mind was filled with unpleasant uncertainties. He knew he was innocent but after more than a year in prison, he had no idea who was guilty.

"I really need Aus," he thought.

He paced the room for what could have been hours, playing out every possible scenario poor Lila could have gone through.

"What did they question her about? Maybe they pressured her into sharing past information about me? Or maybe they questioned Chandler? Had they been there before, and I just didn't know? What if they took her to prison for being an accomplice? No, they wouldn't have done that and if they wanted to do that, they would have done it when it happened, not now. Where did they say they were from again?" He wondered in frustration, "Ugh, I could barely hear."

Riley was exhausted from his lack of sleep and racing thoughts. He sat down on his cold bed and didn't remember falling asleep when he awoke to Aus calling out down the hall, "Room service! Get it while it's hot!"

He was drowsy as he walked to the cell door to see Aus' smiling face. He was happy to see that his eye was healing well, and the swelling had gone down.

"Hi, buddy," Aus said, "How's it going?"

Desperate, Riley couldn't handle small talk.

"Aus, I need answers," he demanded.

"Well, that's great to hear," Aus said loud enough for anyone within ear shot. Then, he reached into Riley's cell and gripped his orange jumpsuit. He pulled Riley in, his face smooshed between the bars and said, "Riley, you have to keep quiet. Don't speak another word without my permission. If anyone would hear you, we'd be done for. I'll be back at midnight."

Aus let go of Riley and he gasped for air. Riley nodded as Aus handed him his tray of food.

He continued down the hall like nothing had happened and called, "Room service! Get it while it's hot!"

Riley took his food tray and went to sit on his bed. He opened it up to find a small piece of chicken, a side of sweet corn and a pile of chunky mashed potatoes.

For the first time since he'd been at Nadirehs, Riley was hungry. His stomach felt completely empty as he smelled the aroma of the corn and potatoes, paired with a scent of hope. He didn't know what Aus would tell him later, but he couldn't wait to find out.

"Four more trips," Riley thought, "Four more trips."

Riley tried to pass the time without driving himself mad. He paced the room, looked out the window to see if he could make out the shoreline, paced some more, tried to lie down for a while, realized he couldn't sleep and got up to do it all over again.

Like any situation, when waiting feels like an eternity, the time finally came, and Riley heard footsteps coming down the hall of the otherwise quiet prison.

He was sitting on his bed and decided to wait there for Aus to ensure he didn't cause any riffs or upset him.

He heard the keys jingling at the cell door and his heart was racing in anticipation for the answers he hoped to receive.

"Evening, Riley," Aus said as he made his way to the chair in the corner of Riley's room. To Riley's surprise, Aus wasn't in his normal, Hawaiian uniform. He was wearing a plain, black t-shirt with dark denim jeans and his long, brown hair was especially frizzy from the island humidity. It was dark in the room with the only light coming from the single bulb in the hanging blue light, but even in the dark and behind Aus' glasses, Riley could tell his eye was still outlined with shades of black and blue.

He sat down and looked at Riley sympathetically.

"I'm sorry for all of the sneaking around and mixed messages," he paused. "Things are very complicated."

"It's alright," replied Riley. "Obviously, a lot has happened, and I don't really know what's going on and I know you're the only person who can help me understand at this point and you've only been around sporadically," he complained.

"I know, I know, Riley," Aus said with frustration. "But you have to understand we're dealing with some very dangerous men here."

Confused, Riley asked, "Men? What men?"

Aus paused and looked at the ground. After a few seconds,

he looked back up at Riley intently and said, "The Desiccant Keepers."

Riley stared back, waiting for more.

Aus continued, "They administer the rules and keep control over all of the uses of silica gel to ensure it's only used for good. Remember how I told you the gel was first used in World War I to absorb vapors and gases in gas mask canisters?"

Riley nodded.

"Okay, well, fast forward to World War II. It's 1942 and the U.S. makes penicillin that successfully treats patients for blood poisoning for the first time. Penicillin becomes essential to the war and saving soldiers' lives and silica gel becomes indispensable in its ability to keep penicillin dry."

"I never really knew what it was used for," Riley added.

"Not many people do," said Aus. "So, it's June 1944, just after the Battle of Normandy. A young U.S. Soldier, Robert Wilkinson, finds himself in a hospital in England being treated for an execrable gunshot wound in his right arm. He's lying on the hospital bed one afternoon when he turns his head and spots a packet on the floor. He doesn't know what it is but with all his might, he reaches down and picks it up because he's interested in anything that could possibly distract him. He holds it in his left hand and kind of flips it around and after a while, he's left just holding it in his fist. He feels it getting hot but before he can think too much about it, he's finds himself standing outside of his home in Grayle, Pennsylvania, with only black boxers on I might add, as I'm sure you've figured out," Aus laughed.

Riley was too focused to smile.

Aus' face turned serious again and he continued, "He thinks it's a dream, but he looks down and his arm is still wrapped from the wound and the throbbing is undeniable. He goes to the front door and knocks. To his surprise, his mother-in-law answers and is shocked and relieved to see him. She welcomes him in and quickly leads him to the bedroom where his wife is very ill. She's been bedridden for weeks and the doctor predicts she only has a few days left to live. Fearing the end of both their lives, the two laid together and said their goodbyes. They fell asleep and when Wilkinson awoke, he was back in the hospital room in England. But, like I'm sure you also experienced, he knew it hadn't been a dream."

Aus paused again, "Remember how I told you that the magic of silica gel only works for those who need it?"

Riley nodded.

"Well, that isn't entirely true, Aus sighed. "You see, silica gel works to take people exactly where they think they need to be. Emphasis on *think*. In your case, you know your family needs your help, so your thoughts are naturally focused there. That's why the gel took you home. But the truth is, if you can learn to manipulate your mind and think hard enough about something or somewhere, it's possible the gel can take you... well, anywhere really," Aus trailed off.

"That's amazing!" Riley exclaimed.

"No, Riley, it's not! I shouldn't have said anything," Aus replied harshly. "The gel is an incredible asset but only when it's used for good. And that's why the Desiccant Keepers are in place.

Riley stared at Aus, again waiting for him to continue.

"You see, shortly after Wilkinson returned to the hospital from his trip home, he made friends with a man named Lawrence Bryant, who'd been drafted into the war only three months prior. At twenty-three years old, Bryant was being treated for a pretty severe gunshot wound in his lower abdomen and Wilkinson believed he wouldn't make it much longer. He decided to share his secret with Bryant, in hopes it would work for him as well and he'd get one trip home to see his family before he died. The gel worked. Bryant successfully made the trip home one day to find out his wife was expecting. Wilkinson had never felt the need to use the silica gel again for travel because he knew he'd lost the love of his life and he had no reason to go back home again. However, he soon realized that Bryant didn't feel the same. Bryant became obsessed with going home and his determination to live increased dramatically. Against all odds, Bryant healed and couldn't help but tell others about his secret travels home. In the small hospital, word spread quickly and after only a couple of days, five of the ten men had successfully taken trips home."

Aus was getting worked up, "It was then that Wilkinson realized that the magic didn't work for everyone. He studied the stories each man shared when they returned back home, and they all had something in common: something monumental was happening in their lives. Whether it was a dying loved one or a newborn child, the gel only worked for those who had a reason."

"Well, that sounds like a good thing," Riley commented.

"Of course, it does. And truly, it was and still is a good thing. But, it's unfortunate that like anything else in this life, a few bad apples can spoil the whole bunch. You see, things didn't get out of hand when the secret spread, and soldiers were using the gel often to go home. It got out of hand when…" Aus paused, visibly upset. "When Blake Towns manipulated the gel for the first time."

Riley was now on the edge of his bed, leaning in anxiously to hear the rest of the story.

"Blake, or BT for short, was one of the unsuccessful soldiers in the small hospital. He had tried numerous times but was never able to travel home. Of course, sad as it is, he had no one to go home to. His parents had died in a car accident when he was only fifteen and his grandmother had taken care of him since. His grandma had died of old age about two years prior and though BT hadn't been drafted, he decided to enlist in the war. He quickly realized he'd made a mistake and he wasn't cut out for battle. He was lonely and depressed and wanted nothing more than to be done with the war, even if it meant dying instead of going home. His depression took a sharp turn for the worst when he heard about others making trips home. He tried day in and day out to hold the gel and go anywhere. His depressed mind had gotten stuck on childhood memories and he constantly replayed experiences he'd had as a kid. From bullies on the playground to teachers he hadn't liked, his anger stretched across all areas of his life. One day, he was fixated on memories from the day he'd decided to enlist. He'd been living in Chicago in a tiny apartment with a friend from high school. His roommate woke up with an incredible headache from the party he'd gone to the night before, so BT decided to walk to the convenience store to grab him some medicine. It was on his way to the store that BT started noticing the recruitment signs for the war. He hadn't thought about enlisting before, but he was lonely and doing nothing with his life, so he started to consider enlisting. He picked up the medicine for his friend and when he got back, he asked him what he thought about it. His friend, still slightly buzzed from the night before, said, 'the more men we got behind us, the better we are,' and BT decided to enlist that same day. During his nearly two years of service, BT replayed that terrible day over and over again in his mind. 'Why'd he let me go? Why didn't he tell me not to do it? Why was he so drunk and stupid all of the time?' he'd ask himself. In his hospital bed, as he once again replayed this vivid day, he gripped a silica gel packet in anger and opened his eyes, shocked to be standing in his Chicago apartment. He saw his roommate, unsurprisingly passed out drunk, lying on the kitchen floor and without thinking, he gripped his throat and strangled him. He looked at his lifeless friend with mixed emotions of shock and sickening pride."

Aus paused again, "Are you keeping up?"

"I think so," Riley replied.

Aus nodded in acknowledgment and went on, "Alright, back to the hospital we go. Bryant had an incredible gift of making friends with anyone and earning their trust. He and BT had flown overseas on the same flight together and when BT checked into the hospital, Bryant had been happy to see his familiar face again. He knew BT was extremely depressed and had been angry since the gel didn't work for him but the day after BT traveled home, Bryant knew something was different. He prodded him, trying to figure out what had happened, until he finally broke him. BT exploded about his trip home to his roommate, and confessed he was overwhelmed by what he'd done. He didn't know for sure if it was real or a dream. Bryant knew it was real but told BT not to worry and convinced him it was only a dream. In fear, knowing it was his fault things had gotten so out of hand, Bryant returned to Wilkinson for help. The two then understood the true power of the gel and knew it needed to be controlled. With only a small population exposed, they knew they needed to rein things in and assume full control as soon as possible. As I already mentioned, ten men had been in the hospital and tried the gel, including Wilkinson and Bryant. Of the other eight men, four had died shortly after their trips home and they spoke with the other three and recruited them to help control the magic. Together they formed the Desiccant Keepers."

"That's only seven," said Riley.

"I know," replied Aus.

"So, what happened? What are we dealing with?" Riley

asked anxiously.

"They never got to talk to BT. After Bryant spoke with Wilkinson, he went back to BT's room and he was gone, not a trace left behind. They obsessively looked for years trying to find him but eventually, considered it a hopeless cause and decided they needed to shift their focus on controlling the use of the gel by everyone, rather than finding one man to stop."

"They just let him go!? After Bryant knew he killed the guy? Did they ever hear anything else about him?" Riley was shocked.

"Over the years, they'd heard about a few sporadic crimes that went unsolved, all with potential ties to BT. They knew he was out there but with such power to manipulate the gel and disappear, they couldn't find him," Aus explained.

The two sat silently for a few moments. Riley had nothing to add as he processed the overwhelming information.

Finally, Aus started again, "As you've probably calculated by now, the men who started the Desiccant Keepers are no longer alive. Well, all except for one but he's ninety-six now and is no longer serving. The board spots have been passed down through generations and it's currently run by mostly grandsons of the original members."

"Are you on the board?" Riley asked.

"I'm not... But my uncle is," answered Aus. "Where exactly did I leave off with my shoe story again?"

"You said your sister called and left a voicemail," Riley answered.

"Ahh, yes! So, she left the voicemail and before I could call her back, my uncle knocked on my door. I was surprised to see him because it was a Tuesday afternoon and he owned the local sporting-goods store, so he was almost always working. He obviously knew I purchased the shoes the day before because I couldn't have afforded them without the family discount, which was one-hundred percent off," Aus smiled. "His plan was to stop by and tell me about the silica gel because he and the board agreed that I deserved it to visit my struggling family. He was shocked, and ultimately concerned, that I'd already figured it out. You see, the board doesn't like it when they don't have total control." He pointed to his face, "Hence, the black eye. I didn't get full permission to share the secret with you and they punished me for that. It was my own fault, I should have waited to tell you, but I knew they'd approve it and I didn't want to wait any longer. I've wanted to help you since the day you arrived. In fact, that's when I made the original request."

"It takes that long to get approval?" Riley asked.

"It didn't used to," replied Aus. "But lately, there's been a rise is suspicious activity and untraceable crimes. Although BT has surely passed away by now, the board is concerned and more uptight than they've ever been."

CHAPTER NINETEEN

It was a perfect, fall day a few years back and the Mines' family was gathered together in California.

Chandler was only four months old at the time and it was the first trip Riley and Lila had taken since she had been born. They were nervous new parents, but Jane had insisted they come home to celebrate Thanksgiving and even promised to make Riley his favorite banana cream pie.

Riley and Lila were chatting in the kitchen when they heard the front door open and an eruption of childlike giggles.

"And cue late arrival," said Riley.

"Oh, stop it," replied Lila as she made her way toward the front hall.

"Hi!" She exclaimed, "How are you two? Keagan, you look amazing, as always," she said as she gave her an inviting hug. "And Kyle, you're so grown up," she said jokingly, pinching his cheeks.

Riley came around the corner.

"Nice of you to show up," he smirked.

Without saying a word, Kyle ran to tackle Riley and the two began to wrestle.

"I guess boys will be boys," Keagan laughed.

After they were done messing around, Riley gave Keagan a hug and said, "It's good to see you."

"Hey, didn't you guys like make a baby or something? Did you forget her?" Kyle sarcastically asked.

"We did… And, we're pretty good at it, I might add. We practice a lot," Riley replied with a wink.

"Oh, stop it," Lila said, slightly embarrassed. "Jane is rocking Chandler by the pool. Come on, let's go out back."

They walked out the large, glass doors leading to the patio.

"Hello, hello!" Jane exclaimed as she got up from the rocking chair. "How is everyone?" She asked, not leaving space for anyone to answer. "I am just so wonderful! All of my favorite people in one place. This is just what I wanted."

"We're happy to be here," Lila responded. "Can I get anyone anything to drink?"

"I'll take a rum and coke," said Kyle.

"Eggnog for me, please," added Riley.

"You have eggnog?" Kyle excitedly asked.

"Of course, I have eggnog," said Jane. "What's Thanksgiving without eggnog?"

"Eggnog, please," Kyle smiled.

"Same for me," added Keagan.

"I'll help you, Lila," Jane replied. "I'm sure Keagan wouldn't mind holding Chandler for a little while."

"Well… if you insist," Keagan beamed as she reached for Chandler.

They walked inside and Jane began getting out the glasses. She set them down and stopped in her tracks as she stared admiringly out the window.

Seeing Jane, Lila said, "I like the two of them together. How long has it been now?"

"Oh, aren't they just perfect for each other?" Jane agreed. "Well, let's see, they started dating when Kyle was a junior in high school, a few months after Warren had passed away. Keagan was truly a lifesaver during that time. Especially, after Riley went off to college. They parted ways when she went to college two years later, but Kyle never dated anyone else. She was headed to Colorado State and he could have gone with her, but he didn't want to leave me alone. After she graduated, she moved back to the area and she was still single. It didn't take long for the two of them to find each other again. Especially, with the help of two meddling mothers," she laughed.

"Did you set them up?" Lila asked.

"Only kind of," Jane smiled defensively. "They've always been perfect for each other and Alexa and I were both heartbroken when they parted ways for college. We always felt they'd end up together, so we just helped push them that direction. I mean a simple summer party was all it took for them to catch up and spark the fire again."

"You dog," Lila said accusingly.

"Seems like it worked out pretty well," Jane said, once again gazing out the window.

"I'd have to agree," said Lila. Lila was an only child, so Keagan was like the sister she never had. They didn't spend much time together, since they didn't live close, but Lila always loved seeing her. "Do you think he'll pop the question soon?"

"Unfortunately, not. I think it will be another year. Keagan has two years left of graduate school and she doesn't want to get married until she's done," Jane replied.

"I guess that makes sense," Lila said. "I can't wait for their wedding!"

"Me either," agreed Jane. She grabbed the tray, now full of drinks, and the two of them headed back outside.

CHAPTER TWENTY

"What do you mean you're not sure if Riley knowingly committed the crime?" Lila asked.

"I know this is shocking," said James. "It's just… I have been researching Riley's case for a while now and I can't get the pieces to connect. Great job, great family, great everything really and then an airport bomb stunt, out of the blue, with absolutely no motives? It doesn't add up."

Lila nodded, suddenly able to breathe knowing they weren't there for Riley.

Sensing Lila's concern, Rebecca started to comfort her. "I know it's a lot to take in, Mrs. Mines. We are here because we want to help you get Riley home. Any information you could share that might help us do that would be greatly appreciated."

"I don't even know where to start," Lila said. "No one has ever asked me anything about it."

"What do you mean?" Conway asked.

"After Riley was arrested, no one asked me anything about him or about the case. I was told he had a trial, but it was kept a secret and I had no chance to be a character witness for him. Everything happened so fast. One day, we're coming home from a family vacation and the next, I'm opening a letter in the mail informing me that he'd be held at Nadirehs for twenty-five years with no chance of parole. Riley has always been my go-to and really, my only friend. With him gone, I had no one to turn to and everyone was scared to ask, so I really haven't talked to anyone about the case at all."

"You're telling me that you weren't *ever* questioned about this case or the events at the airport?" Conway asked.

"That's correct," Lila replied.

"Well, shit," Conway whispered to himself and shook his head. He looked up at James, "Thanks for the invite, Wilde! This case just became very interesting."

"It did indeed," Rebecca agreed.

"What do you mean?" Asked Lila.

James responded, "Mrs. Mines, it is extremely unusual to not question witnesses or family members about an event. And by extremely unusual, I mean it's almost unheard of. The fact that you were never questioned validates all of my concerns and red flags. Something fishy is happening here and there are certainly some games being played."

Lila's eyes began to well, "I… I… I don't know what any of this means," she said, hardly able to breathe.

"I know, Mrs. Mines," said James. "That's why we're here. We need your help. We want to get Riley back."

Lila agreed, "I want that more than anything."

"Okay, then, now that we're all on the same page, let's get down to business," said James. "Could you start by giving us the backstory of the family vacation? Why'd you choose to go to the island, how did you get there, etcetera?"

Lila took a deep breath and thought back to the events leading up to the vacation. She had to think hard because it was a time period she'd worked to forget. For months after Riley's arrest, the thoughts kept her up at night, until finally, one day, she forgot to think about them. Occasionally, a thought would pop in here or there, but she learned how funny life is in the way it seems like some events are the most important thing in the whole world, until one day, you just forget to think about them, and move on.

"Riley's mom, Jane, planned the family vacation for us. Riley's dad died when he was eighteen and since then, Jane held onto her boys pretty tightly. She made it a priority that we all get together for every holiday," Lila paused. "Sorry, am I sharing too many details?" She asked politely.

"Not at all!" James insisted, "In fact, you can't possibly share too many details. This is exactly what we need."

"Okay," she said continuing. "We normally go back to California to celebrate Thanksgiving and Christmas."

Rebecca interrupted, "One trip to celebrate both or two separate trips?"

"Two separate trips," Lila clarified. "We always celebrate Thanksgiving on Thanksgiving Day and Christmas changes because we like to be at home for Chandler, so we normally go closer to New Year's. This trip was out of the ordinary. Jane loves her home around the holidays more than anything and she's always the picture-perfect host. From the decorations, to the food, her home always looks like it should be in a magazine."

Lila paused, her face turning somber. "Jane decided to change the scenery for Christmas for everyone's sake. Although, truthfully, I'm not sure why she chose the island. You see, the island is owned by the Mines' family friends and growing up they would all vacation there together. But, after Warren died, they pretty much stopped going. Jane had been looking for a place to go for Christmas and her friend, Alexa, suggested going to the island again."

Conway interrupted, "Mrs. Mines, you're beginning to ramble a bit. We don't know who all of these people are so we might need some more explanation. Who is Warren?"

"Did you even read the information I sent you, you idiot?" James retorted. "Sorry, about that, Mrs. Mines, most of us have done our research and we know who the family members are and who owns the island…" James shot Conway a look across the room.

"You can really call me Lila. Mrs. Mines sounds too formal," she replied.

"Please continue… Lila," James said with a smile.

"Okay, where was I?" She asked.

"Alexa suggested the island to Jane," prompted Rebecca.

"Oh, yes. Jane wasn't crazy about going to the island, but she *really* didn't want to stay at home and she also didn't want to go somewhere new because she is very particular, and she wanted everyone to have a good time. She knew the island would be especially tough for Kyle, but I guess he said it would be fine. See, these are the parts of the story I am not totally sure about because Kyle is not very forthcoming with information and I didn't get to talk to Riley as much as I wanted and Keagan was always my go to for information and it's been a really hard two years. Wow… That's hard to believe. Anyway… I don't know, maybe we shouldn't have gone to the island. Kyle seemed to be the best he'd been, but it was still a lot and –"

"Sorry to interrupt," said James. "But even I don't know who Keagan is?"

"Oh," Lila said, looking to the floor. "Well, Keagan… um… Keagan Monarch… she is, or umm… well, was Kyle's fiancé," she said through tears.

The officers didn't know what to say.

"I'm sorry," she said. "I just haven't talked about it in a while."

Rebecca got up and moved across the room to console her. "It's okay," she said. "It's understandable you'd feel this way and you've had a really hard year." She put her arm around Lila and rubbed her shoulder.

Lila enjoyed the comforting. After all, she'd felt completely alone for a year.

"So, let me get everything straight here," said Conway. "Keagan's family owned the island and Keagan and Kyle were engaged, correct?"

Lila nodded.

"Did they date while they were growing up? How long were they engaged? Why did they break off the engagement?" He asked.

Rebecca shot him a look for his insensitivity, but he was confused and trying to put the pieces together.

Lila had stopped crying and began to gather her thoughts once again.

"I don't know all of the details, but I know they started dating when they were juniors in high school, soon after Warren died. They had grown up together and were always the best of friends but nothing romantic until then. Then, she went off to college and Kyle stayed home to take care of his mom. They were both still single when she came back from school and with two overprotective and meddling mothers, they ended up together again. They dated for like four more years, I think, before Kyle proposed. I'm not sure on all of my timelines but I do know that he proposed in September of 2019. Kyle set up a beautiful picnic on one of their favorite cliffs with candles, lights, rose petals, the whole shebang and after he proposed, we were all waiting at the Monarch's house to celebrate. They honestly were the perfect couple, and everyone was so glad Kyle had Keagan around. Everyone had worried about his mental health since his dad's death, but Keagan kept him in a good place. A couple of months after their engagement, they were driving home from a movie and got t-boned by a drunk driver. Keagan was in the passenger seat and... and... she never stood a chance," Lila said, crying once again.

"I'm so sorry, Lila. We had no idea," replied James.

"It's okay. I haven't spent much time talking about it and there's a lot going on right now. I'm a little emotionally drained," she admitted.

Warren, who had been sleeping in his rocker in the living room, suddenly awoke and started crying.

"He's hungry," said Lila. "I need to feed him. I also really need a break from this."

"That's fine. It's getting kind of late anyway," replied Rebecca. "Is there somewhere around here we could grab a bite to eat?"

"Yeah," answered Lila. "Your best bet is probably the sports bar around the corner. Take a right out the door and a left at the first street, it will be up on your right. They have pretty good food there. I'd recommend the barbecue wings."

"Thank you," said James. "We will get out of your hair for the night. Are you okay if we come back in the morning? Around 9?"

"That would be fine," Lila replied as she picked up Warren and walked to the front door to let them out.

CHAPTER
TWENTY-ONE

Riley was sitting on his bed, deep in thought, when he heard keys clanking around his cell door. Aus hadn't told him he was going to stop by but after their discussion the night before, and with time being of the essence, Riley half-expected secret midnight visits to become the norm.

Aus made his way inside and sat in his usual chair in the corner. "Okay, Riley," he said. "We've spent too much time talking about me and about the history of silica gel. I mean come on; I sound like a boring high school history teacher. We've got to pick up the pace and focus on you. We need to use your trips wisely. How many did they give you?" He asked.

"I assumed you knew," Riley said, confused. "They gave me five trips."

"Do you have the poem?" Asked Aus.

"No," replied Riley. "I took it with me on my last trip to show my wife and –"

"You what?" Aus asked, shocked.

"I took it with me to show my wife."

"How did you get it through with you?"

"I held it in my hand?" Riley responded, unsure of what Aus was trying to get at.

"Oh, uh, okay," he replied.

"Should I not have showed her?"

"No, don't worry about it. That's okay. If you show people you trust and you're using the gel for good, it's not a problem. What did she say?"

"She wanted to know if it was real and she wanted to know how I was coming home and most of all, she wanted to know if I did it."

"And, did you do it?" Aus asked.

"No, I didn't do it. I still barely know what *it* is. I have absolutely no idea why or how I'm here."

"Good, I didn't think so. Hopefully, we can fix that. To get five trips is pretty generous. Normally, the board only gives like three, so they must really see something here," said Aus.

"Oh," Riley said surprised, "I had no idea. I figured everyone was given five."

"Nope, this is pretty special," Aus said. "Tell me more about your visit."

Riley nodded, "When I arrived, I was standing outside of my home, in only black boxers, of course."

"Isn't that the strangest thing?" Aus laughed.

"Just to be clear, you think the strangest thing about using weird, magical gel that allows people in need to transport anywhere in the world, is the fact that you only have on underwear when you get there?" Riley asked sarcastically.

Aus giggled immaturely and asked, "What do you think girls arrive in?"

"You're stupid," Riley laughed.

Aus busted out laughing and Riley laughed harder. They could hardly control themselves.

"It's not even that funny," commented Riley but Aus could hardly breathe he was laughing so hard.

Finally, Aus said, "Okay, okay. Sorry, for the sidetrack. Sometimes, you need a good laugh," he paused. "Please continue."

"Agreed," Riley smiled. "So, I showed up outside and I knocked on the door and Lila answered. She let me in and gave me a chance to explain myself. I showed her the poem and she believed me. She wanted to know more details, so we sat down in the living room and she asked a couple of questions about the day I was arrested. We barely got to talking before we were interrupted by a knock on the door."

"From who?" Aus inquired.

"Police officers of some sort. I couldn't hear where they were from because I was hiding in the kitchen. I briefly talked with Lila and told her I had to go but they had planted themselves in the living room and she was stuck with them. I have no idea what they questioned her about. Do you think there's any way they could have known I escaped?"

Aus looked at Riley unimpressed, "Riley," he started, "There are obviously safeguards in place to make sure no one knows when you're traveling."

"Uhh, not obvious to me, I guess. What do you mean?" He asked.

"How do you think injured soldiers being cared for in a hospital could disappear for half days or more at a time and no one notice?"

"Come on, Aus. Sometimes, you've got to get to the point faster here, what do you mean?"

"It's a very complicated process and the Desiccant Keepers still aren't exactly sure how it works but in essence, when you take a trip with the gel, the people from where you leave temporarily forget that you exist."

"What?" Riley asked.

"I said it was complicated," Aus said. "It's for your protection. So that, when you up and leave one morning to take a trip home, and a guard walks by, they don't think 'Where's Riley?' No, they just don't think anything at all. They walk by your empty cell and to them, it's always been empty. And as soon as you're back, they walk past the same cell and recognize you."

"How can that be? That's insane," Riley said.

"Let's not get into semantics, Riley. The whole concept is insane. It's just important that we follow the rules and do our part to keep things on the down low."

"Hmm, so, ultimately what you're saying is that there's no way the officers could have been questioning Lila about my whereabouts?"

"Absolutely not," replied Aus.

"Then, why were they there?" Riley asked, raising his voice.

"Keep it down, buddy," Aus whispered. "I don't know why. Obviously, you're going to need to go back and find out."

"Okay, I'll go now. I would have gone already but I didn't have another packet," Riley said.

"I could give you one now but it's late and I'm guessing you're tired. The second you fall asleep; you'll wake back up here and trip number two will be over. Do you really want to waste that?" Aus questioned.

"Aus, I have to go. I'm so worried about her," said Riley.

"Lila is surely asleep right now," Aus replied.

"We have a three-and-a-half-month-old baby. She surely is not," Riley retorted.

"It's up to you," Aus said as he reached into his pocket and pulled out a silica gel packet.

"How does this work now? Do you just give me a packet whenever I want?" Riley asked.

"Pretty much," Aus answered. "Except that you have to wait 24-hours between each trip from the time you get back to the time you depart next."

"Easy enough," said Riley grabbing the packet from Aus. "Wait, so when I hold this packet and leave, you'll temporarily forget I exist?"

"No, I won't," said Aus. "It gets a little confusing. To be named a Desiccant Keeper, you have to serve on the board. Like I mentioned early, the board members have almost always been family. However, there have also been a few close friends who have been named Desiccant Keepers and a handful of honorary Keepers along the way."

"Honorary?" Riley asked, looking for further explanation.

"Yes, honorary. Occasionally, when a Contender, I'll get there in a second, does a great act of duty using silica gel or something like that, who knows the criteria, the board will honor them with a ceremonial induction as a Desiccant Keeper. Contenders are you and me. Once you use the silica gel, you enter the realm of a Contender and you're immune to the effects of the outside world. In other words, if someone you see uses the silica gel, you can literally watch them disappear before your eyes and you'll know they're gone."

"Have you ever seen a stranger use it?" Riley asked intrigued.

"Only once," said Aus. "I was at a restaurant in Dallas and I went to use the restroom. My friend had told me I had something in my teeth, so I went to check it out. I walked in and there was only one other man. I went to the restroom and walked out, only to remember I'd forgotten to check my teeth. I walked back in, no more than four seconds later, just in time to see a splash of water in the corner. When a Contender, or a Keeper for that matter, uses the gel, a small splash of water is left behind. It evaporates very quickly and almost always goes unseen, but it's a sure sign of silica gel use. I'm not sure why it happens. Maybe it has to do with the natural drying agents of the gel in real life or something but it's pretty amazing to watch it happen."

"This just keeps getting crazier and crazier," Riley said,

shaking his head. He gripped the gel in his right hand, looked at Aus and with a wink said, "Prepare to be amazed."

Water splashed in the center of the room and formed a small puddle, no more than a foot in diameter. Aus got up from his chair and stood over the water, watching it disappear in a matter of seconds.

"That kid really is something special," he whispered to himself, shaking his head in disbelief.

CHAPTER

TWENTY-TWO

"Alexa! Over here!" A camera man called as she strolled the red carpet at the premier of her newest movie, *Summer Daze*. Alexa donned a sheer black, floor-length evening gown. It had flowers of gold laced throughout that shimmered when the lights caught them just right. The cut was low in the front with an open back, but Alexa pulled it off well, in a way only a fifty-year-old woman who'd worked hard for everything she'd earned could have. Her silky brown hair shaped her thin face quite nicely in a half up do and laid just past her shoulders. Her physical features were flattering but more than anything her radiant personality made her a woman of infatuation for many.

She smiled to amuse the camera man and scanned the crowd for her family. "They were supposed to be here by now," she thought.

"Mom!" Keagan shouted from a crowd of paparazzi. "They won't let us in!"

Alexa rolled her eyes, "Ugh, this is so ridiculous," she thought. "One second," she replied, "I will get you in."

She quickly walked to the closest security guard and pointed to her daughter and Kyle.

"Will you please let them through?" She asked, "They're with me."

He went over to the crowd of men pushing to get the best

shot and made a path for them to join her on the red carpet. Keagan was wearing a lovely navy dress with long sleeves. The dress was tight at the top and came in at her waist to show off her slender figure.

Through her fake smile, Alexa mumbled, "You see, these things wouldn't happen if you would just ride here with me."

Keagan, also holding a forced camera smile, replied, "Yes but that would take away from our adventures!"

Since she was a kid, Keagan had always been a little wild. Being an only child to her wealthy parents, she always got exactly what she wanted and was rarely punished. Although many of her friends had gotten into drinking and drugs, Keagan had stayed on the straight and narrow. Compared to others her age, Keagan's adventures were far healthier and safer, so her parents tried not to complain too much, even when she drove them crazy.

Alexa turned to look at Kyle and studied his slim-fit black tux.

"You look lovely, Ky —" she paused as she caught a glimpse of his shoes. "Do you always have to wear those things?" She asked.

"Mrs. Monarch, come on. These are my Brays," he said motioning down to his feet. "They're my lucky shoes."

She shook her head and laughed, "I know, I know. Thank you for coming."

"Of course," he replied. "I wouldn't miss it for anything."

"Come on now, let's go inside," Alexa declared. She was a tough woman to say no to. She had built an acting career out of nothing and her presence on the screen was remarkable.

The three of them headed inside to find their seats. Alexa stopped to sign a few autographs while Keagan and Kyle giggled to themselves making snide comments about some of the stuck-up celebrities in attendance.

They sat down in the movie theatre and Alexa turned to them both, "Are you planning to join me at the after party?" She asked.

"I already told you no, Mom. You know we don't really like those things," Keagan replied.

"But Kyle, don't you want to go?" Alexa pleaded.

"Mrs. Monarch, you know I listen to the boss. Whatever she says, goes," he smiled looking at Keagan.

"Kids these days, don't know how to please parents anymore," Alexa said shaking her head.

"Oh, Mom, don't be so dramatic," Keagan said. "We will decide for sure after the movie. Just focus on enjoying your big night!"

The lights flickered, queuing everyone to take their seats for the start of the movie.

"Where is dad?" Keagan asked.

"Oh, you know your father at these things... I arrived with him an hour ago and haven't seen him since. Yack, yack, yack, always chitchatting away. God love him," she laughed.

"There he is," Kyle said pointing toward the front of the theatre. He was slowly making his way back to them, smiling and waving at everyone he passed like he was king of a small-town parade.

"I didn't know Dad was starring in this movie?" Keagan joked.

"Every day is a movie in your father's mind... and he's always the star," Alexa replied. "At least he's a handsome one," she added, smiling as Jay finally approached.

"Your bowtie is crooked," Alexa said as she reached out to fix it. Alexa and Jay had been married for twenty-four years but their love for each other was still burning strong.

Jay leaned into kiss Alexa, "Well, I guess I'm not perfect after all," he said, shrugging his shoulders with a wink.

"Could you please tell your daughter to join us for the after party?" Alexa asked.

"Alexa, darling, she's twenty-six years old, if she doesn't want to go to the party, she doesn't have to go," said Jay.

"Thanks, daddy!" Keagan sweetly replied.

The lights dimmed.

"We'll make the final decision after the movie," Alexa said. She didn't like it when things didn't go her way.

CHAPTER

TWENTY-THREE

"Mom! What the heck?" James yelled into the phone. "When I asked you about Alexa, you didn't think to tell me that her daughter died? Or that her daughter dated Kyle Mines? Don't you know I'm trying to work a case here?!"

"Oh, honey bear. Please, calm down," his mother replied. "I didn't know you needed information like that. How could I have known?"

"Momma, I'm sorry, I don't mean to be angry at you," he replied, lowering his voice. "It's just, I told you there was suspicion surrounding this the case and you didn't tell me anything important," he replied.

"Sorry, baby. I didn't want to make you upset," she said. "It's very sad. The way she died, you know, and I didn't want to put that on you."

"I'm a cop, Mom. That's exactly what I deal with every day. I need pertinent details like this to help me do my job. This new information is game changing for the case," James explained.

"Okay, okay, I get it. You just have to understand that sometimes you do these things," she replied.

"What things?" Asked James.

"You get really, really excited about things and build them up and then, when the time comes or reality hits, you're always really disappointed because it never lives up to your expectations. Like remember as a kid when every birthday you would get so excited because you'd convinced yourself that it was finally the year, we'd gotten you a puppy? And then, when we didn't get you a puppy, you were always devastated, even though you knew your dad was allergic to dogs?"

"I don't need a lecture right now, Mom. I'm just out here trying to do my job and I need any information you have," he replied annoyed.

"Well, I'm going to California tomorrow so I'll see what I can find out," she said.

"You're what?" James exclaimed, raising his voice again.

"I'm leaving for California tomorrow to visit Alexa," she said.

"You have got to be kidding me. You didn't think that that was important to share with me either?" He asked.

"I just shared it with you… didn't I? And there's no need for you to get caught up in crimes and crazy stuff like this," she said.

"Mom, I am a cop! This is my job. Please, please, whatever you do, get as much information as you can and bring it back for me. When will you be back?"

"A week from Saturday," she replied.

"Okay, we will get together then. Fly safe," James said.

"I will. Love you, honey bear," she said.

"Love you, too," James replied and hung up the phone. He was standing outside the restaurant and although snow began to fall, he was hot from the conversation.

He walked into the restaurant and found Rebecca and Conway in the back at a round booth too big for only three people. The quaint place was unsurprisingly empty on a Thursday afternoon.

He approached the table, "I don't even know what to say,"

James said.

"What did she say?" Asked Rebecca.

"Oh, she said she knew that Keagan had died and that she and Kyle had dated but she didn't want to 'upset me,'" he made air quotes, "With the news so she didn't tell me," he shook his head.

"Are you serious?" Conway asked.

"Yep, oh, and she's going to California to visit Alexa tomorrow," he rubbed his face in frustration and pulled his hair. "She's useless. For once, in all of my cases, I finally have someone with an in and she's completely useless."

"How did you end things with her?" Rebecca asked.

"I told her to get any information she could and that I'd like to talk when she gets back."

"When does she get back?" Rebecca asked.

"Next Saturday," he replied. "I figure we can gather as much information as possible from Lila here and then see what we can bring together." James was visibly frustrated.

"It's alright," Rebecca said, rubbing his arm. "You're doing the best you can and we're here to help."

"Gag me," Conway replied.

Rebecca rolled her eyes at him and looked back at James. "We've been here like what, two hours tops?" She asked, "And look at what we've uncovered already."

"But, what if I'm wrong... Again? I could lose my job... I could lose you your jobs... What an embarrassment I would be."

"If it makes you feel any better, you're already an embarrassment in my book," Conway added.

Rebecca shot Conway another look, and to her surprise, James genuinely laughed. "Ahh, you're right. Who cares what people think? I'm starving," he said, grabbing the menu and trying to move on from his brief meltdown.

"I think it's his brother," Conway added.

"You're on board with that theory now, too?" Rebecca asked shocked.

"Yeah, I think he has a motive. I mean, look at the facts. James is right about Riley up and leaving him after their dad died to take care of the house and their mom alone. Then, he has a really tough year and loses his fiancé. I'd be pretty mad at the world, if that were me, and if I wanted to take my anger out on someone, my brother who abandoned me would be a pretty good bet. Plus, he obviously had access to his shoes while they were on the island. I don't know… I'm just saying, that's what I think."

"Yes, but what about –" Rebecca started.

A beautiful, black waitress with flowing braids approached the table.

"Hello, how are you guys doing today?" She greeted. "Can I get you started with anything? Something to drink? Appetizers?"

"Could we please have waters all around, an order of nachos, barbeque wings with extra ranch, sweet potato fries and…" James hesitated as he scanned the menu and pointed to one more item, "And mozzarella sticks."

"Sounds good," she said as she scribbled on her notepad. "Will that be all?"

"I'll take a side salad, please," Rebecca added.

"I'll get that right in for you," she replied with a smile as she walked away.

"A salad? Really?" James said giving Rebecca a look of disapproval.

"Sorry, not all of us like to eat like twelve-year old boys," she laughed.

"I'm kind of with you, Conway," James shifted gears. "Kyle is definitely a top suspect after hearing about Keagan."

"But why would he want to lose yet another person he loved?" Rebecca asked. "Plus, I don't see how that would fit with the other huge piece of the puzzle."

"What's that?" Asked Conway.

"Don't you remember why we're here?"

James and Conway looked at each other, realizing Rebecca had a point.

"That's true," James admitted. "Still not really sure how that fits into the equation at all."

"Can I see that picture again?" Conway asked.

"Yeah," James said as he pulled out his phone and found the photo. "Here it is," he said, leaning closer and flipping his phone so they could all see it.

They studied the picture from the treehouse that displayed a pair of hunter green sneakers. The shoes had white soles and white laces with a distinct "B" logo on the side. The tongue of the right shoe was flipped up to display the handwritten word "Mines."

CHAPTER

TWENTY-FOUR

Lila looked at her watch as she put Warren down in his crib.

"8:50," she thought. "Ten minutes to gather yourself and get it together." She continued the pep talk in her head, "They're here to help you. Well, you're like 95% sure they're really here to help you. But, they're also strangers. And your husband is in prison. And he's teleporting to visit you. Oh my gosh," she thought. "My husband is teleporting to visit me. That's really a thought I'm having right now. I don't even know what's happening anymore."

She walked down the hallway toward the stairs and paused by the children's game room. Chandler was happily playing with her dolls.

"Hi, Chan!" Lila said, "What are you doing?"

"My dolls are going to a party!" She replied excitedly. "They're all dressed up and they're in line now, waiting to get in."

"Wow! It must be some party," Lila said.

"Yes, it's the biggest party of the year," Chandler explained.

Lila smiled; it was just the conversation she needed to calm her nerves for the next round of questioning.

"Hey, Chandler, look at me," she said. "Mom has some

friends coming over and we need some privacy downstairs, can you keep yourself entertained up here for a while?"

Chandler looked up, then back down at her dolls and nodded.

Just then, there was a knock on the door. Lila looked down at her watch.

"9 o'clock on the dot," she thought. "They're prompt."

"Coming," she hollered as she walked down the stairs. She opened the door and welcomed them in.

"Good Morning," said Lila.

"Morning," they replied.

"How was my dinner recommendation last night?" She asked once they'd all found their seats in the living room.

"Delicious," replied Rebecca. "We were all pretty hungry. Thank you for the suggestion."

"Good! I'm glad you liked it," Lila replied.

The four of them sat in silence for a few moments until James finally said, "We have a lot to get through, Lila. A lot of questions and concerns and we know it will be hard for you."

She nodded.

"Are you up for it?" He asked, "Truly, we just want to help you get Riley home."

"How can I know this is real?" She asked.

The three officers looked at each other and Rebecca and Conway nodded, as if they were cueing James to continue.

"Lila, we are here at the risk of losing our jobs," he paused. "Our boss told us to stop wasting time on this case because it's closed and he doesn't think there's anything special about it, but we really feel like something is off. The way everything happened in the airport and the fact that you were never questioned. There are a lot of questionable actions that have been taken involving this case and we want to make things right. What are we doing as police officers if we aren't protecting those who need to be protected? We really want to help you."

Lila half nodded, processing everything James had said. Her eyes looked glazed over but after a few seconds of nodding, the fearful gaze began to change to a look of hope.

"Do you really think you can get him home?" Lila asked.

"We believe he deserves to be home," James replied. "And we will do our best to get him here."

Rebecca and Conway nodded in agreement.

Now fully convinced, Lila asked, "Alrighty then, where do we begin?"

"I think it's safe to say that we are all under the impression that Riley was framed. We believe that someone planted the bomb in his shoe for some reason. Correct? Does everyone agree with that statement?"

Everyone nodded.

"So, I guess to start, we need to know if you feel there was anyone who could have been targeting Riley? Do you know of anyone he'd made enemies with or owed anything to?" James asked.

"Not in the slightest. I've known him almost eight years now and I've never heard anyone say a bad thing about him," she replied. "He honestly is the best man I've ever known and that's a common opinion about him, not a wife opinion."

"Okay," James said. "That's good to know. Shifting gears, a little, back to where we were before we left for dinner, or lunch, or whatever that was yesterday, you said the Mines family frequently visited the island growing up, right?"

"Yes," Lila replied. "They went with the Monarch's pretty often, I guess. Riley hadn't ever mentioned that before though. I only learned about those trips when we were on the island."

"Was that your first time there?" Conway asked.

"Yes," Lila replied.

"Did it surprise you that Riley hadn't mentioned his trips to the island before?" asked Rebecca.

"Uh, not really," responded Lila. "Sometimes, he didn't tell me about things because he'd had such a great childhood and mine wasn't great, so he tried to not make me feel bad. Other times, he avoided old stories because they reminded him of his dad, and he was sad about them. So, no, I would say I wasn't really surprised."

"Had he spoken much about the Monarch family to you before?" James asked.

"Oh, well, yes… of course! Their families are like best friends. I met the Monarchs very early on in our relationship. And then with Keagan and Kyle dating, I've spent a lot of time with them over the years."

"When did they start dating again?" James asked. By now, all three officers had their own note pads out and were writing down everything they thought necessary.

"Like I said yesterday, I don't know exactly," Lila said. "But probably around August 2015? About a year and a half or so after Riley and I met so that's my best guess."

"And since then, how much time would you say you've spent with the family?" James asked.

"With which family? Lila asked.

"The Monarchs," James clarified.

"I don't know… I mean we probably got together with them every time we went out to California. Maybe three times a year since I met Riley back in 2014? But not at all after Keagan died. Things got pretty tense."

"And you didn't know they used to vacation to the island together?" James asked.

"No, I didn't. I don't understand why we're spending so much time on the Monarchs right now?" Lila replied. "How will this help Riley?"

"Yeah, I'm pretty confused as well," Conway piped in. "Let's get back to the basics. Could you tell us about your trip from start to finish? Just the general details, how you traveled, everyone you interacted with, etcetera?"

"Sure, I can do that," Lila replied. "Let's see… We left on December 27, 2019. A car picked us up here to take us to the airport. The driver dropped us off at JFK and we had no delays. The flight was super easy, and the airport was surprisingly not too crowded. Well, not too crowded for JFK at least. We landed in Miami around four p.m. and headed straight for the marina. Originally, we were supposed to meet Kyle and Jane at the airport and go to the marina together, but their flight got delayed by like two hours, so we ended up taking a separate car and boat to the island," said Lila.

"Who picked you up from the airport?" Asked Conway.

"One of the staff members from the island," she replied.

"Do you remember which one?" He asked.

"I couldn't say for sure… Chandler did not do well on the flight and I was very distracted trying to keep her entertained. I wasn't paying much attention," said Lila.

"Do you think if we showed you a few pictures you could pick him out?" Conway asked.

"It's possible," she replied.

"Okay, good to know. Keep going," prompted Conway.

Lila started again, "We took the boat to the island and probably got there around six or seven. Dinner was ready when we arrived and… and I don't really know what you want me to keep saying here. This feels ridiculous. Everything was completely normal the entire vacation and truthfully, I thought it was one of the best vacations we'd ever taken," she was very upset. "I have absolutely no idea what happened the day he was arrested or how the bomb was put in his sho…" she trailed off; her face suddenly concerned.

"What is it, Lila?" Rebecca asked.

"Well, there is this one thing…"

"You can tell us anything," James encouraged.

The officers were on the edge of their seats.

Lila continued to sit in silence, clearly thinking through all the possible effects of sharing her information.

"Spit it out already!" Conway shouted.

James and Rebecca both shot him a look.

"It's okay, Lila. Just take your time. I know this is a lot to talk through," said Rebecca.

Lila nodded, hesitated a second more and finally said, "The shoes he wore that day he almost never wore. I just think it's strange that the one day he decided to wear those, something like this happened."

"What do you mean?" James asked. "Did he not like them? Or why did he never wear them?"

"It's kind of a long story," Lila said.

"We've got nothing but time," replied James.

CHAPTER

TWENTY-FIVE

The theater erupted with applause as the credits began to scroll at the end of *Summer Daze*.

"That was amazing, Mom!" Keagan said, "Great job!"

"Thank you," Alexa replied. "Was it good enough for you to join us at the after party?"

"Mom, please don't make this so hard on me. We just don't want to go. I think we're going to go out for some pizza instead," she replied.

"Oh, I am in for pizza!" Jay piped in.

Alexa shot Jay a look.

"You will be coming with me," she said, then shifted her focus back on Keagan. "If you insist on being difficult, I guess there's nothing I can do about it."

"Thanks, Mom!" Keagan smiled as she gave her a hug. "Truly, I think that was your best performance yet."

"You really were wonderful, Mrs. Monarch," Kyle said as Keagan grabbed his hand and pulled him toward the door.

"Thank you," Alexa replied as they walked away. "Raise her to be strong-willed and this is the thanks I get," she said to Jay, shaking her head.

"The crazy thing is, she's just like you," he smiled.

Keagan and Kyle weaved through guests on their way out of the theatre.

"Why didn't you want to go to the party?" Kyle asked.

"Oh, Kyle, there are so many of those parties and they are all the same. I'd much rather eat pizza with you on the couch in my underwear than keep this stupid, fancy dress on all night and mingle with the oh-so-sophisticated California high society," Keagan said in an obnoxious voice.

"Well, when you put it like that," Kyle grinned. "I can see what you mean."

The second they got outside, Keagan kissed Kyle on the cheek and took off her sparkly, silver high heels.

"Catch me if you can," she teased as she took off running down the sidewalk.

"Oh, you're on!" Kyle shouted as he started running after her. They ran side by side, wind blowing in their hair, until they finally reached the car.

Keagan stopped at the trunk and reached out for Kyle's hand. He grabbed her hand and pulled her in for a kiss. He moved his right hand down her back as his left hand played with her hair.

"I'm too hungry for that," Keagan said, pulling back to look at Kyle's eyes.

He laughed, "You're so demanding sometimes."

"I know," she replied, grinning. "Especially, when I'm hungry."

"What my girl wants, my girl gets." Kyle declared, "Onward to pizza!"

They got in the car and started down the road.

After a few minutes of not talking and listening to the radio, Keagan broke the silence and said, "I'm sorry about my mom."

"What do you mean?" Kyle asked.

"Her comment about your shoes. She knows better than that. I've told her about them before," she replied.

"Oh, I don't mind at all," Kyle replied. "They're my lucky shoes. I wear them where I want and when I want, and the red carpet is always a good occasion." Kyle had always been confident in his style and since his dad died, he had learned to not let people's opinions bother him.

"I know… But I just wanted you to know that I felt bad, Keagan said. "And also, you should know that those are my favorite pair yet."

"Really? These?!" Kyle asked.

"Yes, by far my favorites!" She replied.

"Thanks, babe," he smiled. "Are you going to call and order the pizza?"

"Yeah, I can do that," she replied. "Veggie with half ham?"

"I wouldn't have it any other way," said Kyle.

Keagan pulled out her phone and began to dial the number for the pizza shop.

Just as she put the phone up to her ear, Kyle reached over and yelled, "Keagan! Look out!!"

She turned to the right just in time to see the flash of bright headlights headed straight for her.

CHAPTER TWENTY-SIX

Alexa screamed like a giddy high school girl from the steps of her Beverly Hills mansion as Mrs. Wilde got out of the black limousine in the driveway.

"Debbie! I can't believe you're here!" She greeted.

"Me either!" Debbie said as she reached out her arms, inviting Alexa in for a hug.

"How have you been? How is everything? I've missed you so much," said Alexa.

"Good, good! Things have been good. I'm just so happy to be here. How are you? I know things have been tough."

"Oh, you know me, I'm good! I just keep on pushing," Alexa replied. "Come on, let's go inside, sit down and open a bottle of wine. We'll drink the good stuff though, not the cheap crap we drank in college" she laughed.

They walked inside and Debbie said, "You get the wine and I'm going to use the restroom."

She headed for the stairs to her usual guest suite. Alexa and Debbie were the kind of friends that always felt welcome in each other's homes. If Alexa hadn't been outside, Debbie would have walked right in. They shared the special kind of bond and love for one another that only old friends could.

Alexa and Debbie grew up together just outside of Montgomery, Alabama. They met in kindergarten at Hidden Lakes Elementary School and had been inseparable since. They attended the University of Miami together and went their separate ways after college. Alexa moved to California to pursue her acting career and Debbie stayed in Florida, where she married well and never had to pursue a career. Although they lived on opposite coasts, their friendship never weakened.

"Oh, Debbie," Alexa called as she was halfway to the stairs. "We're putting in some new windows in your usual guest room, so we'll have you stay in the one downstairs. You can just use the guest bath around the corner."

"Oh, okay. Sounds good," Debbie replied.

Debbie walked into the kitchen as Alexa poured them each a generous glass of red wine. They made their way out to the porch and sat comfortably on a large white couch that overlooked the perfectly manicured garden and pool.

"I always forget how beautiful it is out here," said Debbie.

"It might be beautiful but it sure is lonely," replied Alexa.

"I'm sure," Debbie said sympathetically. "Have you thought about moving to a smaller place?"

"I've thought about it. I've even thought about just moving away but we have so many friends here and my career is here," Alexa explained.

"Yes, but you travel all of the time for your job and you can really live anywhere," Debbie said.

"I know… You're right… But it would be so hard to leave. There are so many memories here." Alexa paused, "You know it's almost been two years exactly?"

"Of course, I do. Why do you think I picked this week to come visit? I figured you'd need a friend," Debbie replied.

"She would have been married a year already. Remember how she always wanted to get married on New Year's Eve? And to time the ceremony so that their kiss happened precisely at midnight? She was always such a dreamer," Alexa smiled, holding back tears.

"Yes, she was," Debbie agreed.

CHAPTER

TWENTY-SEVEN

"Happy Birthday, Kyle!" Warren smiled, as he handed him a box wrapped in silver paper with a big, red bow. "I can't believe you're already ten years old... Where did the time go?"

Like most young boys, Kyle immediately began tearing at the paper until he unveiled a black shoe box with a white "B" logo. He opened it to find gray tennis shoes with white soles and a black logo.

"You got me Brays? I have always wanted a pair!" Kyle exclaimed as he pulled them out and immediately began to put them on.

"I know, that's why I got them for you," Warren replied. "The best part is they look just like mine. That way, every time you wear them, you'll know your dad is thinking about you."

After he finished tying them, Kyle jumped up and gave his dad a hug.

Jane walked in carrying a round, chocolate cake with ten colorful lit candles.

"Happy birthday to you, happy birthday to you, happy birthday dear Kyle, happy birthday to you," she sang as Warren and Riley joined in.

"Make a wish!" Warren added.

Kyle blew out the candles and waited anxiously as Jane cut everyone a piece.

"This is the best birthday ever!" Kyle declared after taking his last bite of cake. "Can I go ride my new skateboard now?"

"Of course," Jane replied. "As long as you wear your helmet," she added. "And don't think I won't be out there to check."

"Okaaay, Mom," Kyle said as he ran out of the living room toward the garage.

Sensing Riley's disappointed mood, Warren asked, "Everything okay, Riley?"

He unconvincingly nodded.

"Are you sure?" Warren asked again.

"Why did Kyle get a pair of Brays and not me?" Riley pouted.

"Well, for starters, it's not your birthday," Warren laughed but Riley was unamused. "Oh, Riley, you have so much to learn."

Warren often took opportunities to teach the boy's life lessons and like most children, they didn't realize the wisdom they were given until it was too late to receive more.

"You see, we are all different in the ways we show and accept love," Warren said. "Let me ask you something," he paused, "Would you rather me give you a $20 bill or go out to get ice cream together, just the two of us?"

Riley looked at his dad, thought about it for a moment and then replied, "Umm, probably ice cream."

"That's what I thought you'd say," said Warren. "You see, you would rather spend quality time with me than have me give you a gift. Your brother is very different. He would much rather I give him an expensive gift to show how much I love him than spend quality time with me. Neither option is better than the other, just different. Understanding these love languages helps us get along and better relate to one another."

"I guess that makes sense," shrugged Riley, losing interest

in his dad's lecture. "Those shoes are worth a lottt of ice cream trips," he smiled.

"Yes. Yes, they are!" Agreed Warren.

CHAPTER

TWENTY-EIGHT

Lila was pacing in the master bedroom, soothing Warren, when suddenly, she heard a thud downstairs.

"What was that?" She nervously wondered.

She set Warren down in his crib, grabbed the baseball bat she kept next to the bed and made her way slowly down the stairs.

To her surprise, Riley was calmly sitting on the couch with his feet up on the coffee table, "Hi, beautiful," he said.

Lila's heartbeat slowed with immediate relief.

"Geez, Riley. You scared me to death. How did you even get in?"

"I really have no idea. This time when I traveled, I just landed right inside," he laughed as he got up to greet Lila on the stairs. He hugged her tight, "I've missed you so much."

"I've missed you, too" she replied.

Warren began to cry upstairs.

"Aus told me not to travel back this late but I told him I knew you'd be awake," Riley said gesturing up the stairs toward the crying noise.

"It's hard to not be awake when your baby is always crying and your husband is in prison," Lila said in a sarcastic tone with a layer of belligerence.

"I'm so sorry, Lila," Riley said. "I'm trying my best to get out and while I'm here, I will help as much as I can."

They walked up the stairs and down the hall to the master bedroom. Riley stopped and took a second to really look around the room. When he'd seen it only a week or so ago, he didn't have a chance to take it in. He missed his king bed with the navy-blue comforter he and Lila had picked out together the weekend before they'd moved into their townhouse from some boutique shop on the west side Lila had found. He missed the gold floor lamp in the corner that didn't match anything but that they'd vowed to keep in every place they lived because it was the first item they bought together. He missed the feeling of the fluffy gray carpet between his toes as he walked through the room. And, most of all, he missed going to sleep next to his best friend every night.

"Let me grab you some clothes," Lila said, interrupting Riley's thoughts of the past and bringing him back to reality.

"Thanks," he replied. "I'll try to console Warren."

Riley walked to Warren's white crib that sat next to Lila's side of the bed. He reached in and stuck his finger out, inviting Warren to grab it. "Hi, little buddy," he said in a whisper. "I know we haven't spent any time together and I'm really sorry about that." He continued, "But, I'm your dad... and, I love you more than you could ever know... and I'm doing everything I can to come home, little buddy."

Lila emerged from the bathroom with shorts and a tee shirt for Riley.

"Here you go," she said, tossing him the clothes. He quickly put them on and leaned over the crib to pick up Warren. He held him close and stared down at him with immense admiration.

"He looks just like you," Riley commented, looking up at Lila.

She laughed, "No, he doesn't, and you know it!" She

retorted, "He looks just like you."

"Yeah, I know. I was just trying to be nice," laughed Riley. "He's as handsome as they come… just like his father," he said with a wink.

Lila rolled her eyes and half smiled, the way she always did to show both her amusement and annoyance with Riley's silly comments.

"They're coming back again tomorrow," Lila said as she glanced over to look at the clock. "Or better yet, today," she added seeing it was just after twelve-thirty a.m.

"What have they been asking you?" Riley asked.

"So many things. So many things," answered Lila. "But they're on our side, Riley. They want to help you!"

"Really?" Riley exclaimed, "Why?"

"Well, don't act so surprised if you didn't do it," Lila teased. "James, the sort of head officer, I guess, found the case really interesting and he kept looking into different pieces of it and he felt like things were off. I guess his mom is really good friends with Alexa Monarch, so he felt like he had a connection to the case, since we were vacationing on their island… I don't really know. I just know that he convinced two other cops that things were off, Rebecca and Conway, and none of them think you did it. They want my help to understand everything so that they can build a case for why you're innocent."

"That's incredible!" Riley exclaimed. "I mean… that is really amazing! I can't believe we have people helping us!" Sensing Lila's lack of enthusiasm, he asked, "Is this not good news?"

"It is… but there's a caveat," she timidly replied.

"What is it?" He asked.

"Umm… there's really no easy way to say this but… their top suspect is your brother," said Lila.

"Kyle!? No way it was Kyle! What? That's ridiculous!"

Riley shouted defensively. "Why would he ever do that to me? Where did they even get a stupid idea like that?

Lila hesitated, "There are a number of reasons… and pieces of evidence they've collected that could… potentially… maybe… lead to Kyle."

Riley set Warren back down in his crib and began to anxiously pace back and forth across the room, "Are you kidding me, Lila? What? Do you seriously believe he could have done it? Why would he do that to me? To our family? We've had our ups and downs but through so many tough times we've always stuck together. We always had each other's back. There's no way he would have done that to me," Riley explained.

"I know. I know, Riley. But can you honestly tell me that the thought hasn't crossed your mind?"

Riley stopped his pacing and looked down at the ground. He pulled his hair in frustration and looked back up at Lila, "I mean… I can't deny that the thought hasn't crossed my mind. I was wearing my Brays and those *are* our shoes… he was on the island and had access, I guess… I mean…" He paused. "But, NO!" He shouted, now very angry. "He wouldn't have done that to me!"

Lila always knew when she needed to let Riley be angry. He rarely was, and he never stayed angry for long, but she knew when it was best to just let him get it out. His face was burning red as he processed the new accusations.

After a few moments of silence, Lila said, "I'm sorry, Riley. I know it's not at all what you want to hear. Do you want me to talk you through some of the evidence?" She asked.

Riley sat down on the tufted gray bench at the foot of the bed. He put his elbows on his knees and leaned forward with his hands grasped tight together.

"I suppose that's a good idea," he said reluctantly.

Lila walked to grab her phone off of the nightstand and sat down next to Riley. She put her arm around him and rubbed his back.

"About two weeks ago, James made a trip to the island to see if he could scrape up any evidence. He was trying to get a feel for some of the staff and he wanted to see if anything he found led him to any solid reasons to believe you didn't do it," said Lila. "While he was out there, he found these in the treehouse," Lila explained as she showed Riley the picture James had taken of the hunter green sneakers.

Riley grabbed Lila's phone and examined the photo. "And?" He asked, looking for further explanation.

"And what?" Lila replied, a little annoyed. "What do you mean 'what'? Those shoes are identical to the ones you wore in the airport. It seems a little strange that a matching pair would be left on the island. Don't you think?"

"They're not identical," said Riley.

"Yes, they are! They're the exact same shoes. Same brand, color, style," argued Lila. "They're exactly the same."

"No, they're not," Riley argued. "Those are Kyle's."

"How do you know?" She asked.

"Isn't it obvious?" He asked.

Suddenly very confused, Lila shook her head, "No."

"Have you ever seen me write my name in a pair of shoes before? Or really on anything?" Riley questioned.

Lila tilted her head to the side, "I guess not," she replied.

"Since we were kids, Kyle's clothes have always been labeled. My mom started doing it when we were younger and briefly wore the same size. She wanted it to be easier for us to distinguish whose was whose. As you know, Kyle's a little obsessive compulsive, so it stuck. He's written his name on basically everything he owns since," explained Riley.

"Really? I had no idea," Lila said.

"Yeah, those are definitely his shoes," Riley confirmed. "What did the officers say about the photo?"

"Originally, they didn't even show me the photo. They just asked me to think of anything suspicious involving the case… I really couldn't think of anything… but then I did think about how I thought it was weird you were wearing your Brays on the day of your arrest because you never wore them," Lila said. "And then they showed me the photo."

"Did you tell them the backstory?" Riley asked.

"Yes," she replied.

"Do you honestly think Kyle could have done it? Why else would you tell them that, Lila?" Accused Riley.

"I need you back home," said Lila. "I am willing to do anything to get you free."

"How did you tell it? What details did you include?" He asked.

Lila paused, thinking back to her conversation earlier that day, "I explained to them that Brays were your dad's favorite shoes. I told them that every year for Kyle's birthday, since he was nine –"

"Ten," Riley corrected.

Lila rolled her eyes, "Since he was ten, Warren bought him a pair that matched his. I explained it was their father-son thing and that Kyle had always been obsessed with the shoes and loved to match your dad. Then, I told them how after your dad died, you started getting Kyle and yourself matching pairs for his birthday each year to help him keep the tradition alive."

"You have to know how to show people you love them," Riley smiled.

"I know," said Lila. "I also know that you only ever wear those shoes to please Kyle. He's probably the only one who even knows you have them," she paused. "It's just strange to me that a matching pair, or I guess now Kyle's pair, would be found on the island. Can you please just admit that it's a little strange, Riley?" Lila pleaded.

"Have you asked Kyle about it?" Asked Riley.

"No," Lila said. "No, I haven't called up my brother-in-law, a top suspect in a case against my husband, to ask him about evidence that points directly to him... evidence that three random cops from Florida brought to my house out of the blue to investigate a case that's been closed for a year," Lila had a lot of attitude when she got defensive. "Let's just say, I didn't know how to broach the subject."

"Call him," said Riley.

"What?" Lila asked.

"Call him," Riley said again. "Now."

"It's almost one in the morning," replied Lila.

"It's only ten in California," he retorted.

"What am I supposed to say?" She asked.

"Ask him why his shoes were left on the island and tell him you had cops come by asking about me," Riley said.

"You're acting like this is casual conversation. I've barely talked to him since you've been away!" Said Lila.

"It *is* a casual conversation," Riley replied, "Because he didn't do it. I'm sure he wants me out of prison as much as you do."

Lila stared blankly ahead.

"Lila, please listen to me. I'm confident he wants me out of prison." Riley continued, "I'm sure he'll jump at the opportunity to help free me."

"And what if he doesn't? What if he gets defensive and upset? Or angry? What if he leads us further to believe that he did it? Then, what?" She asked. "Then, what, Riley?"

"All valid questions, babe. All valid questions that we'll never be able to answer... unless you call him," Riley replied.

Sensing Lila was still not convinced, Riley continued to

persuade. "You can put it on speaker, I'll be right here the whole time. That way, we can listen and discern together."

Lila nervously bit her lip.

"We do make a pretty good team," she admitted.

"Yes, we do!" Agreed Riley. He kissed her on the cheek.

Lila waited a second longer before picking up her phone.

"Okay… here goes nothing," she said.

CHAPTER

TWENTY-NINE

The lights were dim in the overly modern restaurant as Alexa and Debbie sipped on martinis at the bar.

"I love chic places like this," said Alexa. "They're popping up all over around here."

"It's wonderful," agreed Debbie. "And I think this martini would still be delicious even if it wasn't my third," she laughed.

Debbie's phone started to buzz, and she looked down to see that James was calling.

"Don't bother me now, Son," she said. "Don't you know I'm trying to have fun?" She asked rhetorically, rolling her head back in a dramatic fashion and declining his call.

Alexa's face saddened and she said, "I wish my kid still called me."

"Oh, Alexa," Debbie said with her foot in her mouth. "I'm so sorry. You're right. I shouldn't complain."

"It's alright," Alexa replied. "I think I'm just feeling these drinks a little and I always get sad when I'm drinking."

Debbie's phone started to buzz again with another incoming call from James.

"Maybe, you should take that," suggested Alexa.

"You're probably right," Debbie replied. "I'll step outside," she said as she stood up, caught her balance a second and made her way toward to the door.

"Tell him I say hello," Alexa called. "Oh, and that I hope he had a nice trip to the island!"

Confused, Debbie looked back at Alexa and nodded.

"Hi, James," she answered the phone.

"Mom!" He exclaimed, "How are ya?"

"Don't play that game with me, James. I know you need something, and I also know you're keeping things from your momma. Alexa just told me to say hello and that she hopes you enjoyed your trip to the island…"

The phone was silent on the other end.

"You didn't think it was important to tell me that you went snooping around my best friend's island?" Debbie continued.

"Momma!" James pleaded, "It's not about her at all… this case is huge for me. It could be the big break I need for my career. I just needed Alexa for access."

"Well, why didn't you ask me then?" Debbie asked.

"You would have said no," James replied.

Unable to defend herself, Debbie shifted gears.

"Why did you call?"

"I wanted to know if you had any updates for me," said James.

"You interrupted my vacation to ask me about evidence?" She asked appalled. "Didn't your momma raise you better than that?"

"Mom, this is urgent. I am in New York and we only have one day left. I need anything and everything I can get to make my time with Lila worth it," he said. "Have you found out anything interesting about the Mines' family to note from your trip?"

"You are sooo demanding," Debbie whined.

James was sitting on the edge of a double bed with a white comforter, in a hotel room at the New York City Hilton. Conway was sitting up against the headboard on the other bed and Rebecca was sitting in the office chair at the small desk.

He muted his cell phone and said to the others, "I think she's drunk!"

"Put it on speaker," Rebecca insisted.

James nodded and the three of them listened in.

"I don't really think there has been anything interesting to note. The only time we talked about the Mines' family was when she brought up that Keagan and Kyle would have been married two years. She said that she felt terrible for Kyle and that she thought he had it even worse than her, you know, with his brother in prison and all. She said they still talk often, and she tries to take good care of him," Debbie said.

The three officers looked at each other, trying to find any ties to the case.

"Thanks, Mom," James finally replied. "Please, if you can, keep digging. I need more information about their family. And I might need to go back to the island. You can ask for me this time, if you'd like?"

"Probably not," replied Debbie. "Talk to you later," she mumbled as she hung up the phone.

"She's so not helpful," James complained as he slammed his phone down on the bed.

"I didn't think it was that bad," Rebecca said. "What else do you expect her to find out? She's on a girl's trip with her best friend and she doesn't want to dig for evidence. She just wants to gossip and catch up. I think it's valuable to know that Alexa and Kyle still talk after everything that happened."

Conway looked up, questioning Rebecca's point, "What do you mean? Why wouldn't they talk?"

"I don't know," she hesitated. "I guess I just don't know what they would have in common anymore without Keagan…"

"But Keagan still is their bond," James replied.

"Yes," Rebecca replied. "I completely agree. My point is that people tend to respond very differently to death. Some people get closer and rely on one other, while others draw back in isolation. When I was in high school, I lost a couple of friends. It was a pretty tragic time for my family and me. I've always been an analyzer, hence the career choice," she smiled. "And I've always watched people. Some would band together through prayer and gift giving, while others would pull back in isolation. I saw families grow stronger because they'd lost a parent and I saw couples become divided because they lost a child. Death is extremely challenging, and it brings out best," she paused, "And worst in people. I think the fact that Alexa and Kyle still talk gives us information about the way they both respond to trials… especially Kyle."

James and Conway nodded, processing the information.

"I guess that's true," said James. "I didn't think about that."

"It gets tricky though," Rebecca said, now pacing the room, "Because if we're assuming Kyle's main reason for planting the bomb would have been Riley abandoning him after his dad died, that would make sense. Kyle likes to stick with others in times of grief and Riley left him alone. However, I would argue that comforting Alexa would be much more difficult than comforting Riley because with their dad, there was nothing they could have done, but with Keagan, Kyle was driving, and even though it wasn't his fault, there's still a level of guilt. So, to comfort Alexa would take a tremendous amount of effort, even more effort than it would take to comfort Riley living across the country."

"You're losing me," admitted Conway.

"All I am trying to say is the way Kyle responded to both scenarios is interesting. I don't feel like his responses align," Rebecca said.

"He's like twelve years older now," Conway argued. "He

was only in high school when his dad died. People change."

"They do," agreed Rebecca. "But not as much when it comes to death. It's more of a natural response. Whether you're fifteen or sixty-five, if you find out you've lost someone, most likely, you will react in a similar way. And in Kyle's case, based on this information and what we've learned from Lila, he didn't respond the same."

"Seems like a stretch to me," Conway rolled his eyes. "Let's just ask Lila about it in the morning," he said as he flipped off the lamp by his bed. In a matter of seconds, he was lightly snoring.

"How does he fall asleep so fast?" Rebecca asked. With only a little light remaining in the room, she made her way toward James and sat on the edge of the bed.

"Maybe I'm just trying to make something out of nothing," she sighed. "It's just… we've been here two days and I feel like we don't have anything. I'm confident he didn't do it, but I have no idea who did. I know you both think Kyle, but I just don't see it," she said shaking her head. "Were you serious about going back to the island?"

James nodded, "Yeah, I think we might need to. I agree. I don't think we've gained anything substantial from being here and we have no real leads. But honestly, if we go back to the island, I'm not sure what we'd find. There's zero reason to believe anyone there had a motive to frame Riley."

"What if someone bribed them?" Rebecca suggested.

"I guess that is a possibility," James replied. "I was hoping to find out something from Lila that could give us reason to believe something like that could have happened. Like someone he's had a falling out with or someone he owed money to. But it sounds like he's genuinely a good guy. I don't know what to think."

"Me neither… I guess we'll see what tomorrow brings,"

Rebecca replied and looked at the clock, "But for now, I need to get my beauty sleep."

James smiled, "You don't need beauty sleep. You're already perfect," he said as he reached his hand over and touched her leg.

Rebecca grabbed his hand and tossed it away.

"You're full of it, Wilde," she teased.

James fought off acting on the thoughts racing through his head.

"Goooodnight," Rebecca smiled, shoeing James off the bed. "You have your nice cot over there," she pointed.

Realizing he had been lost in thought, James laughed.

"I'm still not sure how I'm the one who ended up on the cot. Especially, when I'm the one paying for this idiot," he gestured toward a passed-out Conway.

"Probably because I'm pretty and Conway is a jerk," she replied.

James let out a fake laugh as he got into bed and climbed under the covers.

"Goodnight, Rebecca," he said.

"Night, Wilde!" She replied.

CHAPTER THIRTY

"Hi, Lila," a familiar voice answered the phone.

"Hi, Kyle," Lila replied. "How are you?"

"I'm alright," he responded. "And yourself?"

"Doing great," Lila replied unenthusiastically as she gave Riley a nervous stare, not knowing how to shift the conversation. She had never been good at small talk or beating around the bush.

"Well, that's good to hear," said Kyle. "And how are the little ones?"

"Oh, you know them, they're great. Always keeping me busy," Lila replied.

"Great," Kyle said awkwardly. "So... what's up? I'm assuming you had a reason for calling."

"Yeah, I did... I don't really know how to broach the subject," she awkwardly laughed. "But I have a question for you... um... about your Brays."

"What about them?" Kyle asked.

Riley nodded, signaling Lila to go on.

"Well, I had some officers stop by yesterday and they've been looking into Riley's case. They think something is off and they don't believe he did it. They um... well, they found your matching shoes on the island and I don't think they know they're yours but... I'm not sure... I just wanted to give you a call about it before I would say anything."

"Are you serious, Lila?" Kyle immediately got defensive.

"Do you really think I did it, too? Why does everyone think Riley is so innocent all of the time and that I'm the crazy one? I didn't do it. I swear," Kyle said.

With a sigh of relief, Lila replied, "Kyle, I don't think you did it." She looked at Riley acknowledging the fact that she was fibbing a bit about her previous beliefs. "I want to help make sure your name stays clear."

There was silence on the other end of the line.

"I just need to know why your shoes were left on the island, Kyle," Lila said, trying to spark more conversation. "It looks suspicious since they match the shoes Riley was wearing at the airport and I really don't think they know they're yours but sooner or later, I'm sure they'll figure it out and that won't look good for you. Please, let me help you."

There was still silence on the other end. Lila and Riley looked at each other, shrugging back and forth, not knowing what to say next.

Kyle finally spoke up, his voice sounded shaky, "I was wearing them the night Keagan died. Before we got hit, we were talking, and she told me how they were her favorite pair of Brays I'd ever owned… and you know I've owned a lot."

Lila could tell he was smiling at the memory.

"After the accident, I couldn't get myself to wear them. They reminded me so much of her…" he paused.

After a few moments of silence, Lila encouraged, "It's okay, Kyle. Take your time."

He took a deep breath, "Keagan and I always stuck together on the island. Riley was often too cool for us little kids, so we learned to entertain ourselves."

Riley nodded, agreeing with Kyle's statement.

He continued, "We formed a club together on one of our trips. It was pretty exclusive," he laughed. "And like all kid clubs, you needed a password to get in. We always met in the treehouse and thanks to Keagan's ability to sweet talk the island staff, she always brought the snacks. No matter what time of day it was, she brought pizza. I swear that girl could have lived off only pizza," he smiled. "We coined ourselves the 'Pizza Society,' and our secret meetings became a tradition on the island," Kyle paused.

Lila waited patiently for him to continue.

"I know everyone thought we started dating after my dad died but the truth is, I knew I wanted to marry Keagan long before that. We kept our island adventures quiet... after all... what happened in the Pizza Society, stayed in the Pizza Society. We shared so many memories in that island treehouse..." he paused, again. "Including our first kiss... It was the summer before second grade, and I remember it like it was yesterday. The sun was shining in on her beautiful blonde hair and I asked her if she wanted to be my girlfriend. Of course, she said, 'yes.' Then, she looked at me and in the most matter of fact tone I've ever heard, she said, 'Since I'm your girlfriend now, you could probably kiss me' and I did. She was always so sure of everything she wanted.... I'm sorry... I haven't talked about her in so long... I'm getting carried away. I guess you don't need to know all of this."

"No, it's okay," Lila insisted. "Thank you for sharing! I'm sure it feels good to reminisce a little."

"Yeah, it really does," he agreed. "Well, here's the part of the story that gets kind of embarrassing... when we went on vacation, I told Riley to bring his green pair of Brays because those were Keagan's favorites and Riley never cared which pair we matched. In fact, I don't think he ever even wore his Brays, unless I was around," Kyle laughed.

Riley smiled and nodded at Lila.

"True," he whispered.

"The last day we were on the island, I went out to the

treehouse with my shoes. I had the chef make our favorite pizza: veggie with ham on half. I brought it out there with me and I sat on the edge... wait, did you see the treehouse when you were out there?"

"I didn't," replied Lila.

"Oh, Lila! The treehouse is absolutely magnificent," Kyle exclaimed. "I need you to fully understand this magical moment." When Kyle was passionate about something, his enthusiasm was incomparable. "Lila, this treehouse sits on the far back edge of the island. You have to walk on the paved paths and wind your way back until you find the tree with the red ribbon on it. When you get to the ribbon, you take a right off the path and cut through the trees. It's not long until you reach a small cliff with a wooden suspension bridge leading to a huge palm tree. The bridge sits over the white sandy beach below and connects to the porch of the house. You have to remember; this is the Monarch's island we're talking about, so it's hardly a treehouse at all... it's more like a mini mansion. You walk across the suspension bridge and enter onto the wrap-around porch. This level of the house circles the entire tree and has a wooden fence with slats. A spiral staircase winds around the trunk and up to the second floor of the house. The level it leads to is the heart of the house and is enclosed with wooden walls and glass windows. In the center, the trunk has wooden slats that form a ladder to the roof where there's a door that pushes up and open. If you're brave enough to climb the ladder, you can sit on the roof, with your feet hanging off the edge and look out at the ocean for miles in every direction."

"That sounds amazing," said Lila.

"I know. Quite honestly, I'm not sure why Keagan and I were the only ones to take advantage of the view," Kyle replied.

"So, you brought your pizza out to the treehouse," Lila said, prompting Kyle to continue with his story.

"Yes," Kyle replied. "I went out to the treehouse with our favorite pizza and Keagan's favorite shoes of mine in hand. I just wanted a moment for myself. I climbed up to the top, like we always used to, and I sat with my legs hanging off the edge. I ate my half of the pizza and left the veggie only half for Keagan... I was looking for closure. I wanted to go to our favorite place in the world one last time and share a moment with my best friend. Since her passing, I hadn't been able to wear the shoes anymore. And since I knew I'd never wear them again, I thought it would be nice if I left them there for her. I thought they deserved to stay in our favorite spot forever."

CHAPTER
THIRTY-ONE

Lila came strolling down the stairs wearing light pink, silk pajama pants with a matching pink top. She was wrapped up in a fluffy white blanket with her hair pulled back in a loose ponytail.

"Wow! I love you," Riley said as he looked up at her from his laptop.

"You're ridiculous," she replied.

"And you still don't know how to take a compliment," he grinned.

He got up and greeted her with a kiss on the cheek. Lila pulled him in and began to kiss him passionately.

"Ewe," Lila heard Chandler say from the kitchen.

Lila stopped kissing and looked confusingly at Chandler and then back at Riley.

"Breakfast is served, my darling," he smiled.

Lila squinted her eyes at Riley, wondering what he was up to.

"Remember what I told you to say, Chan," Riley prompted. Chandler nodded.

"Surprise!" She exclaimed. "Happy Birthday, Mom!"

"It's not my birthday," Lila laughed.

"Daddy said since he missed it last year, we could celebrate this morning! He woke me up early and we made all of this food for you," she explained.

The large table was covered with far too much food for the four of them. The feast included French toast, pancakes, eggs, strawberries, grapes, bananas, fruit juices and more.

"This is way too much food for us!" She laughed, "Unless Warren here is about to start pulling his weight."

"No, Mom," Chandler corrected, "Warren won't eat this food."

"Right, Chan? Mom is crazy," Riley said.

"Mmhhm," Chandler agreed.

Lila shook her head. She was grinning ear to ear.

"Alright," she said. "Let's dig in!"

They sat down at the table and began to serve up plates with their eyes much bigger than their stomachs. As they started to eat, Riley tried to remember the last time he'd enjoyed such a large meal. His mind flashed back to the day he was arrested and the spread they'd enjoyed on the boat ride that morning. Suddenly, he lost his appetite.

"Are you alright?" Lila asked, sensing Riley's changed spirit.

"Yeah," he said. "Just not super hungry."

"Then, why did you make this huge meal?" Lila asked.

"I looked at the clock earlier and it was five a.m. I was getting tired and needed to distract myself from falling asleep, so I came up with this birthday idea. I woke Chandler up and we got to work right away making anything she wanted. I thought I could take a little time to show you my love... after all, I have missed a year of spoiling you," he smiled.

"I have so many reasons to love you, Riley Mines," Lila replied as she took a spoonful of whipped cream from her plate and flirtingly licked the spoon.

"Could I have a bite of that? Pleaaase," Riley sweetly begged.

Lila scooped up another spoonful and went to feed Riley. As soon as she got close to his mouth, he blew the whipped cream and it splattered on her face. Chandler exploded with laughter.

"Oh, you are still so cruel!" Lila laughed. "Don't encourage him," she pleaded with Chandler.

They laughed and laughed and for the first time in over a year, things felt good. Things felt really, really good.

The laughter quickly ceased, and Riley and Lila were pulled back into their sad reality when they heard a knock at the door.

"It's only seven and the officers aren't supposed to be here until nine... who could that be?" Lila asked Riley.

Riley shrugged, "I have no idea."

"Okay, well... why don't you take Chandler upstairs and she can show you her new dolls?" Lila suggested.

"Will you, Chan? Will you please show me your new dolls?" Riley asked.

"Yes!" She exclaimed as she grabbed her dad's hand and pulled him toward the stairs.

Lila, realizing she was still in her thin pajamas, grabbed the blanket she'd brought downstairs and wrapped herself in it. She hesitantly made her way to the door.

She peered out the window. Instantly relieved, she opened the door with a smile.

CHAPTER

THIRTY-TWO

Faces blurred passed as Kyle stood at the end of the receiving line. He'd barely eaten in days and he could hardly keep himself upright.

Everything had happened so fast. One moment, he was laughing with the love of his life and the next, she was gone.

He couldn't sleep, he could barely breathe, and every thought was interrupted by another more painful than the last.

"How are you holding up?" Riley asked as he put his hand on Kyle's shoulder.

Slightly startled, Kyle replied, "I don't even know anymore. I know it wasn't my fault, but I can't help but feel guilty. I mean what if we'd left a minute later? What if I had taken a different route? What if we'd gone to the after party instead? What if we hadn't gone to the premier at all?"

Riley pulled Kyle gently from the end of the line, realizing he couldn't handle it any longer.

"It's not your fault, Kyle. There's nothing you could have done and you're going to drive yourself crazy if you keep thinking of ways to change the past," Riley said as he led him out of the crowded room and into the back hallway where there were a few black, folding chairs. "Take a seat. There's too much going on right now and understandably, you're overwhelmed. Let me get you something to eat."

Kyle nodded and Riley left him to go grab some food.

Riley made his way through the crowded room and over to the small kitchen where light appetizers and desserts filled the counters. To his surprise, he was the only one in the kitchen. He looked down at his watch and saw the time.

"I guess we are nearing the end," he thought.

He grabbed a small, paper plate and started to pile on cheese cubes, crackers, carrots with ranch dip, two chocolate chip cookies and a bite size brownie. His mind flashed back to his father's funeral and the enormous spread of upscale delicacies it had had. Being a famous chef, his father had many friends who volunteered to provide the food. Although the memory made the food in front of him look pitiful, he didn't care.

He thought, "I guess it doesn't matter. No one wants to eat at these things anyway."

His stomach growled loudly.

"On second thought, maybe I do want to eat."

He started preparing a second plate for himself. As he grabbed a few carrots, he heard a toilet flush, followed by voices coming from the other side of the wall. He wasn't paying much attention until he faintly heard Kyle's name. He moved closer to the wall and put his ear up against it to try to listen in.

"It's dreadful," the woman said. "And to think that dumb boy is the reason she's gone."

"He should be the one who's gone," the other woman replied. "It's not like he does anything anyway."

Furious, Riley dropped the plates of food and stormed to the back hallway to get Kyle. He flung open the door and found Alexa and Kyle sitting together.

"Are you okay?" Kyle asked, seeing that Riley was flushed and had failed to bring back the food.

"No, I'm not," he replied. "Let's get out of here. I don't have time for people who disrespect my brother. Plus, I am hungry, and I need something better than that garbage."

"What happened?" Alexa asked.

"I overheard some women talking and blaming Kyle for Keagan's death. They said he should have been the one to die!" Riley's face was now burning red with anger. "Who says that? Don't they know he's hurting more than anyone?"

Alexa shot him a look.

"Sorry, you *both* are hurting more than anyone," he quickly corrected. "We can't change what happened and we can't blame anyone other than the drunk idiot who ruined everything."

The room fell silent.

"It's almost over anyway," said Riley, gaining his composure. "Let's find Mom, Lila and Chandler and get out of here."

Kyle nodded.

"I'll talk to you later, Mrs. Monarch," he said as he stood up to leave the room.

They found the girls and made their way out of the funeral home.

In the parking lot, Riley suggested, "Kyle, why don't you ride with mom and meet us at Los Molcajetes? Is that good with you? I figure you're always up for a beer and some chips and queso."

"That's great," Kyle replied as he walked to the driver's side of Jane's car.

"Why don't you have Mom drive?" Riley asked. "You're pretty emotional right now."

"Damn it!" Kyle exploded. "Does no one think I can drive? I didn't do it! It wasn't my fault! None of it was my fault." He sat down, leaned his back against the tire and put his hands on his face.

Riley looked at Lila, signaling her to put Chandler in the car.

"I'll go with the two of you," Jane said as Lila picked up Chandler. The three of them made their way across the parking lot.

"That's not what I meant at all, Kyle. I'm sorry," Riley said as he joined Kyle on the ground. "There's nothing I can say that will make things better right now... nothing at all... but you know what?"

Kyle took his hands off of his face to look at Riley.

"What?" He asked.

"I seem to remember the wise words of a young man when Dad died." He paused, "When Dad died, you reminded me that there is a bigger and better plan than anything we could possibly understand or imagine. You wrote down a quote for me and I've kept it in my wallet ever since."

Riley reached into his pocket and pulled out a brown, leather wallet. He opened it up and grabbed a folded piece of paper out from behind a couple of twenty-dollar bills.

He held the piece of paper out so both of them could read it:

The universe is but a vast and undeniably intricate design that no human being can truly explain. Of all of its complexities, the greatest, I believe, is love. Love is but the one emotion strong enough to keep men and women alive while simultaneously, a lack of love is strong enough to tell those same men and women to end their lives. Without love, we cannot feel pain. We cannot feel the emptiness of life without love and we can't understand the depth of our love until it is taken away. It is this pain of lost love that builds us up and grows our hearts so we might spread this same love to others. And if we're lucky, love again.

Kyle smiled, "I gave that to you when Dad died?"

"Yeah," Riley laughed. "I have absolutely no idea why. Seems like it's more for intimate relationship love but I respected your efforts at the time."

The two of them busted out with laughter.

"I cannot believe I gave that to you!" Exclaimed Kyle. "That's hilarious."

"But it's true," said Riley encouragingly. "Whether it's the love of a parent, friend or partner, the loss of love is never easy. It feels like the weight of the world is inside your chest. Tasks like breathing, before subconscious, feel unmanageable. Loss of love is truly a terrible feeling and… I'm so sorry," Riley said.

After a long pause, Kyle said, "I don't think I can stay here."

"You can move to New York with us," Riley quickly suggested. He had always been a problem solver and liked when he could provide viable solutions.

"I don't need to leave forever…" Kyle paused. "I do love it here and I know mom needs me. I just… I think I need a break," he explained.

"Absolutely… a change of scenery," Riley agreed. "I think that's a great idea and we'd be happy to have you."

"I'll think about it," Kyle replied. His stomach growled loud enough for both of them to hear. "I think my stomach finally caught up with me. I haven't really eaten the past couple of days," Kyle admitted.

"I know," said Riley. "Let's go get some food." He jumped up and reached down to assist Kyle.

"I'm about to smash some chips and queso," Kyle yelled as he gripped Riley's hand and stood up.

"Bout to smash," Riley sang as he pumped his fists.

They laughed like only siblings do at their inside joke.

When Riley stopped laughing, he looked sincerely at Kyle

and offered a hug.

"I love you, bro," he said, patting Kyle on the back.

"I love you, too," Kyle replied. Without staying serious for too long, Kyle pulled back and put his hands around his mouth like a megaphone. "Bout to smash!" He yelled.

CHAPTER

THIRTY-THREE

"Jane!" Lila greeted as she opened the door and greeted her with a hug.

"Mom?" Riley thought to himself.

Before Riley could respond, Chandler went racing out of the game room and down the stairs.

"Grandma!" She called.

"Is my Mom really here?" He thought. His heart was racing, "Surely, she can't know I'm here."

He tried to listen quietly but could barely hear the muffled conversation downstairs.

Suddenly, Chandler shouted, "Dad! Aren't you going to come say hi to Grandma?"

Lila didn't know what to say. She had never been good at lying.

Unfazed, Jane responded, "Oh, sweetheart, your Dad isn't here."

"Yes, he is," she confidently replied. "We were just playing upstairs together."

Jane looked at Lila for an explanation.

"What's going on here?" She asked.

Riley thought of the poem, "Trust only those who come to you... I'm sure it would be okay," he encouraged himself.

He slowly emerged from the hallway and stood at the top

of the wooden staircase. "Hi, Mom," he hesitantly waved.

Jane looked at Riley, then at Lila and back at Riley. She started to hyperventilate, unable to comprehend the situation.

Riley started to walk down the steps and Jane put her hand out to stop him from getting any closer.

She finally caught her breath to form a sentence, "What are you doing here?" She asked.

"It's a really long and unbelievable story, Mom. I need you to trust me," Riley replied. He was now at the bottom of the stairs.

Jane kept her hand up in defense.

"I don't know. I don't know what's happening," she replied.

"Let me explain it to you," Riley calmly pleaded.

"It's okay," Lila added. "Everything is okay." She put her hand on Jane's back and led her toward the living room.

Riley bent down to Chandler's eye level.

"Hey, Chan," he said. "Will you please go play with your dolls?"

"But grandma just got here!" Chandler whined.

"I know but it would make Daddy really happy. Would you please?" He asked.

Chandler sighed, "I guess." She turned and dragged her feet all the way up the stairs.

Riley turned toward the living room and took a seat on the dark green, wingback chair.

He looked across the coffee table, trying to meet his Mom's sad, green eyes. She looked thin. Thinner than the last time he'd seen her. Her hair was now grayer than its normal brown and her cheeks were wrinkling, below her eyes, more than he'd ever seen before.

Riley thought about everything she'd been through. From her husband to Keagan to himself. Although he was still alive, to her, he assumed he felt dead. There was no way to communicate and the last time she'd seen him, he was being tased in an airport.

"Not exactly my most flattering moment," Riley was lost in thought.

"Did they release you?" Jane asked.

"I would have called you the minute they released me," Riley replied.

"Did you escape?" Jane asked.

"Of course, I didn't escape, Mom," he said. "You know it's impossible to escape Nadirehs and you know I'm too much of a rule follower to do that anyway."

"Did you do it?" Jane questioned.

Riley stared across the room, still trying to meet his Mom's eyes but she was only looking at the ground.

"Will you please look at me?" He begged. Hesitantly, she looked up, a small piece of hair covering part of her left eye. He stared sincerely at her. "I promise I didn't do it," he said.

The conversation was tense and uncertain. Jane had always told Riley that trust was like a dam. When it's built solid, even the strongest storms can't tear it down but when there's a crack in the foundation, the smallest rain can cause a flood. He felt the flood.

"That's what I want to believe, Riley," she replied. "I just don't understand. I've spent the past year of my life trying to replay the vacation and the day and everything and I always come up short. I have nothing. I don't get it."

"Me either," said Riley.

"What are you doing here? How are you here right now? How can I trust you?" Jane asked. The anxiety of the reality of him being there was paralyzing to her.

Lila stood up and quickly made her way to the kitchen. She opened a drawer and pulled out the brown paper that Riley had left only days early. She'd taken the liberty of taping the pieces together. She delicately held the paper and took it to the living room.

She set the poem on the coffee table in front of Jane and she moved to study it carefully.

> *The game is dangerous, but the reward is great.*
> *If played correctly, you'll change your fate.*
> *Trust only those who come to you and above all else, whatever you do,*
> *Don't share your secret or abuse your power, after all you only have sleepless hours.*
> *With only five trips to clean your slate, you don't have any time to wait.*
> *Think smart, not hard and with every flight, always come back to the hanging blue light.*

After reading it, Jane sat still for a few seconds, processing everything.

"Did the prison give this to you?" She asked.

"No… well, not exactly," Riley answered. "The head guard did… But he gave it to me in secret. There is a whole world and a complicated system I still don't fully understand, nor do I really care…. all I know is I've been given five trips to prove I'm innocent."

"How many have you taken?" Jane asked.

"This is trip number two," he replied.

"How do you travel?" She questioned.

"It's the strangest thing… you know those packets in shoe boxes and bags and things? The little white ones that you're not supposed to open?" Asked Riley.

Jane nodded.

"I hold one of those, tight in my hand, for five seconds and close my eyes, when I open them, I am wherever I need to be," he explained. "And then, when I fall asleep, I wake back up in my prison cell."

"You weren't kidding about unbelievable," Jane replied. "Can anyone do that?"

"Not really... I don't think... It's complicated... again, I don't really understand it all. I just know that every second of every trip is valuable and I need to clear my name," he responded.

Jane took a deep breath and Riley could almost feel the dam repairing itself.

"This is honestly crazy... but I want you home with your family more than anything... how can I help?" Jane asked.

"Actually... that's why I called you here," Lila interrupted.

"You what?" Riley asked.

"I called you here because there are officers visiting from Florida and they're trying to help clear Riley's name. I figured you could help," Lila replied, looking at Jane and ignoring Riley's confusion.

"Wait, why did you come in the first place?" Riley asked.

"Lila invited me. She called me last Tuesday and asked if I would come visit. She said she had tickets to a play and that she'd like the company," Jane explained.

Riley nodded, trying to make sense of the situation. Before he'd gone to prison, Lila and Jane hardly spoke. They'd always gotten along but they never made plans together.

"Interesting," he said, looking at Lila. "Care to explain?"

"You came to visit... and it was weird... and I was overwhelmed," Lila replied. "I wanted someone around I could trust. I've pretty much lost all of my friends and I needed someone... little did I know, the officers would show up, too, and the timing would work out perfectly like this. It's really pretty weird how the timing has worked, don't you think? I mean the poem does say, 'trust only those who come to you' and it's like everyone is coming to you. Next thing you know, Kyle will be here," Lila joked.

As if on cue, there was a knock at the door.

The three of them looked blankly at each other.

"I'm sure it's the cops," Lila said.

"It's only 8:30," Riley replied.

"They're probably just anxious to get started," Lila said.

"Should I talk to them?" Asked Riley.

"I don't know… that seems like we're asking for trouble," Lila responded.

"Should I hide upstairs? What if I hear something that I can help with?" He asked.

There was another knock on the door.

"One second!" Lila called.

"I don't know. I don't know, Riley. Do what you think is best…" Lila said.

"I guess I'll just wing it," he replied. "I mean, isn't that what I've been doing this whole time anyway? He said as he stood up from the chair and swiftly ran up the stairs.

Lila walked to the front door and opened it with a smile.

"Good morning," James said. "Everything alright in here? Sounded like some commotion."

"Morning," Lila replied. "I have a four-year-old daughter and a three-and-a-half-month-old son, it always sounds like commotion," she laughed.

James smiled, "Sorry, we're a little early this morning. I hope that's alright."

"It's no problem at all," Lila replied as she gestured for the officers to head inside. "This is my mother-in-law, Jane Mines," she said, motioning toward Jane, seated on the white couch.

Jane stood up to greet them and reached out her hand.

"Nice to meet you all," she said as she shook each of their hands.

"She just arrived from California this morning," Lila added. "I thought she could be a good addition to our discussion… seeing as she also believes her son is innocent."

The officers nodded.

"I think that's a great idea," James said. "Thank you for coming all this way, Mrs. Mines. We don't have much time today, seeing as we need to leave for the airport in a few hours, so I thought we could jump right in?"

James paused and waited for everyone to take their seats.

"Alright," he started. "As I've shared with Lila, my mother is very good friends with Alexa Monarch. In fact, I actually remember going to a party at your house when I was a kid."

"Really? Who's your mother?" Jane asked.

"Debbie Wilde," he replied. "They were childhood friends and then went to college together."

"Oh… yes. I've heard a few stories about their college days," Jane laughed.

Wasting no time, James continued, "Well, I talked to my mom yesterday. She is actually visiting Alexa in California right now and since you were vacationing on her island before the incident, I asked her to do a little digging. She really wasn't interested in helping me at all, but I asked her to see if she could find anything out about your family or any possible motives someone would have had against you or-"

Jane interrupted, "Has she found anything?"

"Nothing solid," James replied. "The only thing she really had to share was that it's rumored Kyle did it. She said she still stays in touch with him and feels bad for all of the backlash and accusations he's received around town."

"Would you agree with that statement, Mrs. Mines?" Conway asked.

Jane nodded, "Yes, it has been a really difficult year for him. I take that back.... It's been a difficult two years for him. He had it rough after the accident with Keagan. People were saying it was his fault, which it wasn't, and I don't even understand how people could think that... and then, after Riley's arrest, people started to come up with the wildest reasons why he would have tried to frame Riley. Like 'Riley abandoned him when their dad died' and 'Riley moved away and built a successful career and left Kyle to take care of their mom and the house' and 'Riley was barely there for Kyle after Keagan died,'" she mocked. "All ridiculous accusations, not even close to the truth. In fact, they're the opposite of the truth. People only see what they want to see. They saw that Riley moved away after Warren died but they didn't care to recognize the fact that he stayed around four months longer than he originally planned to help take care of us. They saw that Riley stayed in New York and built a very successful career but not that he came to visit us all of the time. They saw that Riley didn't stay around long after Keagan's visitation and funeral but not that he invited Kyle to come live here for six months," she was very emotional now, tears welling as she continued her final thoughts. "The two have always been the best of brothers and the best of friends. They've both grown up to be amazing men. Amazing men who are there for each other in the best and worst of times and amazing men who would never, ever do anything to hurt one another."

The room was silent. It had been abundantly clear to the officers that Riley was innocent, but they just weren't sure about Kyle. However, after Jane's monologue, the room felt different.

Riley had been listening intently upstairs and smiled at his

Mom's explanation.

"I've missed her," he thought.

Lila broke the silence, "I couldn't agree more," she said. "Especially, after speaking with Kyle last night."

"You spoke with Kyle?" Rebecca asked, shocked.

Lila nodded.

They all stared at her, waiting patiently for her to expand.

After a couple of seconds, James decided she needed some prompting.

"What about?" He asked.

"Um… I called to ask him why his shoes were in the treehouse…" she replied.

"What do you mean his shoes?" Questioned Conway.

"Well… you know how the shoes have 'Mines' written inside on the tongue?" She asked.

They nodded.

"Well… Riley never did that with his shoes… he never labeled them…" she explained. "But Kyle always did."

The officers sat quiet, trying to piece new information together.

"Why didn't you tell us this when we first showed you the photo?" Asked Conway.

"I… Uh…" stumbled Lila.

"She didn't know until I told her this morning," Jane piped in, realizing Riley had most likely given Lila the information.

Riley was becoming anxious as he heard Lila and Jane stumbling around the conversation. He crawled to the edge of the stairs and slowly, tried to sneak a peek of the group. He saw the three officers, spread out on the white sofa, looking across the coffee table at Lila and Jane seated on the brown leather couch. Riley had imagined very rugged and unapproachable officers interrogating his wife. He was pleasantly surprised by their normal demeanor.

Lila looked toward the stairs and Riley quickly jumped back.

"When the boys were young and started wearing the same size, we decided to write 'Mines' on all of Kyle's clothes and shoes to help differentiate. Kyle was very protective about his things. He has a little OCD and the thought of him accidentally wearing Riley's shirt, even though it was the exact same, drove him crazy. We just felt it would be easier and help prevent a lot of problems… even after they stopped wearing the same size, Kyle never stopped marking his belongings," Jane explained.

"I guess I don't understand what this information is supposed to prove," Conway stated.

"I think it shows us a number of different things," deducted James. "First of all, we see that Kyle left his pair of shoes on the island, which seems like convenient timing to send his brother home with the laced pair and —"

Lila interrupted, "That's not why he left them there."

"Then, why?" Rebecca retorted.

"He told me the long version of the story… but in summary, they were Keagan's favorite pair of shoes and the treehouse was their secret hideout. They spent hours there when they were kids and even shared their first kiss there, years before they started dating. He took his shoes to the island to ceremoniously leave them there for her. It was a sentimental gesture and he asked Riley to bring the same pair because they always matched. If Kyle was going to plant a bomb in Riley's shoe, I don't know why he would do it in the matching pair and then bring them along and leave them there as evidence. Either he's a terrible criminal or he didn't do it," Lila argued.

"It really does seem pretty weird though… I mean that's super coincidental timing," Conway contended.

"You are all basing your knowledge and assumptions on false pretenses," said Jane. "What you don't understand, and what I think you ignored the first time I said it, is that Riley was really the only person there for Kyle after Keagan died. Kyle moved to New York to be with Lila and Riley for six months. You don't turn on someone who took care of you during such a critical point in your life. When you lose someone, you grip on even tighter to those who are there for you. You don't plant bombs in their shoes and send them to prison," Jane was becoming more defensive with each word. "Now, I know I just arrived, and I've missed a lot, but I bet I can be of some assistance here. However, if we spend another minute talking about the possibility of my son being guilty, I'll walk out right now and not give you anything to work with," she threatened.

Knowing Jane's potential with helping to solve the case, James complied, "I'm sorry to have upset you, Mrs. Mines. We can move on and talk about other suspects... of which we have limited leads. Our next... and only remaining suspect, is Benjie Mendoza, one of the island staff members."

Jane and Lila nodded, agreeing to move on and discuss Benjie.

James opened the brown, leather folder he'd been carrying and pulled out a picture. He handed it over the coffee table to Lila.

The photo featured a Filipino man, in his mid-twenties, with khaki pants and a blue, floral button down. His skin was naturally tan, and his hair was dark and slightly shaggy at the top.

"Do you recognize this man?" He asked.

"Uhh... I don't think so," answered Lila.

"Do you?" James asked, looking at Jane.

Lila handed her the photo to get a better look. She studied it and shook her head, "I've never seen him," she agreed.

James looked at Conway and Rebecca and then back at Lila

and Jane.

"That's very interesting," he replied. "As I said, that's Benjie Mendoza. He's the nephew of Salvador Mendoza, who is the manager of Alexa's island. The Mendoza family has run the island for nearly forty years and –"

Jane interrupted, "Oh, I am familiar with the Mendoza family. I know Salvador very well from the time we've spent on the island... but that young man has never been there before."

"I visited the island a couple of weeks ago and he was working. That's where I took this picture... when I was there, he was most often working at the pool and he brought me a number of drinks. In fact, I didn't learn too many other worker's names, but it would have been nearly impossible for me to not have known his... he was the most accommodating staff member by far."

"I'm telling you, that boy has never been on the island. He couldn't be more than twenty-five years old and I know the whole family... I watched the kids grow up. Salvador and Rosie have two sons, Daniel and Matthew, and Salvador's brother, Elijah, and his wife, Mary, have two kids, Jonathan and Carolina. Those were the only children living on the island and Benjie would have been around their same age. If he had been on the island, I would have known... I'm really good with remembering names and faces and he has never been there. I'm confident in that," Jane explained.

"That seems pretty strange..." commented Rebecca.

Upstairs, Riley's eyes were getting heavier by the second. He tried to think of the members of the Mendoza family, but he hadn't paid much attention over the years.

"Come on, Riley," he thought to himself. "You have to stay awake."

"It does seem pretty strange," concurred James. "I ran a

background check on him, and everything came back clean. I didn't think to look at when he moved to the island. I assumed he'd always been there like the rest of them."

"Well, we did say we thought it would be beneficial to go back to the island…" Rebecca said. "Maybe, this gives us a good lead to investigate?"

"Yeah, I'm just not exactly sure how to get back… I don't think I want to ask Alexa again and I wouldn't want my mom to ask," James said.

"Why not?" Rebecca inquired. "Doesn't she know you're looking into the case? I'm sure she wouldn't mind."

"Ehh… I'm with James," Jane agreed. "I know I just got here but I don't think Alexa would like him asking to go back right away. She can be very protective and controlling." She paused, "But… I bet she would let me visit."

"Plus, I'm sure the Mendoza's would be more willing to talk with a longtime friend and confidant, rather than new visitors," Lila quickly added.

"She makes a good point," said Conway.

"I could join you," Lila suggested. "I probably need a break and the island air sounds pretty nice right about now."

"That would be nice," replied Jane. "I could tell Alexa you needed a little getaway. I'm sure it wouldn't be a problem at all."

Everyone nodded, seeing the plan seamlessly coming together.

"How quickly do you think you could go?" Asked James.

Even the excitement of the rising plans couldn't keep gravity from pulling down on Riley's heavy eyelids.

"I could call her today and I'm sure we could get on a flight… What? As soon as this evening?" Jane asked, looking at Lila.

"I think we could manage that," Lila said. "I can call my

mom to watch the kids. She only lives two hours away and she jumps at any opportunity to spend more time with them."

"Well... what are we waiting for?" James asked. "Let's put this plan into action."

CHAPTER

THIRTY-FOUR

Riley slowly opened his eyes to the sound of rattling keys. He stretched out his arms and yawned, trying to reorient himself with his surroundings. He rubbed his eyes and the hanging blue light above him came into focus.

"Dang it," he mumbled. "I really thought I could stay awake."

His prison cell door opened and Aus emerged, wearing a uniform top Riley had not seen before. It was cream colored with a pattern of yellow, red and green flowers.

"New shirt?" Asked Riley.

"Thanks for noticing! Yes, it is," replied Aus. "My sister sent it to me for my birthday."

"Wait, when was your birthday?" Riley asked.

"Yesterday," said Aus. "January eighth."

"Oh, well, happy late birthday!" Riley said enthusiastically.

"Thank you but I've never been too into birthdays" Aus replied. "Plus, I really don't care this year with everything else going on. I've been watching your cell like crazy waiting for you to get back. How did it go?"

Riley shook his head, "Aus, it was crazy. There's so much information and at the same time, nothing at all. The police seem to think my brother did it, but Lila and I really don't think that's possible and neither does… my mom."

"Did you talk to your mom?" Aus asked surprised.

"Yeah… I guess Lila had called her a couple of days ago when the police first came and invited her to visit," Riley said.

"How was she? Did you tell her about the gel?" Aus questioned.

"Yes, and I think she took it about as well as I could have expected. After the initial shock wore off, she was ready to help me out. I do have another question about how the gel works though…" he hesitated.

"Go on," Aus said.

"Well, you said when I leave here, people forget that I exist… but, what happens when I am out in the world? Like, how can my family know and remember me and my visits? Does everyone recognize and remember me?" Riley asked.

Aus nodded, "I figured it wouldn't be too long until you asked that… honestly, it's not an exact science. The Desiccant Keepers have been trying to figure it out for years. The best theory to date is that those who need you, as much as you need them, recognize and remember you but those who are not needed are not affected. For instance, when I went home to visit my family, it was a time of deep sadness and we all needed each other. Therefore, I was able to share about my travels and they were able to understand because they needed and wanted me there, as much as I needed and wanted to be there. In your case, your family needs you and wants you to be home and you need to and want to be home. There have been different situations over the years and a few exceptions but based on the way I understand it… I believe you could go home and walk the streets of New York City without any issues. No one would recognize you and if they did, it would mean they were on your side. Again, it's a very complicated process. I was only given two trips to see my family, so I didn't really have time to think about it. If I were you, I definitely wouldn't test it."

Riley nodded, "I guess that makes sense. So, what do you

think about the cops? Do you think they would be safe to confide in?"

"My assumption would be yes but it's all trial and error at this point. It's only been eighty years since the first use of silica gel for travel. It's still considered relatively new in the big scheme of things."

Riley sighed, "This is all very difficult to understand."

"I know," Aus agreed. "What's the latest? Have they found anything else?"

"They found a pair of shoes on the island that matched the shoes I wore to the airport on the day of my arrest. I think they assumed my shoes were switched out with the pair they found but that's not the case. My brother and I have matching shoes and the pair left on the island were his," Riley stood up and began to pace the room. "My brother admitted to them being his shoes and in summary, he left them there as a sentimental gesture, no connection to the case. My mom showed up and made a compelling argument against the accusations toward my brother and I think the cops agreed to move away from that theory. But I can't be certain because I was getting really tired when I was listening in. I know one of the officers, James, I think, showed Lila and my mom a picture of a man from the island but neither of them recognized him. I faintly remember them offering to go to the island to investigate more –"

Aus interrupted, "Who's them? Lila? Your mom? The cops?"

"Lila and my mom. I think she was going to call Alexa and see if they could take a quick trip out there. I am not sure what they intend to find, I guess they want to question the man in the picture…" Riley suggested.

"That would seem to make sense to me," Aus concurred.

"The thing I don't understand is what the man on the island would have had as a motive. I went to the island as a kid, but I never did anything to make anyone upset. It had also been at least ten years since I'd been to the island before that last trip," said Riley.

"Maybe, someone bribed him," Aus replied.

"I guess that's a possibility," acknowledged Riley. "I have run myself mad trying to think of anyone who would have had it out for me. I'm not a perfect man, but I don't have any inkling of who could have framed me."

Aus shook his head, "Alright, well, we've got three more trips to work with, right? I'm confident we can get something together. It sounds like you have a lot of people working hard for you."

Riley agreed, "I really do." He walked to the wall where he kept his trip tally and added another black mark. "I really have to wait another twenty-four hours?" He asked.

"I'm afraid so," replied Aus. "Come on," he said as he stood up from his usual corner chair and gestured for Riley to follow him to the door.

"Keep quiet," Aus instructed as he locked the cell behind them. They started walking down the hall and took a sharp turn into what looked like an unlocked cell identical to Riley's. To his surprise, there was a staircase where he expected the bathroom to be and they started to walk down them. Aus led the way through an alley of staircases and hallways, up and down, left and right, it was dark, and Riley had no idea how Aus could possibly know where he was.

"We're almost to my place," said Aus. "We can kill some time there this afternoon." Aus led the way up one final staircase and opened a small wooden door. The light came streaming in as they ducked to exit the alleyway. "Welcome to my crib," Aus joked.

"That was crazy," Riley commented as he walked toward the window to see the prison perched up on a cliff about fifty yards away.

"Those secret passageways will get ya," said Aus.

Riley looked around and admired the small, quaint hut. It was exactly what he would have pictured for Aus. Everything down to the green, floral couch perfectly matched his easygoing personality.

"Make yourself at home," Aus said, motioning toward the couch. "Do you like to bake?" He asked.

"I used to," Riley replied. "My dad was a professional chef and we used to bake together. I don't think I've even used an oven since he passed."

"I'm sorry for asking," Aus apologized. "I was planning to do some baking this afternoon. I eat almost all of my meals in the cafeteria because it's easy and free, but I find something soothing about baking, so I almost always have sweets around my place. Plus, what else am I supposed to do besides eat my sorrows away when it's late… and I'm bored… and I think about how sad I am to be stuck on an island working at a prison?" He forced a laugh.

"I always assumed you enjoyed your job," commented Riley.

"Oh, I do. Truly, it's been a good gig. I really only get sad when I start to think about having a family or getting… I feel like I gave up that part of my life for this," Aus explained.

"Have you ever thought about making a change?" Asked Riley, "How old are you?"

"Turned forty yesterday," Aus replied.

"Are you kidding?" Riley said, "You have loads of time!"

"Yeah," said Aus, "It's just hard to make a change."

"Oh, it's absolutely terrifying to make a change," agreed Riley. "I remember my move to New York City like it was yesterday. It was December 29, 2009 and I was on a red eye out of LAX. I sat down on the plane, looked out the window and tried not to cry. I was leaving my family and my home behind for what I hoped would be a great adventure. But the moment I began the adventure, all of the worries and doubts filled my mind. Would I be okay? Would I make friends? Would I find success and happiness? It was the most terrifying flight of my life, but I look back at that moment and it changed everything for me. I started my business in New York, I met my wife, I had my children… I could have let fear get the better of me and walked off the plane but instead, by making that one decision, my life changed forever."

"You make a compelling argument… I've never really talked to anyone about my fears before," Aus admitted.

"I wouldn't assume a prison would be the easiest place to share your feelings," Riley laughed.

"That is very true," agreed Aus. "Maybe, I'll think about making a change," he shrugged. "But for now, I'm going to think about what dessert to make," he laughed, patting his stomach.

"I think you need a birthday cake," suggested Riley.

"Nah, I don't need that," replied Aus. "What about peanut butter brownies?"

"A man after my own heart," joked Riley. "Brownies sound delicious."

"Brownies it is!" Exclaimed Aus as he pumped his fist. He made his way to the kitchen cupboard where he pulled out a metal mixing bowl. "Would you like to help?" He asked Riley.

Riley shook his head.

"Strange as it may be for two grown men to make brownies together in a small kitchen, located on an island home to the world's most inescapable prison… I'd love nothing more than to pass the time with some baking right now."

Aus let out a big laugh as Riley joined him in the kitchen.

CHAPTER

THIRTY-FIVE

The sun was setting as the boat reached the shore of the island. Per usual, Salvador was standing on the dock to greet his guests. Salvador was a large man at six-feet four-inches tall and two-hundred-and-thirty-pounds wide. His skin was dark and a stark contrast to his light blue button-down shirt. He had short brown hair cut slightly longer than a buzz.

"Hello, beautiful ladies," he greeted with open arms gesturing toward the island behind him. "Welcome back! What a pleasant surprise."

"Hi, Salvador," replied Jane. "Thank you so much for having us! Especially, on such short notice."

"Of course! You're always welcome on the island. Let me have someone grab your bags for you and I'll show you to dinner... Benjie!" He called.

Lila and Jane immediately looked at each other.

Seeing their looks, Salvador asked, "Is that alright?"

"Oh, yes," Jane said. "That would be lovely."

A young man, identical to the one in the picture, emerged from the mansion. As Benjie made his way to the dock, Salvador helped Lila and Jane off of the boat.

"Good evening," Benjie greeted. "I'll unload your bags from the boat and put them in your rooms," he said as he hopped aboard.

Salvador instructed, "Follow me, ladies. We have a special

table already set for your dinner. We're under strict orders from Alexa to ensure you have a relaxing time."

"Sounds perfect," Jane replied. "Is Benjie new to the island?" She asked.

Surprised by Jane's enthusiasm for investigating so quickly, Lila played along.

"Yeah, I don't remember him from last time," she commented.

"Uh…" Salvador paused, clearly thinking. "Yes, he is fairly new. I'm trying to think back to the last time you were here. When was that?"

"The end of December and beginning of January a little over a year ago," Lila answered.

"Ahh, yes. He must have started just a couple of weeks after you came. My son, Daniel, decided to pursue another opportunity on the mainland and we needed to fill his spot. My older sister, Marie, never wanted to work on the island. Benjie is her son and she thought it would be good for him, so she agreed to let him try it out. He's done a great job so far and it's been fun having him around," Salvador replied enthusiastically.

"How lovely you get to enjoy so much family time on the island," Jane commented. "What is Daniel doing now?"

They arrived at a small table under the gazebo by the pool. Salvador pulled out Jane's chair and answered, "He's taking classes at the University of Miami. He applied and didn't think he would get in but once he did, he couldn't pass up the opportunity."

"Good for him," she replied, "That's wonderful."

"I am a proud dad for sure," Salvador said beaming. "What would you like to drink?"

"I'll take your finest merlot, please," Jane said.

"I'll have the same," Lila added.

Salvador nodded and walked around the pool toward the

outdoor kitchen.

"How romantic," Jane laughed, gesturing toward the table set for two and ocean view.

"I haven't had a day away from Chandler and Warren since Riley was arrested. I will take romantic," Lila smiled. "I will take anything right now to relax. I love them both dearly… but boy are they needy."

Salvador returned and set the wine glasses on the table. "Enjoy," he said.

"Cheers," Jane said, picking up her glass and holding it out to Lila. "To freeing a man, we both love."

"Cheers," Lila replied, clinking her glass with Jane's.

They sat in silence for a few moments, sipping their wine.

"That's pretty strange timing with Benjie… isn't it?" Jane asked.

"Yes, it's definitely odd," Lila replied. "Hardly seems like a coincidence to me that Daniel would leave, and Benjie would come within a few weeks of the incident."

"Especially, since staffing changes are very few and far between here," Jane said. "But I just don't know what the connection would be. Say it was Daniel… Why would he do that to Riley?"

"My guess is someone would have had to bribe him," said Lila.

"Right," Jane agreed. "But who?"

"I have no idea," Lila replied. "I feel like if we could get to Daniel, then maybe, we could get some answers."

"Why would Daniel tell us anything?" Jane asked.

"I don't know… he wouldn't, I guess" she replied defeated. "Do you think he's close with any of his cousins? Maybe someone would have more information than Salvador?"

"It's possible," Jane replied as Benjie approached the table with a basket of bread.

"Hot, fresh bread for the ladies," he said as he placed the basket on the table. "Your dinner tonight will be a Caesar salad, followed by a salmon fillet with jasmine rice and grilled asparagus and topped off with baked Alaska for dessert. The first course should be out shortly. Is there anything else I can get for you at the moment?"

"That sounds great," Lila smiled. "I think we're alright for now."

"How long have you been working on the island?" Jane asked, abruptly switching subjects.

"I started here at the end of last January," Benjie replied. "So, I'm getting close to a year."

"That's nice. Did you just want to join the family business?" Inquired Jane.

"Not exactly," Benjie said, his body language shifting into a more comfortable, conversational stance. "My crazy cousin, Daniel, decided to up and leave the island and he kind of left everyone hanging. My mom pretty much forced me to fill his spot and it was supposed to be temporary… they said he'd be back in a couple of months, but it's been almost a year and there's no sign of him coming back."

"Oh, wow. I'm sorry to hear that. Has anyone spoken with him?" Lila asked.

"His brother, Matt, talks to him on occasion and visited him one time a while back. From what I understand, he spends most of his days drunk at a hotel bar in Miami Beach. Must be nice to not work and lay around on the beach all day with no responsibilities and a cocktail waitress to deliver you free drinks," he mocked.

Lila and Jane looked at each other, confused about the new information.

"I thought Salvador said Daniel was attending the

University of Miami?" Lila questioned.

"Oh, that whole spiel? Yeah, he's embarrassed. He thought it was some fling with a sugar momma that would come to an end but clearly, it has not," Benjie replied annoyed. His whiny imitation picked up again and his body movements were now very animated, "So, next time you find yourself at the Perennial Hotel, be sure to say hello to the drunk Mendoza lying on the beach."

"Benjie!" Salvador called from the pool deck. "Quit gabbing and let them relax," he insisted.

"Evidently, I've got to go," Benjie said. "Carolina will be serving you your food. Enjoy your time on the island."

"Thank you, Benjie," Lila and Jane said simultaneously.

As he walked away, Jane whispered to Lila, "You don't know how helpful you've been."

"What should we do with that?" Asked Lila. "Should we go to the hotel?"

"I don't know what to do... Maybe, we should call James and see what he thinks? We're not detectives by any means and we've gotten pretty lucky already," suggested Jane.

"That's a good point," Lila replied. She could see Carolina walking out toward the table with salads in hand. "We can call him after dinner... for now, let's just try to enjoy this beautiful view and some delicious food."

CHAPTER THIRTY-SIX

Riley paced back and force in his prison cell, wondering what time it was. Yesterday, after they'd finished eating the entire pan of brownies, Aus told him he'd stop by in the morning, around eleven, with the third silica gel.

He looked outside and concluded it had to be getting close to eleven, based on the sun. He paced and paced, not knowing how to make the time go faster.

He sighed a heavy sigh of relief when he finally heard footsteps down the hall.

"Good morning, Riley," Aus said unenthusiastically as he opened the cell door.

"Is everything okay?" Asked Riley.

"Yes," Aus replied. "It's just that... after you left last night, I was thinking about all of the information you shared and how Lila and Jane might go to the island... and I am just worried that they won't be in New York when you get there... I would hate for you to waste a trip."

"I thought about that, but I figured the gel would take me where I needed to be. Isn't that what you said? Like if I need to be with Lila, it will take me to wherever Lila is?" Riley clarified.

"Not exactly," Aus sighed. "As I've explained before, the gel has some real quirks and limitations. It takes people where they need to be, but it only works for people who need to be home... I know that doesn't really make sense but it's the only way to try to explain it."

Riley closed his eyes tight, thinking through the information.

"So... what you're telling me is that I could use this gel and go home to no one? And if I fall asleep before they'd get back, I forfeit the trip?"

"Unfortunately, that's correct," Aus replied.

Riley grabbed his hair and pulled it out of frustration.

"How can I possibly know when they'll be home?" He shouted.

"I don't know," Aus said, shaking his head.

Riley talked out loud, contemplating his thoughts, "I'm not sure how quickly they were planning to leave. If I head out today, they might have already left but if I wait until tomorrow, that gives them even more time to prepare and leave for a trip... Then, on top of that, who knows how long they'll be gone. I guess it makes the most sense to try as soon as possible to catch them. Otherwise, I think I'd have to wait a week and try my luck," he paused. "AHH," he screamed. "What do I do?"

"Please keep it down, Riley," Aus calmly replied. "I know this is not the ideal situation but at least you have a chance to get out. Things could be much worse. In my opinion, I think you either go right now and hope to catch them or wait a week. Any option in between allows for too many variables."

Riley nodded, "I think you're right. I'll go now. I don't want to wait any longer."

"Are you sure?" Aus asked.

"Positive," he replied, reaching out his hand impatiently.

Aus reached into his left pocket, pulled out the silica gel and set it in Riley's hand.

Aus grabbed Riley's shoulders and looked seriously at him, "Make it a good trip," he said. "You only have three trips left and we need to get you out of here... I'm wishing you the best,

Riley Mines."

"Thank you," Riley said as he moved to stand in the middle of the room. He closed his eyes and counted, "One, two, three, four, five." With a splash of water, he was gone.

Riley stood nervously, keeping his eyes closed. Something felt different.

The breeze against his bare chest wasn't bone chilling cold and the ground beneath his feet didn't feel like the New York City sidewalk or the hardwood floors in his home. He wiggled his toes and felt sand slide between them.

"Where am I?" He thought, too fearful to open his eyes.

He felt something hit his stomach and instinctively, he opened his eyes. He looked down at the ground and saw a lime green, foam football.

A young, boy with bleached blonde hair and pale skin, red from the sun, was running toward him.

"Sorry about that, sir," he apologized. "My friend needs to learn to throw," he laughed, pointing across the beach.

Riley hesitantly picked up the football and handed it to him.

"It's alright," he said in a trance, still not looking up.

"Thanks," the boy said as he grabbed the football and ran back to his friend.

Riley took a deep breath and built up the courage to examine his surroundings. He looked up and laid his eyes on the vast, blue ocean continuing for miles in either direction. He slowly turned around and fixed his eyes on an all-glass building standing thirty stories tall.

"Where am I?" He wondered.

He scanned the bustling beach, filled with tourists, looking back and forth, until a light blue towel hut caught his attention. There was a white sign, posted in front of it, with black words that read, "Towels Available for Perennial Hotel Guests Only."

CHAPTER
THIRTY-SEVEN

"Okay, according to Lila and Jane's information, Daniel Mendoza spends his days drunk at this hotel bar," James said as he opened the door leading into the lobby of the luxurious Perennial Hotel, located on the North Shore of Miami Beach. "We only have forty minutes left of our lunch break, so we need to act fast."

The lobby featured white marble floors with thirty-foot high ceilings that boded gorgeous hanging lights of all colors. Straight ahead were windows that covered the East wall and overlooked the pool deck out to the ocean. The room was light and airy with an aroma of saltwater.

"This place is amazing," commented Rebecca.

"It really is," agreed Conway.

"A little too amazing, in my opinion, for a general island staff member to have planted himself for a year," James said.

"Maybe, Alexa pays them reaaally well," Conway laughed.

"Or maybe, he's just living it up and doesn't care about racking up debt," Rebecca suggested.

"Both possibilities, I guess," James replied as he continued toward the glass wall. "I'm assuming the best place to start is the main hotel bar," he stated. "I've been here before, it's on the second floor."

Rebecca and Conway agreed and started to follow James

toward the elevators.

On their way, they walked past the large glass windows. Rebecca admired the swimming pool, stretching fifty yards wide, with its inviting blue water. She looked longingly at the white, plush lounge chairs surrounding the pool and daydreamed of a life in the lap of luxury. Her eyes followed the winding path to the right of the pool that led down to the waterfront. She stared out at the water and stopped dead in her tracks.

"Oh my gosh… oh my gosh," Rebecca panted.

James and Conway, who were a few steps ahead, stopped to look back.

"What is it, Rebecca?" James asked.

Rebecca could feel her heart pounding inside her chest.

"I see him," she replied.

"Daniel?" Conway exclaimed. "Where?" He asked, quickly moving to the window to get a better look.

"No," Rebecca shook her head. "Riley," she said pointing toward the beach.

"What?!" Conway and James replied simultaneously.

"Look!" She said as she pointed toward a man in black boxers looking lost on the beach. "That's him!"

"It can't be him," Conway argued. "There's no possible way!"

"It sure does look like him though," James agreed as he stared out the glass.

"I swear it's him," Rebecca insisted.

"And how do you suppose we find out?" Asked Conway, "Just walk up, tell him we're the police and ask if he's an escaped convict?" He suggested obnoxiously.

"I don't know but it's him!" Rebecca replied.

"Well, we're going to need to figure out our plan pretty soon because he's on the move," James said as he pointed toward Riley starting to make his way south on the beach.

Rebecca took off at a dead sprint out of the lobby doors and down the sidewalk leading to the sand.

James and Conway exchanged panicked looks.

"What is she doing?" Asked Conway.

"I don't know, but I'm following her" James shouted as he took off running.

Rebecca was far too fast and athletic for James and Conway to catch her. She maneuvered around the hotel guests with ease and was quickly on the beach.

"Rebecca!" James called, "Rebecca!"

Hearing the commotion, instinctively, Riley turned around. He stared back at the three officers, now running toward him, and recognized their faces.

"No way," Riley thought to himself.

"Riley," Rebecca called as she got closer to him. She stopped about five feet away and caught her breath. "You're Riley Mines, aren't you?"

Riley stared back at her, not knowing how to respond.

He thought back to Aus' words, "No one can recognize you, unless they're on your side."

James and Conway were now standing behind Rebecca staring in disbelief at Riley. His blue eyes looked bright and wide as he stared back at them.

Riley replied with three words that he knew had the power to completely change his fate, "Yes, I am."

Completely caught off guard, the officers looked blankly back at him.

In an effort to conceal his knowledge, Riley broke the silence.

"And who are you?" He asked.

"I'm Officer Rebecca Good," she gestured toward the others, "Officer Luke Conway and Officer James Wilde."

Noticing the attention, the group had now garnered on the beach, James suggested, "Why don't we go inside and find a space a little more private to converse?"

Riley nodded.

James led the group with Riley in the middle and Conway and Rebecca in tow to ensure he cooperated.

Riley sensed their tension, but he didn't feel threatened or anxious, he knew he needed them to clear his name.

"Aus said I could only travel home. This is crazy. I don't even know where I am," Riley's mind raced. "Did the gel take me to these people? I'm so confused... Okay, calm yourself, Riley. They only recognize you because they're on your side. It's going to be okay. Make this trip count."

He continued his personal pep talk as he followed James into the hotel. The four of them made their way up a grand, marble staircase to the second floor of the hotel where a few ballrooms were located. The floor was quiet, and James found a spot with a black, leather couch and a couple of cream-colored accent chairs.

James and Rebecca shared the couch, while Conway and Riley each took their own chair.

"Truthfully, I have no idea where to start with this," James said. "What are you doing here? Did you escape Nadirehs? Isn't that impossible? Also, are those boxers? Why are you wearing boxers?"

Riley was nervous. He wanted to trust them but couldn't find the words.

"It's okay," Rebecca encouraged. "We want to help you. Just tell us how you got here."

Riley took a deep breath.

"I didn't escape," he replied. "It's going to sounds crazy... but I 'traveled' here," he said using his hands to signal quotation marks. "And when I 'travel,' for some reason, I show up in boxers."

"What do you mean you 'traveled'? Rebecca replied, copying the sign.

"It's a long explanation… but basically, I've been given five trips to teleport to help clear my name," he hesitated for a few seconds before continuing. "And if we're really being transparent here," he paused again. "During my last trip, I was upstairs while you were talking to my wife and my mom in Manhattan."

The officers sat motionless as they tried to process the information.

"I'm sorry. Maybe, I'm just misunderstanding you…" Conway replied aggressively. "You're trying to tell me that you've been teleporting," he shook his head. "That you have five trips to teleport to clear your name." Conway scratched his head, "Well, if this isn't the biggest pile of bullshit I've ever heard, then I don't know what is."

"Hear him out, Conway," Rebecca argued. "We're in this deep anyway… we might as well give him a chance."

"Thank you," Riley said, looking at Rebecca. "The head guard at Nadirehs came to me with a poem. The physical poem is at my house in New York… I left it with Lila. But I have it memorized," he paused. "The game is dangerous, but the reward is great. If played correctly, you'll change your fate. Trust only those who come to you and above all else, whatever you do. Don't share your secret or abuse your power, after all you only have sleepless hours. With only five trips to clean your slate, you don't have any time to wait. Think smart, not hard and with every flight, always come back to the hanging blue light."

"How do you travel?" James asked.

"Do you really believe this guy?" Conway doubted.

James shifted his gaze toward Conway.

"Why else would an escaped convict be out casually walking on Miami Beach with no clothes on and agree to sit down with three officers? If I escaped from prison, I probably wouldn't choose to do it so publicly."

"Miami!" Riley thought, relieved to know where he was.

"You make a good point," Rebecca commented.

"Oh, get a room," Conway rolled his eyes. "We have less than thirty minutes until we need to be back at the office. You know Hillsteg will have something to say if we're gone too long."

"Call him and tell him we got food poisoning," demanded James.

"You know we can't do that," said Rebecca. "Not after we all took off the same time last week… he might get suspicious."

James replayed the poem in his head.

"You only have sleepless hours," he said aloud. "What exactly does that mean?"

"I have from the time I arrive until I fall asleep at the place I'm visiting. This is only my third trip and the last two were to my house. Whenever I fall asleep, I wake back up in my prison cell. In it, there's a blue light above my bed, hence the hanging blue light portion of the poem."

"When did you get here?" James asked.

"Seconds before you spotted me," Riley replied.

"Good," said James. "I live just around the corner. It's —" he paused to look at his watch. "Twelve-thirty now and we're off at five. You can spend the afternoon at my place, and we can talk more tonight."

"Okay," Riley replied, not having a better suggestion himself. "Sounds good."

"And we can call Lila and Jane," Rebecca added. "They're on Alexa's island right now. I'm sure they'd want to know you're here. Maybe, they'd be able to come later."

"Really?" Riley asked.

Rebecca nodded.

"Come on," instructed James. "Let's get out of here."

CHAPTER

THIRTY-EIGHT

The harsh slap of a hand against Aus' face was the only sound in the otherwise silent room. Aus was on his knees with his hands tied behind his back. He shut his eyes tight and looked down at the floor as he absorbed the pain. His face was quickly turning red from the impact.

He slowly tilted his head back to look up at the rich, green eyes of Duke Wilkinson.

Duke was the grandson of Robert Wilkinson. He stood tall and relatively slim with light blonde hair that complimented his fair skin tone. He looked fairly young for being in his mid-forties.

Duke straightened his black tie, unrolled and buttoned his sleeves and lightly brushed the chest of his tuxedo, signaling he was finished with the beating.

He began to pace back and forth in the dimly lit room. The walls were covered in multicolored, dark stones and the floor was smooth cement. The room was shaped in a perfect circle, with only walls and no door. In its original build, it served as a dungeon that could only be accessed from the top. Lining the perimeter of the room were seven large, golden chairs with red velvet padding. Each throne was occupied by a man in a tuxedo. Above each chair, a gold plate was engraved with a board member's name.

Aus looked around the room from left to right, studying each name plate carefully; making sure to avoid eye contact with his disappointed uncle.

Chance Briggs
Colton Sterling
Micah Bryant
Duke Wilkinson
Miles Beckham
Hansel Westley
Maclan Andrews

"I didn't think we'd have to do this again, Aus," Duke taunted brashly. "But it seems you still haven't learned the proper way we do things around here."

"I don't know what you're talking about!" Aus called out.

In the nearly nine years Aus had been a Contender, he'd never thought about sharing his gift. A Contender is given the right to share the gift of silica gel only once in their lifetime, as partially determined and controlled by the Keepers. Aus had been saving his one chance for something special and when he met Riley, he knew it was meant to be.

Aus tried to stay out of the Desiccant World as much as possible and only spoke of current events when his uncle brought them up. In nine years, he'd managed to stay under the radar but in the last ten days alone, he'd been summoned to headquarters twice.

When the Desiccant Keepers were formed, they understood the importance of establishing a monarchy. They created a charter outlining the laws and established a formal meeting place.

They deemed manipulation of the gel acceptable only for Keeper meeting purposes.

During his time in the hospital, in 1942, Lawrence Bryant read about an abandoned castle located somewhere off the coast of Scotland. The men agreed it would become the Desiccant Keeper headquarters and they studied the photograph for days before attempting to manipulate the gel.

On the first of August, the men gathered around and attempted to make the trip together for the first time. Only two were successful. They didn't have time to waste, with some men healing, some heading home and others being sent back out to battle, they knew they needed a plan.

They determined that the first of every month would be a mandatory meeting day. It wasn't until December of that year that every member successfully made the trip.

"Maclan!" Duke shouted. "Play the screen!"

Maclan was an athletic man with dark brown hair and brown eyes. He was Aus' father's brother and the family resemblance was undeniable.

Maclan stood up from his chair and made his way to the wall behind him. He wiggled a stone out from the others and grabbed the small piece of tattered cloth out from hidden behind it. He whipped the cloth open, walked to the center of the room and brushed it out on the ground in front of Aus.

Light suddenly shot out from the fabric and projected a screen that covered the entire ceiling. A video of Riley appeared. It pictured him walking along the beach with officers running after him.

Aus continued to watch as Riley turned and went inside with the officers. The footage showed Riley getting into a car with them and ended with him sitting in an unfamiliar room, alone, twiddling his thumbs.

The screen went dark. Maclan picked up the cloth and put it back in the wall behind the stone.

"Let me ask you something, Aus," Duke said. "Does that

look like Riley's home in New York City to you?"

"I've never been to his home," Aus replied.

Duke moved quickly and put his face inches away from Aus'.

"This is not the time for humor," he replied, spitting on his face. "Don't you understand what this means?" He screamed. "He's manipulated the gel. We've lost control!" His face was red with anger.

Micah stood up and made his way to Duke. Micah's inviting hazel eyes and silky black hair combed to the side exhibited a calming presence. His tuxedo accentuated his slim build and his graceful gate made him the most approachable man in the room.

"Why don't we let Aus explain himself?" He suggested.

"Oh," Duke sang obnoxiously. "Yes, let's have the inadequate idiot tell us of how he's messed everything up. I'd love to hear it from his perspective." Duke turned and fluttered to his chair. He sat down with a childlike grin, tapped his fingers together, put his elbows on his knees and rested his chin on his hands. "Please, do tell!" He begged.

Aus hopelessly looked back and forth across the room. Although the beatings had been grating, he still knew giving Riley the gel had been the right thing to do.

"Riley is special," Aus started. He spoke slowly, "He is kind and intelligent and his intentions are good. As you know, Riley was wrongfully accused of a crime he didn't commit and placed in my prison on Nadirehs Island. He spent nearly a year rarely leaving his cell and looking hopeless before I decided he was truly innocent. As we can all recall, I didn't wait for permission to be granted and I gave him a gel early. My wrongdoing... not his," Aus paused to collect his thoughts. The men were unamused, all blankly staring back at him.

"Clearly, I don't know as much about the powers of the gel

as you do but I know that Riley's..." Aus hesitated. "Well, Riley's different," he explained. "Think about your ancestors. Think about their struggles to travel to this very castle and the practice it took them. I'm sure many of you struggled your first time as well."

A few heads nodded around the room and Aus felt the mood shift slightly.

"I simply gave Riley the backstory of the gel and explained the dangers of manipulation. Of course, I told him the story of BT, just like my uncle told me when I was given the gel," he said, looking at Maclan for confirmation.

Maclan nodded.

"I didn't tell him anything more than that and when Riley left for this trip, he was planning to go home. I spoke with him right before he left, and he understood the risks of wasting a trip if his family wasn't home. I can almost guarantee Riley was as shocked to be standing on that beach as you were to see him there," Aus said. "It's not my fault," he pleaded.

Unconvinced, Duke accused, "There's something you're not telling us."

Aus knew the dangers of Riley's untapped power and wanted to keep him safe. He'd heard horror stories from his uncle of men who'd threatened the Desiccant Keepers power over the years, and he didn't want Riley to become one of them.

Duke jumped up, swiftly made his way to Aus and grabbed his neck.

"Tell me," he demanded with his grip growing tighter.

Aus struggled to breath and his face started to turn red.

"He took something with him," Aus gasped.

Duke let go, knowing Aus was now willing to cooperate.

"On a trip?" Duke asked.

Aus nodded.

"Yes, the second time he traveled," He paused. "He took the poem home to show his wife. When he got back and told me about it, I played it off like it wasn't a big deal. I didn't want him to think it was abnormal," he said, shaking his head.

Duke began to pace back and forth around the room again.

"Thank you for your loyalty," he said sincerely to Aus. "I can see that you don't want to make enemies with us and for that, I am truly grateful."

"What are we going to do?" Shouted Briggs.

Briggs was the youngest Keeper and had only been on the board six months. He was twenty-four years old and as entitled as they come. He was undeniably handsome, and his family was extremely wealthy. His overly tanned skin matched his perfectly toned body and shaggy, brown hair. His appearance exemplified that fact that he'd never worked a day in his life and that he would never have to.

"Can someone please get the kid under control?" Hansel asked.

Hansel was the eldest Keeper and was nearing the end of his time of service. He was in his late sixties and his gray hair, wrinkled skin and large glasses showed every ounce of his age. His tux fit slightly tighter than his counterparts and the few extra pounds in his midsection didn't help. Although he tended to be grouchy, when he spoke, all of the members listened with the utmost respect.

"Let us not overreact. It's not as though we haven't seen something like this before. How quickly you've forgotten that one among you has the same ability. If the skill is used for good, then there is simply no threat at all."

Duke replied, "Of course, Hansel. I am sorry for disregarding your abilities. However, you're a board member and you were raised to one day be a Keeper, which leaves little cause for concern. Riley on the other hand doesn't know the strengths he has. If Z would find out..." Duke paused.

"Who's Z?" Aus asked.

The Desiccant Keepers gasped and Maclan shook his head, once again disappointed by Aus' actions.

"Who's Z?" Duke repeated back to Aus with screeching disapproval. "Z is short for Zade Towns, the grandson of BT. In recent months, we've seen a rise in sporadic, untraceable crimes and we have reason to believe Z is on the move. Unlike the actions of his father and grandfather, he seems to be acting in a more purposeful way. He's chasing power... If he learns of Riley's skills, there's no telling what he'll do to recruit him."

"Riley has no interest in the Desiccant world," Aus replied. "All he wants to do is go home to his family. He wants his normal life back, nothing more."

"I sure hope that's the case," replied Duke.

Micah calmly spoke up again, "The odds of Z finding out are so, so very slim and you know that, Duke. I think at this point it would be best if we come up with a plan to ensure we keep Riley out of our world." Micah directed his attention to Aus, "Have you told Riley about some of the strange travel we've seen?"

"I haven't told him anything specific, but I've mentioned that the gel can be very finicky, and it's not fully understood," Aus replied.

"Perfect," Micah said. "So, Aus will reinforce the idea that we've seen occasional flukes in travel and that when Contenders are truly deserving, the gel can take them somewhere besides their home. If he tells him that and Riley truly only cares about getting home, then he'll probably never think another thought about it."

"I agree with Micah," Hansel replied. "You're overreacting. We don't have reason to believe that Riley is suspicious at this point and I think we can keep it that way. Are you confident you can relay the message to him?" He asked Aus.

"Yes," Aus replied. "I'm telling you... he's just a normal guy who's thankful for the opportunity to potentially clear his name. His end game is nothing more than getting home."

"We are counting on you, Aus," Duke said sternly as he tossed him a packet of silica gel. "I hope I don't see you again anytime soon."

CHAPTER

THIRTY-NINE

Riley sat uncomfortably in an oversized black shirt and baggy gray shorts on a tan, linen loveseat, in an unfamiliar living room. James' home looked like a collection of oddities, from what Riley assumed, were his grandparent's hand-me-downs. The furniture was nice and had been well taken care of, but it was very outdated. The only new item was his television. A TV that was much too large for the space.

"How did I end up here?" Riley wondered, left alone with his thoughts for the first time since he'd landed in Florida. "I thought Aus said I could only travel home?" He shook his head. "Maybe, it's because I really need to be here. I mean... everyone I need help from is here. Why would the gel send me to a place I'd be alone? It makes more sense for me to be here anyway..."

Riley was used to killing time in prison and he'd learned to cope with being alone. He looked up at the gold-rimmed analog clock on the wall across from him. "At least I know what time it is here," he smiled to himself.

The officers had called Lila and Jane on the way to James' house and they said they would leave right away. He figured it would be at least an hour, so he knew he had some time to waste. He flipped on the television and stopped on the first sports channel he found. It was showing a rerun of a Knicks' game from the previous year.

"I guess that's one benefit of prison… I don't know who wins," Riley laughed. He found himself lost in the game and for the first time since he'd been locked away, he relaxed.

He was focused on the game when a knock on the door startled him.

"Riley!" A familiar voice called.

Riley jumped up and quickly went to the front door. He opened it to greet Lila and Jane with open arms.

"How did you know to come to Miami? How did you know we were her?" Jane asked as they walked in the door and made their way to the living room. Riley sat down once again on the loveseat and Lila joined him. Jane made herself comfortable on the matching sofa.

"I didn't," replied Riley. "I used the gel and expected to go home. I even thought I might waste a trip if you had left already but when I opened my eyes, I was standing outside of some hotel on the beach. Next thing I knew, the cops were running at me. Luckily, I caught a glimpse of them from upstairs last time I was in New York, so I wasn't too nervous. And according to the poem, I can trust those who come to me. We talked for a bit at the hotel, but they needed to get back to work. That's when they called you and they took me back here to wait."

"So, they found you outside of the Perennial Hotel?" Lila asked.

"Yes!" Riley replied, "I could not remember the name… How did you know that?"

"We told them to go there," Lila explained. "How much do you know about our plan?" She asked.

"Not much… I barely overheard you talking about Benjie and visiting the island," he answered.

"Okay, so to catch you up, we ended up going to the

airport with James, Rebecca and Conway yesterday afternoon to see if we could get on their same flight back to Miami. Luckily, it wasn't a problem at all, and Alexa was nice enough to let us visit the island. Your mom called her and explained that she'd come to visit me and deemed I needed an immediate break because I'd been working so hard taking care of the kids. Speaking of them, they're with my mom, so they're in good hands… we landed in Miami around six-thirty last night and went straight to the island. During dinner, we met the newest staff member, Benjie. We started a conversation with him, and he was an open book. He shared that he'd started working on the island at the end of last January when Daniel decided to up and leave. According to Salvador, Daniel is studying at the University of Miami," she paused. "But, according to Benjie, he spends his days getting drunk off free cocktails at the Perennial Hotel. We called James last night to suggest they look for him at the hotel and he said they would go on their lunch break today. I can't believe you landed at the hotel and ran into them… That's crazy!"

"Wow," Riley replied. "That is wild… what are you hoping to find out from Daniel? Do you think he did it?"

"We're not really sure… but we have a theory. We're assuming he was bribed to plant the bomb and keep quiet. If they paid him off enough to not work the rest of his life, then I wouldn't blame him for abandoning the island and taking it easy on the beach every day," Lila said.

"So, what's the plan? Just ask him if he was paid off? Why would he possibly answer that?" Riley asked.

"That's the part we're not sure about. Hence the reason we wanted the cops to handle that part," Jane chimed in.

"I guess I kind of ruined that," Riley said.

"You didn't ruin anything," Lila said, kissing him on the cheek.

"Good," Riley replied. "Hopefully, the cops will have a good plan when they get back tonight."

"I hope so," agreed Lila. "They have done well so far so I am sure they will."

"How long do we have until they get back?" Jane asked.

"It's almost two," Riley said looking at the clock on the wall. "They said they'd be back around five… so like three hours."

"Alright," Lila replied. "I guess we'll just hang out until they get back."

"Orrr… we could get ice cream," Riley suggested.

"Ice cream?" Lila questioned.

"I haven't had ice cream in almost four-hundred days," Riley whined.

"Are you crazy?" Exclaimed Jane. "Your face was plastered everywhere when you were arrested. You want us to just parade you out and about on the streets?

"No, no, sorry… I should have explained," Riley replied. "Silica gel is very interesting and there are many rules and complexities that I don't fully understand. Aus, the prison guard, has explained the most important rules to me and one of them is how people in the outside world view Contenders… Contenders are people traveling with the gel. Evidently, only people who are on my side will recognize me. Anyone else, will just see me as a new and unfamiliar face. It's all very strange…"

"So, you're saying that if we go out for ice cream, no one will think anything of you?" Jane confirmed.

"That's correct," Riley said. "I don't know much about it, but it almost seems like silica gel…" he paused, deciding how to explain his thought. "It's like it functions in a different world."

"I don't know…" Lila commented. "That seems pretty weird… but you know you don't have to do much to convince me to get ice cream," she smiled. "But only if you're positive…"

"I'm positive," Riley replied.

"I hate to burst your bubble, but we don't have a car," said Jane.

"That's alright. I saw an ice cream shop on the way here. It's not too far to walk and I would really enjoy the fresh air," Riley replied.

"Well then… to ice cream!" Lila declared as she stood up and moved to the door.

They walked outside into the sticky, Florida air and began to make their way to the shop. With each person they passed, their nervous tension decreased and soon enough, they were enjoying their afternoon adventure.

"Smells like chocolate and happiness," Riley commented as they walked in.

A young man came out from behind the swinging, metal door that led to the kitchen. He was wearing a white, paper hat with his curly, red hair bulging out at the bottom. His green t-shirt displayed a triple-scoop ice cream cone with the words "Agowa's Ice Cream Parlor" printed above it.

"Welcome to Agowa's," he said unenthused, looking at the floor. "What can I get scooped for –" he looked up and stopped mid-sentence. "Hey, I know you!"

Their stomachs dropped.

"I knew this was a bad idea," Jane thought.

"Oh no," panicked Riley.

"Jeffery?!" Lila exclaimed, "How are you? What are you doing here?"

Jeffrey lifted up the countertop and walked to hug Lila.

"I've been down here for a number of years now. My dad always wanted to open an ice cream shop, so when I left for college, my parents decided to move to Florida and go for it.

After I graduated, I moved down here too and I help them out every once in a while, when they need it."

"That's so great! I can't believe it's been so long," said Lila. "Oh… I'm sorry, let me introduce you. This is my husband, Riley, and my mother-in-law, Jane," she gestured toward them both. "And this is Jeffrey. I went to high school with him and we were in the drama club together."

Riley and Jane's stomachs released the tight knots they'd been in, and they smiled at Jeffrey.

"It's nice to meet you," Jeffrey replied. "As you can see, Lila's theatrical efforts were a little more successful than my own," he said jokingly, motioning around the ice cream shop.

Lila laughed, "It's so good to see you. Do you like it down here?"

"Oh, yeah," Jeffery answered. "I love the weather and the people and everything about it. It's great. What are you doing here?"

"We're just on vacation. It's nice to escape New York in the winter," Lila replied.

Jeffrey nodded, "I can understand that. Well… I don't mean to hold you guys up, you came for ice cream and that's what you'll get," he said. "It's on the house!"

"You don't have to do that," Lila said.

"Of course, I do!" Jeffrey replied, as he made his way back behind the counter. "Whatever you'd like."

Jane smiled, "Thank you! That's very nice. I'll take a dish of mint chocolate chip, please."

"You got it," said Jeffrey.

"And I'll do a cone with moose tracks," Riley added. "And let's make that a double."

"Absolutely," Jeffrey replied, as he began to scoop up the orders. "And for you, Lila?"

"I'll take a dish of rocky road with some whipped cream,

please," Lila answered.

"Of course," Jeffrey said as he finished Riley and Jane's requests and handed them over the counter. He worked on Lila's and topped it off with an extra helping of whipped cream. "It was so great to see you," he said as he handed it to her. "And nice to meet you both as well. I hope you enjoy your time here," he smiled.

"It was great to see you, too," Lila said. "Thank you, again!" They sat down at a white, metal table outside.

"Geez," Riley said. "I about had a heart attack in there. I thought he recognized me at first!" He exclaimed.

"I thought the same thing," Jane replied.

"Oh gosh," Lila said. "I didn't even think about that!"

"It's all good. I am just glad he didn't... and glad I can enjoy this amazing ice cream," Riley took a big lick and then stared lovingly at the cone. "Oh, how I've missed you."

Jane and Lila laughed. It was nice for the three of them to have some uninterrupted time to together and not stress about what their lives had become. They chatted for a while and the time passed quickly.

Before they even knew it, Lila looked down at her watch and exclaimed, "It's 4:45 already! We should head back. They'll be home anytime."

"Time really does fly when you're having fun," Riley replied.

They walked back to James' house and less than five minutes later, James, Rebecca and Conway arrived.

James led the way through the front door. "Lovely! The whole gang is here," he said, genuinely excited. "My mind hasn't stopped racing all afternoon and I think I have a plan for this evening." He continued, "I still think it's best if the three of us," he motioned toward Rebecca and Conway, "Go to the hotel. I don't have reason to believe Daniel would freely offer information, but I think with the threat of the law, he might cooperate."

"I don't know…" Rebecca chimed in. "I'm not convinced that's the best plan."

"Why?" James asked.

"I feel like if he was bribed, which we're assuming he had to be, then don't you think they would have paid him off well? Or at least they're watching him? Why after more than a year would he crack to some local police officers?" Rebecca responded.

"She makes a good point," Conway agreed.

"Do you have a better plan?" James asked defensively.

"Maybe, I do," answered Conway. "I've been trying to put myself in Daniel's shoes. He's obviously sad and for whatever reason, after the incident, he felt it was best to get off the island. Maybe, because of guilt? Maybe, because he was told he had to? Maybe, he just made so much money that he wanted to go blow it and live it up? I don't know… but one thing I do know, or can almost guarantee, is that he wasn't instructed to get drunk on a beach every single day."

"What if he likes to drink?" Asked James.

"He might," Conway said, "But think about it. If you paid someone to commit a crime and keep quiet, would you want them drunk all day, every day? Always in a vulnerable state to give away your secret? I wouldn't." He continued, "Which is why I believe he feels guilty about it. My assumption is he thought he was tough enough to handle it but after everything happened, he couldn't stand the reality of the life he'd built for himself."

The room was quiet.

"That is an interesting theory," Rebecca replied. "But how do you think we'd get that out of him?"

"I don't think *we* would," he answered. "I think *you* would."

"Me?" Rebecca exclaimed. "What do you mean me?"

"As a good-looking, single man," Conway started.

"Gag me," Rebecca whispered.

"I'm in my most vulnerable state when I'm intoxicated and turned on," Conway continued.

"Are you kidding me, Conway? This better have a point," Rebecca demanded.

"It does," Conway replied. "I'm just saying… if I were drunk and a pretty girl started asking me questions, I don't know that there's anything I wouldn't tell her."

"So, what are you suggesting?" Lila asked.

"I think a little undercover work might be in the cards tonight," he said, looking at Rebecca. "Put on a tight dress, talk him up all night, take him back to his room and close. By close… I mean get the answers, of course. The rest is up to you," he said with a wink.

"You can't seriously think this will work," Rebecca replied appalled. She looked at James for back up.

James gave an unsure smile.

"I'm sorry, I don't actually think it's the worst plan…"

"You can't be serious!" Rebecca shouted.

"All in favor of my plan?" Conway asked, raising his right hand.

James raised his hand first, followed by Riley, then Lila. The room stared at Jane and after a few seconds, she slowly raised her hand.

"Guess you better start getting ready," Conway smugly said. "Make sure it's something nice."

"Ugh. Am I supposed to go home now to change?" She asked annoyed. "It will take me an hour to get home and back in the traffic right now."

"I'm sure I have something that will fit you," said Lila. "Come on. We can take a look."

Lila stood up and reached for Rebecca's hand to get her moving. She grabbed her purple suitcase by the front door and turned to James, "Where's your bathroom?" She asked.

"There's a guest room down the hall and to the right," he replied. "It has a bathroom attached."

"Thank you," Lila said as she walked down the hall with Rebecca in tow.

"How did you know where we were?" Conway asked Riley.

"What do you mean?"

"I mean, how did you know we were going to be at the hotel at that exact time?" Conway clarified.

"I didn't," Riley replied. "I had no idea... I expected to open my eyes in New York like the previous three times."

"Wait," James chimed in. "I thought you said this was your third trip?"

Riley replied, "Well, it's my third trip since I was given the five trips to clear my name. Before that, I had a sort-of 'accidental trip' if you will."

"Why do I feel like nothing you say adds up?" Conway asked disapprovingly.

Riley answered, "Probably because it doesn't. I barely know what I'm doing right now, and I don't know how much I'm allowed to share. All I want to do is clear my name and I believe you three can help me."

"We can and we will," James declared. "Don't listen to him," he said, gesturing to Conway. "He's always pessimistic."

Conway rolled his eyes, "Just realistic."

Ignoring Conway, James continued, "I like this plan. I think there's a good chance he'll share something of value with Rebecca and that could give us our next step. I feel like there has to be a tie to him and the case. He was on the island... and he would have had plenty of access. The question is why?"

"I'm not sure," Riley said. "I've spent the entirety of the

last year thinking through every scenario… anyone I could have wronged… anyone who would have wanted revenge… and not that I'm perfect but I don't believe I did anything so bad to someone that they'd plant a bomb in my shoe. I mean, how ridiculous does that sound? A bomb… really?!" Riley said distressingly.

"I'm tired of talking about it all," Jane said, frustrated. "I don't think there's anything we can do at this point but wait to see what Rebecca finds out. Let's quit talking in circles."

No one felt compelled to argue.

"I could turn on the television while they're getting ready?" James suggested.

"That's great," Jane replied.

James flipped on the TV and turned on a mindless sitcom. The four of them were lost in the show when they heard the guest room door open.

A few seconds later, Lila came walking down the hall and said, "Voilà," as she stepped out of the way and motioned toward Rebecca.

Rebecca emerged wearing a black dress with one strap over her right shoulder. The dress hugged her tight down to her mid-thigh and accentuated her curves. Her long, brown hair was half-pulled back in a loose braid with flowing big curls. Her look was complete with silver, dangling earrings and strappy black high heels.

They stared in awe as she made her way into the living room.

"Damn," Conway whispered.

Rebecca shyly looked down at the ground.

"I think it's too much," she admitted.

James encouragingly replied, "It most certainly is not. You look amazing, Rebecca. Any guy would be lucky to have you."

She smiled back at him.

"Get a room," Conway commented, rolling his eyes.

"You did a fantastic job, Lila," Riley said. "Surely, Daniel will want you, Rebecca."

"We shall see…" she nervously said. "What exactly is our plan here?"

"I think it's best if the three of us go," Conway said, motioning to Rebecca and James. "I think it's too risky to bring Lila and Jane, and obviously Riley, in case he would recognize your faces. I don't want to send Rebecca completely alone, so I think we should grab our own table at the bar to be safe." He looked at Rebecca, "Ideally, you'll be able to get all of the answers you need at the bar and not have to make any moves upstairs."

She nodded and looked down at her dress. She rubbed her hands down her hips and for the first time, realized how nicely the dress fit her.

"Maybe, I can fool him after all," she smiled.

"You've got this, Rebecca," Lila said as she made her way to sit by Riley on the couch.

"We're counting on you," Jane added.

Riley nodded, "Yes, we are."

"Let's go," Conway instructed. "The earlier in the night we get there the better."

"I'll drive," James said. He got up and made his way to the front door and Rebecca and Conway followed.

"We'll be back soon," James said as he closed the door.

CHAPTER FORTY

The lights were dim as Rebecca made her way into the hotel bar.

The room was modern and swanky with a large, circular bar in the center. The countertop was made of cement and its metal base glowed from the blueish-white colored lights shining up on it from the floor. Light brown, leather chairs surrounded the bar and in the center of it all was an impressive display of top shelf liquor. Glass windows lined the back wall of the bar and ran the length of the balcony, exhibiting gorgeous, waterfront views. On the weekends, it was nearly impossible to get a spot outside but on a lowly, Monday night, real estate was far less competitive.

James and Conway had gone in ahead of Rebecca to scope out the premises and ensure Daniel was present. As expected, he was seated alone at the bar.

Rebecca immediately recognized the familiar face of the Mendoza boy. His dark, brown hair was cut shorter on the sides than the top and looked freshly combed. His naturally brown skin was dark from days spent under the sun and a stark contrast to the coral, button down shirt he was wearing.

Rebecca straightened her dress and took a deep breath.

"You can do this," she encouraged herself as she made her way to the bar.

She sat down, leaving one seat between her and Daniel and grabbed the cocktail menu.

"Look cool and unamused," she coached herself.

Daniel glanced up and she felt him staring. She looked to her left, out of the corner of her eye and offered a soft smile. Daniel smiled back.

The bar tender, who looked as if he belonged in the 1920's with his suspenders, bowtie and curled mustache, approached Rebecca with a drink in hand.

"A mojito for you. Compliments of the man over there," he said gesturing toward James and Conway. James gave a small wave and smiled.

To ensure Rebecca worked in her best state of mind, they'd payed the bar tender to deliver her mocktails all night. The first drink was club soda, garnished with mint and lime.

Rebecca turned to see James wave and rolled her eyes as she turned back around.

"Thank you," she said to the bar tender, clearly annoyed.

"Is everything alright?" Daniel asked.

Rebecca couldn't believe she'd already garnered his attention.

She shook her head, "He's my ex… he's always trying to win me back."

"Wow," Rebecca thought to herself. "I just made that up… maybe, I'm not half bad at this."

"Exes," Daniel sighed. "What are we gonna do with them?"

Rebecca chuckled and nervously stared down at her nails, not knowing what to say next.

"So, what brings you here alone on a Monday night?" Daniel asked.

"Wow… he's going to make this really easy," Rebecca thought relieved.

"I was supposed to go out with some friends, and they canceled last minute. I figured I shouldn't let a good dress like this go to waste," she smiled.

"No, you absolutely shouldn't," he replied. "You look stunning."

"Thank you," she replied. "I'm Elizabeth, by the way."

"Nice to meet you, Elizabeth." He got up from his chair and reached out his hand. "I'm Daniel," he said as he sat down in the chair that had been open between them.

"It only seems fair to ask you the same question," Rebecca said. "What are you doing here alone on a Monday night?"

"I live here," Daniel replied with a sly smile.

"You live here?" Rebecca asked, confused.

"Well, sort of," he replied. "Things are complicated, and I guess you could just consider this is a longer than expected pitstop."

Rebecca nodded, "How long have you been living here?"

"Oh, gosh…"

He squinted his eyes and looked up, clearly thinking. "I guess I officially moved in last February," he said, unsure of himself.

"That's crazy!" Rebecca exclaimed, "You've been living at this five-star hotel for almost a year now? It must cost you a fortune."

Daniel laughed, "Oh, I don't have to pay… I have connections."

"Must be some connection," Rebecca said, shaking her head. "Don't you get lonely living in a place like this? How can you get to know anyone?"

"I try not to think about it," Daniel replied.

Rebecca apologized, "I'm sorry for bringing it up."

"It's alright."

The two sat in silence for a few moments.

"I have a terrible idea," Rebecca finally said, feeling bold and motivated.

"What's that?" Daniel questioned.

"Well, since you're lonely," she paused, "And I'm lonely," she paused again. "We could try to not be lonely and drink together?" She suggested as she raised her glass.

Daniel grinned, "Now, that is an offer I can't refuse." He raised his glass. "Cheers! To a night without loneliness."

"Cheers," Rebecca said as they clinked their glasses together. She stared into Daniel's green eyes. "He really is good looking," she thought. "Ugh... stay focused."

"Excuse me," Daniel said, trying to get the bartenders attention. "Two tequila shots over here," he ordered.

"Coming right up," the bartender responded. He turned and went to the other side of the circle.

"Chad is the man!" Daniel said to Rebecca, talking loud enough for him to hear.

Chad came back around the bar and smiled at Daniel.

"You've got to keep this one under control," he said looking at Rebecca. He sets the shot glasses down in front of them with a couple of sliced limes to the side.

Rebecca grabbed the shot and the lime and nervously smiled at Daniel.

"Tequila, huh? That's pretty aggressive," she joked.

"I need to know you're committed to this night of loneliness," he replied.

She smiled, "To a night of loneliness."

They clinked their shot glasses together, tapped them on the bar and kicked back the shots.

The fresh taste of cold water ran smoothly down Rebecca's throat. She closed her eyes tight and pretended it was tough to swallow. She bit hard into the lime and shook her head.

"Woo!" She called out.

"Refreshing," Daniel teased. He paused before continuing the conversation. "So, Elizabeth... what do you do for a living?"

"I'm a therapist," she replied. "And yourself?"

"I'm in between jobs at the moment," he answered. "Hence, the extended hotel stay."

"I guess that makes sense," Rebecca nodded. "What did you do before?"

"I worked in hospitality," he said. "Are you from around here?"

"Yeah, I grew up about twenty minutes from here in Wotila," she answered. "What about you?"

"I grew up on an island just off the coast," Daniel replied.

"That's nice," Rebecca said casually.

Daniel looked at Rebecca for a few seconds and then shook his head.

"You're very different," he said.

"What do you mean?" She asked, slightly offended.

"I don't know," he paused. "When I tell most girls that I grew up on an island they're immediately fascinated… and all you said was 'nice.'" He answered gesturing quotation marks with his hands.

"Uh oh," Rebecca thought. "I need to act more interested. I'm not supposed to know he grew up on an island… that normally *would* be very interesting. Ugh, get it together!" She frustratingly thought to herself.

"Sorry," she said, batting her eyes. "It's just been a long day and I'm distracted. It is really cool that you grew up on an island. How did you swing that?" She smiled.

"My family worked on it," he replied. "Do you know who Alexa Monarch is?"

"The actress?" Rebecca questioned.

"Yeah," Daniel answered.

Rebecca nodded.

"She owns the island and my family has taken care of it for

years. It's a full-time job, so we lived and worked there," he explained. "It's wasn't a bad gig."

"Doesn't sound like it," she agreed. "So, why'd you leave?"

Daniel laughed, "Oh, it's a long story… and I'd definitely need a few more drinks before I shared that."

"Families are tough," Rebecca replied.

"Yes, they really are," Daniel agreed. "Hey, Chad," He called. "Could we get two mint juleps over here, please?"

"Mint juleps?" Rebecca questioned. "We just did tequila shots and now, you want to move to mint juleps… What is this? The Kentucky Derby?" She laughed.

"I love a good mint julep," Daniel defended. "So, sue me. Plus, Chad here makes the best."

Rebecca laughed.

"When you spend your days living at a hotel and drinking often… you have to get creative," Daniel said. "I've been on a mint julep kick lately."

"You know the first time I ever had a mint julep?" Rebecca prompted.

"When?" Daniel asked.

"I was studying abroad in Ireland when I was a junior in college," she explained. "My internship was across from a distillery called Hulsting's. I went there every Monday night with my coworkers and the drinks were amazing. My go-to was there spicy mint julep."

"Wow," Daniel said. "I wish you'd told me that before I ordered you one. Chad's probably won't compare to your fancy, Ireland mint julep," he pursed his lips obnoxiously.

"I'm sure it will be fine," Rebecca replied.

"Who knows what it will even be?" She thought, unsure of Chad's ability to make a non-alcoholic drink look like a mint julep.

Just when her doubts crept in, Chad emerged from the

other side of the bar with two identical drinks in hand.

"Wow," Rebecca thought. "Looks like he knows what he's doing."

Chad set the drinks on the bar in front of them.

"Thank you," Rebecca said.

"Would you want to sit out on the balcony?" Daniel suggested.

"That would be lovely," Rebecca replied. "It's a beautiful night."

Daniel stood up from his barstool and reached his hand out. Rebecca took hold of it and used him to balance as she stood to her feet. She wasn't used to wearing high heels.

Rebecca expected him to let go of her hand when she got her balance but to her surprise, he kept holding it and led her outside.

"I can't believe this is working," James whispered to Conway.

"I told you," he replied.

Daniel and Rebecca made themselves comfortable out on the empty balcony. They sat down in chairs facing out toward the water and the calming sound of crashing waves was the only background noise. Although they were facing the wrong way for the sunset, the sky was still filled with shades of orange and pink.

"Yeah, I, uh… I love to c-come out here around this time of night," Daniel slightly stumbled through his words.

"He must have been drinking for a while before I got here," Rebecca thought. "I wasn't expecting him to become intoxicated so quickly."

"It's beautiful," Rebecca replied. "I grew up only twenty minutes from the water, but I did not get to spend enough time out here."

"That's too bad," Daniel said. "I look at it every single day but it's just not the same anymore."

"What's not?" Rebecca asked.

"The island was so much better," he said sadly.

Rebecca didn't feel it was a good time to push him.

"So, how many siblings do you have?" She asked, changing the subject.

"I have one brother named Matthew," he answered. "And then two cousins who are basically my siblings, Jonathan and Carolina. We all grew up together. We're as close as they come."

"That's nice," Rebecca replied.

"How about you?" He asked.

"I have an older sister named Claire," she replied. "She's seven years older and the exact opposite of me, so we've never been very close."

"Siblings are a gift," Daniel said. "I'd do, do everything I could to get c-closer to Claire if I were you."

"That's a pretty bold statement for having just met me," Rebecca chuckled.

"I'm sorry," Daniel said. "You're right. I totally crossed the line. It's been a long year… I miss my family."

"Couldn't you go visit them?" She asked. "You said they aren't far."

"I also said it's complicated," Daniel replied.

Rebecca didn't respond. They sat listening to the waves for a few minutes and sipped their drinks.

"Man… first dates are awkward," Daniel finally said.

"Oh," Rebecca was shocked. "I didn't realize we were on a first date?"

"Yeah," Daniel confidently replied. "I think it shifted to a first date when we moved to the balcony. I think I'd consider inside our meet-cute."

"You are really a bold man," Rebecca commented.

"I know," Daniel replied. "I barely know who I am anymore and I'm always trying to be clever."

Rebecca could tell he was genuinely being honest.

"Are you always this sad and open on first dates?" Rebecca asked.

"No," Daniel answered. "Like I said, there's something different about you. Maybe, it's the whole therapist vibe."

"Maybe, so," Rebecca agreed.

"I've never seen a therapist before though, so maybe, I'm just making things up," Daniel replied.

"Well… I could give you a taste. We could play the get-to-know you game I normally play with my clients if you want?" Rebecca suggested, "I mean, it seems appropriate if this truly is a first date," she smiled.

Daniel grinned, "Sure."

"Well, let's see here," Rebecca said. "What's your favorite color?"

Daniel rolled his eyes, "That's the first question you ask in a therapy session?"

"Oh," Rebecca replied. "I guess I forgot to mention that I'm a child psychologist."

"I see," Daniel laughed. "Blue."

"Ahh, mine is purple," said Rebecca. She paused before asking, "What's your favorite memory?"

"Wow, that's quite the jump," Daniel replied. "It's probably more so a collection of memories." He continued, "Growing up, when guests weren't on the island, my parents would let us swim in the main pool. It's absolutely amazing. It's this gorgeous infinity pool that overlooks the ocean and I swear it goes on forever. Plus, when you're young, everything feels so big and this pool felt like a world of possibility. We'd pretend to be pirates or dolphins… we'd play for hours and make up countless games. On the best days, my mom would deliver us all ice cream sundaes poolside with brownies, vanilla ice cream, hot fudge, whipped cream and a strawberry on top. I hated cherries, so my mom always made mine special," Daniel smiled.

"That sounds lovely," Rebecca replied.

"It was," Daniel said, still reminiscing. "Damn… we're only two questions in," he said. "You're good."

Rebecca smiled, "I try my best."

"What's your favorite memory?" Daniel asked.

"It's easy for me," Rebecca replied. "When I was eight, we went to the pumpkin patch as a family. Claire was fifteen but for one simple day, she wasn't acting too cool for me and our family had the best time. I remember taking my first hayride, spending far too long looking for the perfect pumpkin to carve, drinking apple cider and eating cinnamon sugar donuts. It was one of those days when everyone was simply happy."

"That sounds like a good day," Daniel concurred as he sipped the last drink of his mint julep. "You better keep up," he teased, pointing to Rebecca's half empty glass. "I'll go get us another round and when I come back, I expect you to be finished."

"Aye, aye, Captain," Rebecca obnoxiously saluted. "Actually, would you mind getting me a mojito instead?"

Daniel paused before heading in the door.

"Are you hating on my mint juleps?" He asked.

Rebecca thought, "Actually, I just don't want you accidentally drinking a mocktail."

"Just not as good as Ireland," she teased.

He shook his head and replied, "You got it."

Alone with her thoughts, Rebecca planned her next steps. "I can ask another fun question, then I can move into something a little more serious about his past and then maybe I can lead into why he left. Is that too forward? I don't know…

this is so much pressure. I really can't believe it's working at all." Her mind raced until finally, Daniel returned with two drinks in hand.

He placed Rebecca's on the table, "Alright, so what's next?" He asked.

"What is your favorite food?" She replied.

"Oh, it's mac and cheese. Hands down," he answered.

"Really? Mac and cheese?" Rebecca questioned.

"Oh, yeah. Throw some little hot dogs in there or some peas and it's game changing," he chuckled.

"Well, that's cheap, I guess," replied Rebecca.

"What about you?" Daniel asked.

"Definitely granola bars," she answered.

"You're kidding," Daniel said. "Surely, you're kidding."

"Nope," Rebecca replied. "I seriously love granola bars. There are so many different kinds and they always come in handy. You can go sweet or savory, up your protein, get your daily fiber... truly, granola bars are a treat for any occasion."

"That is so weird!" Daniel exclaimed and busted out in laughter.

Rebecca laughed too.

"I know," she said. "I really love them though."

"I'll say it again, Elizabeth. You are very different," Daniel smiled.

"Okay, let's switch gears," Rebecca said. "We're going to dive a little deeper."

"How can anything get deeper than granola bars?" Daniel joked.

"If you could describe your family in one word, what would it be?" She asked.

Daniel sighed.

"Loyal," he confidently replied. "They're loyal to the core."

"That's a good word," Rebecca commented.

"Yeah," Daniel half agreed. "However, in the wise words of Cicero, 'Nothing is more noble, nothing more vulnerable, than loyalty.' Loyalty leaves too much room for betrayal, in my opinion."

"Wow, that's a good point," Rebecca replied.

"What about your family?" Daniel questioned.

"Caring," she replied. "They are always going above and beyond for others to make sure they're well taken care of.

"That's nice," Daniel replied.

"It really is," Rebecca said. "I can't really complain about my family. I wish I was closer to my sister but other than that, I'm super lucky."

"Sounds like it," Daniel replied. "I'm lucky, too." He hesitated, "I just screwed it all up."

Rebecca nodded, giving him the opportunity to share more.

"That loyalty will get you," Daniel said.

"Do you want to share?" Rebecca sincerely asked.

Daniel pounded the remaining half of his drink and stood up. He paused, catching his balance and then walked to the railing and stared out to the water.

"He's really feeling it," Rebecca thought as she set her drink down on the table and joined him at the railing.

"I haven't talked to anyone like this in over a year," Daniel sighed. "Every girl I've met here has only been interested in money. Not a single one has asked me anything more than surface level questions about myself. And here you come in on a random Monday night and I'm just an open book." He paused, "Life is weird."

"Yes, it is," Rebecca agreed. "I'm sorry it's been a tough year for you."

"It's okay. It's all my fault anyway."

"Do you want to talk about it?" She asked.

"I can't," Daniel said. "It would only get me in more trouble."

"Oh, no," Rebecca thought. "This might be tougher than I expected."

"You know what, no. Screw it," Daniel said angrily, throwing his arms up. "Things can't get any worse than they already are, so I might as well tell someone."

"Or not," Rebecca thought, optimistically.

Daniel sighed and closed his eyes.

"I won't share everything… but I'll get a little off of my chest."

"That sounds great."

"You see, I was given a task on the island… a very important task from Alexa Monarch herself."

"That's impressive," Rebecca commented.

"Yes, it was," Daniel agreed. "It was the first time she'd given me a task directly and she said she'd make it worth my while. It wasn't unusual for her to ask specific tasks of us on the island and she often paid out great bonuses for big requests, so I didn't think much of it. I blindly agreed and later found out it was much more extensive than I'd expected. I felt uncomfortable… but remember that thing I said about loyalty?"

Rebecca nodded.

"I'd promised Alexa I wouldn't tell anyone, and my family treated her like family. I had to respect her wishes and stay loyal."

"That sounds like a lot to handle," said Rebecca.

"It was," he replied. "And it would have been fine. I could have completed the task and moved on with my life, no problem." He paused, "But I messed it up."

Rebecca's stomach dropped.

"What happened?" She prompted.

"I mixed it up," he answered. "I was supposed to swap out one item and I swapped out the wrong one. It ruined everything."

Rebecca nodded, intently listening.

"I'm not sure I fully understand…"

"How can I explain this?" He mumbled to himself. "Okay, so you know how I said my mom would swap out the cherry for a strawberry on my sundaes?"

"Yes," said Rebecca.

"Well, I basically was supposed to deliver the strawberry topped sundae to one person and the normal sundae to another, but I mixed them up. The wrong person got the strawberry sundae… on a much larger scale than ice cream."

Rebecca could hardly believe what she'd heard. She'd just uncovered pertinent information for the case.

"Wow, that sounds terrible," she said, trying to play it cool. "Did she fire you because of it?"

"No," he shook his head. "She paid me to go away. She didn't want my family finding out or thinking anything was suspicious. She told me she'd pay for anything I needed, as long as I didn't go back. I told my parents I'd met the girl of my dreams when I was ashore one day and that I was running off to follow her…. they believed me," he smiled. "In fact, they encouraged me."

"They sound like wonderful people. I'm sorry you've lost touch with them."

"It's okay," Daniel replied. "Now, I just spend my days drinking alone and talking to any pretty girl I see," he looked up at Rebecca.

She smiled softly, "Thank you for sharing. I know it took a lot for you to share all of that."

"Thanks for listening," Daniel replied. "It kind of felt good to get that off my chest." He shook his head, "I would give anything to go back."

Rebecca held back the rush of solutions that came to mind.

"You're just Elizabeth," she reminded herself. "Maybe, Rebecca can help him later."

"Uh, oh," Rebecca said as she covered her mouth with her hand. "I don't feel so well."

"Do you need to sit down?" Daniel asked.

She nodded.

"I never drink this much," she admitted, sitting back down in her chair. She rubbed her face, "This was not how I expected my night to go."

"Can I get you anything?" He kindly asked. "Water?"

"I'm okay," she replied. "But I might have to cut our night of lonely drinking short."

"That's alright," Daniel said. "Maybe, we could share a night of not lonely dinner some other time?"

Rebecca felt guilty looking at Daniel, knowing she'd betray his trust soon.

"That would be nice," she replied. "I think I need to get out of here."

"I'll walk you downstairs," Daniel said, reaching for her hand.

"That's alright," Rebecca said. "I can handle it."

"Are you sure?" He double checked.

"Yeah," she nodded, stood up and pretended to catch her balance.

"Could I get your number before you leave?" Daniel asked, handing his phone to Rebecca.

"Of course," she said as she typed it in the keypad.

When she was finished, Daniel grabbed her arm and led her to the door.

"It was a pleasure meeting you, Elizabeth. I hope you feel better."

"Thank you," Rebecca replied. "I had a great night."

She walked inside and left the bar. James and Conway watched as Rebecca walked through and Daniel stayed out on the balcony.

"What's happening?" Conway asked.

James replied, "I don't know. Do you think she got anything? That seemed really fast."

"Too fast," Conway replied. "There's no way."

They got up and raced toward the door. They'd planned to pick Rebecca up at the gas station across from the hotel to ensure Daniel wouldn't see them together.

James and Conway hopped in the car and drove across the street. They pulled into the station and up to a pump. They could see Rebecca waiting at the stoplight to cross the road.

They waited patiently until Rebecca opened the door to the backseat. With the sound of her door closing, the conversation erupted.

"Did you get anything?" Conway asked.

"What did you find out? That seemed really fast," commented James.

"Was he nice? Was the conversation weird?" Conway continued.

"There's no way the plan worked," James said, defeated before Rebecca even got a word in.

The two finally calmed down and stared at Rebecca, waiting for her to answer.

"It wasn't for Riley," she said, still slightly in shock.

"What wasn't?" Asked Conway.

"The bomb," Rebecca replied. "It wasn't intended for Riley."

They stared, anxiously waiting for her to continue.

She gulped, overwhelmed by the information.

"It was intended for Kyle."

CHAPTER FORTY-ONE

"Ugh," Alexa sighed as she hung up the phone. "So needy."

"Who was that?" Debbie asked.

"Jane Mines," Alexa replied. "She wanted to visit the island last minute. Something about Lila really needing a break."

"I think I'd need a break, too, if I were alone with two kids under age four and my husband was in prison," commented Debbie.

"Good point," Alexa replied. "She's been so hard to talk to since the accident. She's always sharing memories."

"I think it's nice you have each other to reminisce with though," Debbie said. "Don't you think it would be sadder to never think about the good times?"

"I don't know," Alexa said. "It's been two years and not a single day has gone by without me feeling like I could have changed the night."

"You couldn't have changed anything," Debbie comforted her. "If it was in the cards, then it was going to happen one way or another."

Alexa sat quietly on the red sectional, in the living room, next to Debbie. After a few moments, she asked, "Did I ever tell you that Jane and I set Keagan and Kyle up?"

"I don't think so," Debbie said. "I guess I always figured they found each other, since they grew up together."

"Well, they did," answered Jane. "They always had a

connection and they even dated a little in high school, but they parted ways when Keagan went to college. Jane and I always wanted them back together, so when Keagan moved home after college, we arranged a summer party. They started talking again and the rest was history."

"That's hardly setting them up," Debbie laughed. "But what a blessing for Keagan to have experienced love like that in her too short life."

"I guess," Alexa half agreed. "But without that love, she might still be alive."

"As Tennyson said, 'Tis better to have loved and lost than never to have loved at all.'"

"Do you always have to look at the positive? Sometimes can't you lament and be angry with me?" Alexa asked, annoyed.

Debbie replied, "Alexa, you of all people should know I can lament and be angry with you. You know I've done and will do anything for you." She hesitated before continuing, "Have you thought about seeing someone? They might be able to help with your grief… maybe, they could help you move forward."

Alexa replied, "How can I move on when nothing has changed?"

"Maybe," Debbie hesitated. "Maybe, it's you who needs to change."

"Oh, I don't need to change. Someone needs to pay!" Alexa angrily demanded.

"What are you going to do? Try again?" Debbie questioned.

"I don't know," Alexa replied. "I've thought about it…"

"I don't think you should press your luck."

"Ugh, maybe, you're right," Alexa agreed, calming down. "I think I've been especially on edge lately because of your meddling son."

"He's honestly terrible at his job," Debbie replied. "I don't know how he was ever hired to be a cop," she said shaking her head. "I'm not too worried about him."

Alexa looked down at her hands and nervously began to pick at her fingernails.

"I hope so…" she said. "I guess there's nothing we can do but wait this whole thing out," she paused. "And of course, relax with wine in the meantime."

She reached toward the white, marble coffee table and picked up the bottle of red wine. She topped off the two crystal glasses that had been sitting near the edge of the table. She handed one to Debbie and lifted her glass.

"Cheers!" She said, "To infinitely filled wine glasses and loyal friends."

CHAPTER FORTY-TWO

The front door flung open and a barrage of undecipherable conversation filled the room.

Riley, Lila and Jane nervously exchanged glances, trying to interpret the officers' moods.

"Had they been successful? Did they get new information? Did they fail miserably? Is this a hopeless cause?" Riley's mind turned with wandering thoughts.

The officers continued their banter until Lila finally reached her limits.

"Hello!" She shouted, "Could you please fill us in?"

"I'm sorry," James said. "Yes, we will fill you in. Rebecca, would you like to share?" He prompted.

"Daniel was an open book," she started. "I was honestly surprised at his openness and vulnerability. I think it's because of the immense loneliness he's felt over the past year."

They stared blankly back at Rebecca, waiting for her to get to the point.

"Based on Daniel's comments and our previous knowledge… I believe we can confirm that Alexa bribed him to plant the bomb."

"What?!" Lila exclaimed.

"Why would she do that?" Jane shockingly asked.

"I've never done anything to her," commented Riley.

"Yeah, why in the world would she have it out for Riley?" Lila asked.

"Well…" Rebecca paused.

"Well, what?" Jane asked.

"She wasn't after Riley."

"What do you mean?" Riley questioned.

"She was after your brother."

The room was silent.

Riley could hardly breathe. Over the past year, he'd played through every possible scenario and not once, not once, had he thought of the possibility of him not actually being the target. It made sense… he couldn't believe the thought had never crossed his mind.

"Why would she go after Kyle?" Jane broke the silence.

"You know why, Mom," Riley calmly replied.

"He didn't kill her. The drunk driver did! Why would Alexa do such a thing? He's done nothing to her… he misses Keagan, too."

"I know," Riley said as he stood up and moved to the couch next to Jane. "It's not his fault. We all know it's not his fault. He misses her more than anyone."

Jane began to cry, and Riley rubbed her back, consoling her.

"What exactly did he say?" Riley asked, looking at Rebecca. "How do we know for sure?"

"He told me that Alexa had asked him to perform a task. He said this wasn't out of the ordinary for the island and that Alexa would often require specific things to be done and give bonuses to those who did them. It was the first time she'd asked Daniel directly, so he was excited and happy to oblige. She asked him not to say a word to anyone and he said his family valued loyalty, so he couldn't break his promise. He found out the task was much bigger than he expected but he didn't have a way out. He didn't give me specifics of the task but it's safe to assume it was planting the bomb."

Rebecca paused and looked around the room to ensure everyone was following.

She continued, "He told me he couldn't share all of the details, so he'd give me a broad idea of what happened. He explained it as having swapped the wrong item. He said it was like having two sundaes and one had a cherry on top and the other a strawberry... that's a whole other story I don't need to get into, but you get the idea. There are two different sundaes and he's supposed to swap one out, but he accidentally swapped the wrong one out." Rebecca shook her head, still processing everything she'd learned. "Then, after his mistake, Alexa paid him to go away and that's why he's living alone at the Perennial. She didn't want the Mendoza family or anyone else finding out."

"Wow," Lila replied first. "I can't believe he told you that."

"I know," Jane added. "He's being paid to keep quiet and some random girl walks into a bar, and he gives... that seems pretty strange."

"Normally, I would agree with you, Mrs. Mines," interjected Conway. "However, we've seen this before with bribery. At some point, a person comes to terms with the fact that their life will never go back to normal if they keep living the lie. It's not surprising to me that after a year, Daniel is vulnerable and willing to share. He's probably figuring that, at this point, things can't get much worse."

"That's how I felt when I first got the gel," Riley chimed in. "I remember thinking to myself, 'What's the worst thing that could happen?' I was already so alone, so I decided the risk of further consequences was better than my current state. Maybe, that's what he figured."

"It makes sense," Conway agreed. "And it's great news for us. We were talking through next steps on the car ride back and we think we can use Daniel. We think if we can figure out a way to protect him, we can get the evidence we need."

"How can you protect him if he planted the bomb?" Asked Lila.

"That's where it gets complicated," answered Conway. "At this point, it sounds like bribery motivated Daniel, but we need to know if there's anything more. If Daniel felt threatened, that adds a new layer. If Daniel did something in the past that Alexa blackmailed him for, it gets murky. We need to know exactly what Alexa required of Daniel and why... to do that —"

"We might have to fudge some things and hope it all works out for the best," James interrupted, knowing they might not approve of all they had planned.

The room fell silent once again, each person deep in the process of organizing their thoughts.

"So, what do we do next?" Lila asked.

"I gave Daniel my number," Rebecca answered. "I think we wait for him to call."

"We don't know how long that will take," Riley said.

As if on cue, Rebecca's phone dinged, signaling a text. She picked it up and smiled.

"Apparently, no time at all," she said. She read the message aloud, "It was a pleasure to meet you tonight! I hope you feel better soon. – Daniel."

"He didn't waste much time," James commented.

"Someone's jealous," Conway teased.

"Probably not the time," Rebecca shot Conway a look.

"So, now what?" Lila questioned.

"I think we need to set him up," James said. "Rebecca can plan a date and we'll be waiting for him when they get back. We'll give him the option to work with us and potentially, save himself... or we'll go after Alexa, with the knowledge we have, with no guarantees what will happen to him."

"Isn't that us blackmailing him?" Lila asked.

The officers exchanged glances.

"It is," James finally answered. "But at this point, there really are no other options. If we want Riley out of prison, we might have to walk the ethical line along the way."

"When are you going to set up this meeting?" Lila inquired.

"Do you ever run out of questions?" Conway asked, annoyed.

"No," Lila bluntly responded.

"I think as soon as possible," James said. "Maybe, tomorrow night?" He suggested, looking to Rebecca for confirmation.

"Yeah, that would make sense to me," she replied. "I see no reason to waste any more time."

"What time do you guys fly out tomorrow?" James asked.

"Our flight leaves at four," Lila replied.

"And when do you head back to California?"

He looked at Jane.

"Thursday morning," she answered.

"How quickly do you think Kyle could make it to New York?" James questioned.

"I'm sure he could fly out tomorrow," Jane said.

"Good," said James. "That's good. If we could have you all together in New York and us together here, I think that will help us move more quickly."

"Wouldn't it make more sense if we were all in California? Close to Alexa?" Lila asked.

"She makes a good point," Rebecca agreed.

"Yes," James said. "I think we will all need to be in California at some point, but I don't know if that's totally necessary right now."

"Plus," Riley added. "I'm still not sure how I arrived here... so I can't commit to making a trip to California.

"If by tomorrow night, the four of you are in New York

and the three of us are here with Daniel, I think we'd be in good shape," James concluded.

"What time is it?" Riley looked at the clock on the wall. "10:30," he answered his own question. "Once I arrive back at Nadirehs, I have to wait twenty-four hours to travel again," he said. "If I fell asleep right now, the earliest I could get to New York is 10:30 tomorrow night, and that depends on successfully getting a silica gel packet between now and then."

"I think it's okay if you arrive later," James said. "There is a lot we can accomplish in the meantime, and it might be good for Kyle to arrive before you. That way, Lila and Jane can fill him in on everything and give him a heads up about your mysterious traveling."

Riley nodded, "So I should fall asleep like... right now?"

The officers nodded.

"That's probably best," said Conway.

"I'm pretty wide awake," Riley laughed. "I have a few things on my mind at the moment," he said sarcastically.

"I can warm you up some warm milk," Jane offered.

"Thanks, Mom," Riley said. "But I might need something a little stronger at the moment... anyone have melatonin?"

"I don't," James replied. "There's a drug store around the corner. I can run and grab some?"

"I think I have some in my purse," Lila replied.

"You just casually carry melatonin around with you now?" Riley asked.

"Believe it or not, I still think about you," she smiled.

Riley stood up and walked to give Lila a kiss on the cheek as she fiddled around in her purse for the melatonin.

"Here you go," she said, handing it to him.

"Thanks, babe," he said as he popped the tabs in his mouth and swallowed.

"Did you just dry swallow those?" Lila asked, disgusted.

"Babe, I've been in prison for a year. I've dealt with much worse."

"You can use the guest bed if you'd like," James suggested.

"That would be great."

Lila stood up and gave Riley a tight hug.

"I love you," she said softly.

"I love you, too," Riley replied.

They kissed and then he made his way down the hall and into the guest room.

"Where should I go with Daniel?" Rebecca asked, staring blankly at her phone.

"I don't know," James said. "Pick your favorite restaurant."

"And I'd make it an expensive one," Conway added. "Sounds like he has the means."

"Uh… I have no idea," Rebecca was defeated. "I don't do this."

"What about The 800," Conway suggested.

"What's that?" Rebecca asked.

James and Conway stared at Rebecca with dropped jaws.

"You've never heard of The 800?" James asked.

She shook her head.

"It's only the best steakhouse in town," said Conway enthusiastically. "It's on the top floor of the Luxe Hotel and the floor slowly turns to give customers 360-degree views of the ocean and the Miami skyline. Its timeless style, paired with its classic flair, is truly magnifico," he said putting his fingers to his lips and blowing a kiss.

"You'd think he was the owner," Lila laughed.

"It sounds wonderful," Rebecca agreed. "Do you think it would be too much to suggest that? Especially, considering we're setting him up?"

"No," Conway replied. "Never."

"You could just let him pick the place," Jane suggested.

"I'll do that," Rebecca jokingly rolled her eyes. "Men," she sighed.

Jane and Lila laughed.

"I should probably call Kyle," Jane said.

"Maybe, you should book his flight first and then call him," Lila recommended. "You know he'll be fine with whatever you book."

"That's true," Jane replied. "I'll grab my laptop and look up options."

"I'll grab it for you," Lila offered. "I want to check on Riley anyway."

She stood up from the couch and walked to their bags by the front door. She unzipped Jane's black, leather backpack and pulled out her laptop. She handed it to Jane before making her way down the hall to the guest bedroom.

She quietly opened the door and peered inside.

With mixed emotions, she announced, "He's already gone."

CHAPTER

FORTY-THREE

"Ahem," Aus cleared his throat.

Startled, Riley awoke and sat up on his bed. He rubbed his sleepy eyes until Aus' bruised and cut face came into focus.

"What happened to you?" Riley asked.

"It's irrelevant," Aus casually replied. "What's more important is what happened to you? How was your trip?" Aus asked, playing dumb.

"Good," Riley replied with a yawn, still trying to wake up.

"I'm going to need more than 'good,'" Aus replied, making air quotes.

"I know," answered Riley as he rubbed his face again. "I... uh... I didn't go home," he said hesitantly.

"What?!" Aus asked, acting surprised. "Where did you go?"

"I landed in Miami," Riley replied. "Remember the officers I told you about?"

Aus nodded.

"I landed at a hotel where they happened to be and then I found out that Lila and my mom were on the island. They came ashore and we all worked together," Riley said. "Aus, it's really starting to make sense and I think we have some potential evidence. I might actually clear my name."

"Really?" Aus replied. "What did you find out?"

"Apparently, the man who planted the bomb was bribed by Alexa Monarch."

"The movie star?" Aus questioned.

"Yes," Riley confirmed. "That's whose island we were staying on." He continued, "Evidently, he was supposed to put the bomb in my brother's shoes and mixed them up. I'm not sure on all of the details… but I do know that my brother and I have matching shoes and that we both brought them to the island. Daniel, the guy who messed it all up, semi-confessed to one of the cops."

"That's crazy!" Aus exclaimed.

"I know," Riley agreed.

"Why does Alexa have it out for your brother?" Aus asked.

"The Monarchs have been lifelong family friends of ours and Kyle was engaged to their daughter, Keagan. They were out one night and got hit by a drunk driver. Keagan was in the passenger seat and she died on impact," Riley explained.

"I'm sorry," Aus replied. "That's terrible."

"It is," Riley agreed. "And apparently, Alexa thought it was Kyle's fault."

"Was he drunk?" Aus asked.

"No!" Riley shouted, defensively. "The other driver was drunk and completely ran a red light. My brother did nothing wrong."

"Then, how can she blame him?"

"The same way someone can rationalize placing a bomb in someone's shoe. She has to be certifiably insane," Riley shouted. He took a deep breath before continuing. "I distinctly remember being at the funeral and hearing some women whisper about Kyle being responsible for Keagan's death, but I never thought Alexa felt that way. Last I knew, Kyle and Alexa still spoke on a regular basis." Riley shook his head. "They both lost one of their favorite people. It only made sense for them to turn to each other for support."

"What are you going to do?" Aus inquired.

"I'm planning to go back," Riley paused and looked around the room. It was still very dark and there was no sign of the sun rising outside. "What time is it?" He asked.

"A little after 11," Aus said as he looked down at his watch.

"Wait, what? Were you waiting on me?" Riley asked, confused.

"Yeah," admitted Aus. "I had nothing better to do."

"Well then, I'm planning to go back in twenty-four hours," Riley said. "The officers are supposed to work on getting more information from Daniel and my mom is supposed to fly Kyle out to New York. I'm planning to meet my family back at home, so that we can be together and communicate with the officers pretty easily."

"That seems like a good plan," Aus replied.

"Yeah, it does," concurred Riley. "I'm sorry," he said, staring with a disgusted look at Aus' face. "I can't let it go. Could you please tell me what happened to your face? Tell me it wasn't the Desiccant Keepers again…"

"It's a good thing you're planning to go home again, Riley," Aus said. "They don't like it when things don't go their way."

Riley's stomach turned with guilt.

"Is that," he pointed at his face, "because I went to Miami? I didn't do it on purpose!"

"I know you didn't," Aus replied. "That's what I explained to them."

"Then, why did they beat you?" Riley questioned.

"Well… they did this before they let me explain," Aus half-heartedly laughed. "They told me that in very rare instances, when a Contender is truly deserving, they can travel somewhere besides home. This is extremely rare and when it happens, they're on edge. So, they took it out on me and it's not a big deal," Aus said. "I'm just glad it was worth it and that you gathered some information on the trip."

"Aus, I am so sorry," Riley apologized. "I feel like I've caused you more trouble than you bargained for with this whole traveling thing…"

"Stop that, Riley. Right now," Aus aggressively combated. "I get one shot to pass on the gel and I know I chose the right one. Look at everything you've already uncovered." Aus spoke passionately. "You have two more trips to get out of this place and I would take a beating every, single day if it meant setting you free."

Riley looked down and slightly nodded his head. He knew Aus meant every word he said but he still felt responsible for Aus' tribulations.

"So…" Aus said, trying to lighten the mood. "How was the weather in Miami?"

"It was nice," Riley replied. "We enjoyed a walk outside to get some ice cream –"

"You went out? Riley, I told you not to test your boundaries…"

"I know but Aus… it had been over four-hundred days since I'd had ice cream."

Aus shook his head.

"I guess I can't be mad, since everything worked out okay… How was the ice cream?"

"Amazing," Riley smiled. "So… when you see the Keepers, where are they?"

"At their headquarters… they work out of an abandoned castle off the coast of Scotland."

"Do they live there?" Riley inquired.

Aus hesitated, "Uh, no," he answered.

"Then, how do they get there?" Riley questioned.

"Oh, no," Aus thought, concerned with Riley's increasing

curiosity. "This is the opposite of keeping him in the dark." He had never been good at keeping secrets.

"Uh... they just travel there... like by planes... trains... automobiles," Aus said, unsure of himself.

Riley knew he wasn't telling the truth.

"How do they get there, Aus? Do they manipulate the gel?"

"Uh... no."

"Aus."

"I mean... yeah... they do. They're the Desiccant Keepers. They can do whatever they want," he justified.

"I thought you said it was nearly impossible to manipulate the gel... and that only BT could do it?" Riley accused.

"Ahh, Riley! Why are you doing this to me?" Aus complained. "I can't give out too much information. Right now, all you need to know is that you have two more trips to clear your name. It's a dangerous world, Riley. The best advice I can give to you is to stay out of it."

"Well, if that's the case, why are you so involved?" Riley accused.

Aus stood up quickly and before Riley could comprehend what was happening, he was pinned against the wall above his bed.

"I'm protecting you. That's my only job. I don't care what you do after your trips are over but until then, you listen to me. You're the only Contender I'll ever have and it's on me to keep you safe and out of trouble. Play by the rules, Riley, or you'll bring us both down."

Riley gasped for air as Aus released his grip. He couldn't breathe, so he nodded, acknowledging Aus' wishes.

"Thank you," Aus said as he made his way back to the metal chair in the corner.

"I'm sorry," Riley apologized. "It's been a long couple of days and I'm running on very little sleep. My mind is wandering and I'm anxious," he explained. "I don't want to get either one of us in trouble."

"I know you don't," Aus responded. "I'll let you get some rest. I'll be back in," he paused and looked at his watch. "Twenty-three hours and thirty-five minutes."

"Three trips down, two to go," Riley replied.

Aus walked to the wall where Riley kept the tally of his trips.

"You missed one," he said as he added a new black line. "I'll see you tomorrow."

"See ya," Riley replied as Aus left his cell.

Riley rested his head on his pillow and pulled his blanket over him. His mind began to wander.

"What else don't I know?"

CHAPTER FORTY-FOUR

"Uncle Kyle is here!" Chandler yelled. She had been patiently staring out the front window, awaiting his arrival.

"Uncle Kyle!" She shouted as she ran out the front door to greet him getting out of the car.

"Chan, Chan!" He exclaimed as he scooped her up into his arms.

"Chandler, it's freezing out there and you don't have on any shoes," Lila reprimanded as she stood at the door. It was lightly snowing, and the ground had already collected a thin layer.

"Ahh, she's alright," Kyle said. "It will make her tough."

He carried Chandler up the stairs and into the house.

"Hi, Mom," Kyle greeted as he hugged Jane.

"And Lila," he said, embracing her.

"Uncle Kyle! Uncle Kyle! Do you want to see my new dolls?" Asked Chandler, excitedly.

"Yes! Of course!" Responded Kyle.

"You can show them to him later, honey," said Lila. "How about you give Warren a bottle and let us catch up for a bit?"

"Really?" Chandler asked.

"Yep," Lila replied. "Let me go grab it and I'll get you all set."

"Okay!" Chandler said. "I feed Warren sometimes, Uncle Kyle. I'm really good at it."

"That's awesome, Chan! You're a good big sister."

Chandler made herself comfortable on the white loveseat and Lila returned with a bottle. She handed it to Chandler and then picked Warren up from his play mat on the floor and placed him in her lap. With immense focus, Chandler began feeding Warren his bottle.

"Good job, sweetheart. We'll be right over here," she said, motioning toward the dining room. "Let me know when he's done and if you need anything."

Chandler nodded as she sweetly stared down at her little brother.

Lila, Jane and Kyle sat down around the large, dining room table.

"Can I get you anything to eat or drink?" Lila offered. "Have you had dinner yet?"

"What's going on?" Kyle replied, ignoring her question.

Jane and Lila looked at each other, unsure how to start explaining.

"You remember my call about the officers stopping by and asking about your shoes, right?" Lila asked.

"Yes," Kyle answered, annoyed at the obvious question.

"Well, we've been working with them... they came to me because they had reason to believe that Riley was innocent and they wanted to look further into the case," Lila said.

Kyle nodded.

"Yes, I inferred that," he said bluntly.

"The whole case is very strange. It's weird how there wasn't really an investigation and it's strange what little information was collected. It's not hard to see that in many spots of this case, bribery could have been involved," she continued.

Kyle agreed, "Yes, I've thought about that possibility before."

"So, we went back to the island," Lila said.

"When?" Kyle was surprised.

"The last two days," she answered.

"There was a potential suspect on the island and the officers decided it would be best for us to try to do some undercover work," she explained. "Benjie Mendoza was one of their top suspects, but we didn't recognize him, so our main goal was to learn about him. What we didn't expect was that he would lead us right to who we now believe was the mastermind behind it all."

"Who?" Kyle questioned.

"Alexa," Jane answered before Lila could.

"What?" Exclaimed Kyle. "You flew me all the way out here to tell me something ridiculous like that?"

"Oh, we're not even close to ridiculous yet," Lila murmured.

"Why would Alexa do that to Riley?" Questioned Kyle.

Lila and Jane exchanged nervous glances.

"She wasn't doing it to Riley," Jane hesitated. "She was after you."

Kyle, who'd been anxiously leaning on the table, slouched back with his mouth wide open.

"Oh," he said coldly.

Lila continued, "We ended up talking to Benjie on the island. He only started working there a year ago, after Daniel Mendoza up and left. Supposedly, Daniel said he left to pursue a woman he'd met, and the family thought it would be a short fling, so they asked Benjie to fill in. But, a year later, he is still on the mainland and they essentially don't talk to him. Benjie told us that last he knew; Daniel lived at the Perennial Hotel and spent his days drunk on the beach."

Jane chimed in, "So, we shared this information with the officers and decided it would be best for them to go find Daniel. They went there... gosh, I guess that was only yesterday morning… my days are all messed up and that's when they ran into R –"

Lila interrupted, "And that's when they confirmed that Daniel was at the hotel. So, they formed a plan for Rebecca to go undercover and try to flirt information out of him. Which she successfully did and that's how we found out it was Alexa who paid Daniel."

"Who did they run into?" Kyle asked, ignoring Lila and staring at Jane.

She didn't answer.

"Mom," Kyle replied. "You said, 'and that's when they ran into' and then, Lila cut you off. What aren't you telling me? Who did they run into?"

"We have to tell him eventually," Jane said.

"They, uh…" started Lila. "They ran into Riley."

"WHAT?!" Kyle called out. "What has gotten into you guys? This is all so ridiculous and absurd!" He continued, "Do you hear yourselves right now? You honestly think Alexa Monarch, the woman who I still actively communicate with, whose daughter I was engaged to marry, attempted to plant a bomb in my shoe. And, in your efforts to uncover said obscene accusations, you ran into my brother, who's been housed at the most inescapable prison in the world for the last year?" He yelled and threw up his hands, "I don't even know how to respond to this. You're both insane!"

Kyle got up and began to pace in the dining room.

"We know how this sounds," Lila replied. "We've had a few days to process."

"It sounds like you just found this out yesterday," Kyle argued.

"Well, we've been working with the officers for almost a week now…" She paused. "And… I, um… I've seen Riley a few other times."

"This is ludicrous!" Kyle laughed in denial. "What do you mean you've seen Riley? Are you talking about some kind of alternate reality you're imagining living in with your husband? Or what? My brother is in prison. You haven't seen him!" He shouted.

"Mom! He's done eating," Chandler called.

"Coming, honey," Lila said as she stood up from the table and walked to the living room.

"Will you do mommy a favor and go play upstairs?" She asked Chandler as she grabbed Warren.

"Do I have to?" Chandler whined. "Uncle Kyle just got here!"

"Please," Lila begged. "You can play with Uncle Kyle later," she promised.

Chandler huffed and ran to the stairs.

Lila kept Warren in her arms and swiftly moved to the kitchen. She opened a drawer and pulled out the carefully taped brown, paper bag. She brought it to the table and set it down in front of Kyle. He studied the words:

The game is dangerous, but the reward is great.
If played correctly, you'll change your fate.
Trust only those who come to you and above all else, whatever you do,
Don't share your secret or abuse your power, after all you only have sleepless hours.
With only five trips to clean your slate, you don't have any time to wait.
Think smart, not hard and with every flight, always come back to the hanging blue light.

"What is this?" Kyle asked.

"Riley brought it to me," Lila answered. "I didn't believe him either and I still don't fully understand. All I know is that he's used three trips so far and he's planning to come back tonight."

"Where did he get this from? How is he escaping Nadirehs?" Questioned Kyle.

"The prison guard," Lila replied. "He uses silica gel packets to travel."

"What's silica gel?" Kyle asked.

"You know, those little packets that come in new shoe boxes and stuff," Lila said. "They're white with black lettering and super toxic."

"I never knew that's what they were called," responded Kyle.

"Yeah, I didn't either, until Riley told me," Lila admitted with a humble laugh.

"So, he uses those to travel? Are they like... magic?" Kyle raised his eyebrows.

"We're not entirely sure," Jane answered. "But at this point, we don't really care because all we want is to get Riley home."

"I want him home, too," Kyle agreed. "I miss calling him randomly to catch up and sharing dumb jokes. I still text him things I think are funny and forget he can't reply. It's crazy to me that it's been a year already. I feel like I've been in a funk since it happened and still haven't processed any of it."

"I completely agree," said Jane.

"Same," added Lila. "I think it's because none of it made sense. It was impossible to process because it was all completely wrong and out of character. We didn't get any sort of closure."

"True... Can we go back a second? So, you're saying that

Alexa was really after me?" Kyle asked.

Lila and Jane nodded.

"She still communicates with me all of the time and acts like everything is normal," Kyle defended. "How can you know for sure?"

"That's the information we received from Daniel. He confirmed that Alexa paid him to perform a task. He then said that he messed up the task and because of it, she paid him to go away," answered Lila. "At this point, it's still just an assumption that he mixed up yours and Riley's shoes, but we have a very strong case."

"That does seem to add up…"

"Right now, the officers are supposed to be meeting with Daniel and attempting to collect more information. Once Riley gets here, we'll call them and see what they've found out," Jane explained.

"When will Riley be here?" Kyle asked.

"He has to wait twenty-four hours between trips, and he left a little after 10:30 last night, so I'm assuming he'll be here around 10:45," Lila said.

Kyle looked at his watch.

"Okay, so we have about four hours," he said.

"Yeah," replied Lila. "I was thinking I could make some dinner in the meantime. Does spaghetti work for you?"

"Spaghetti would be great," Kyle answered. "This has been a lot to take in." He paused, "I really think the only way to refresh would be to take my adorable little niece out for ice cream," he pleaded.

"What is it with you Mines' boys and ice cream? It's freezing out and I'm about to make dinner," Lila replied. "How about you play with her now and after dinner we all have ice cream together? We have plenty in the freezer."

Kyle flung his head back and pouted like a little boy.

"Fine," he mumbled, standing up from the table. "Chandlllller," he hollered as he ran up the stairs.

"I think that went better than expected," Jane said after Kyle was gone.

"Not too bad," Lila replied. "He's either on our side or still in denial... both of which are better than completely disagreeing with us."

"That's true," said Jane. "Can I help you with dinner?"

"Honestly, if you could take Warren, I'd greatly appreciate it," Lila replied. "Cooking dinner by myself right now sounds like a dream."

"Of course," Jane replied. "I think I'll take him upstairs and we can watch Kyle and Chandler play. Does that sound like fun?" She asked Warren as she grabbed him from Lila.

"Thank you," responded Lila.

They stood up and went their separate ways. Jane stopped when she reached the bottom of the staircase. She could hear Lila attempting to control her heavy breathing.

"Hey, Lila," Jane called.

Lila turned around, her eyes welling, "Yes?"

"Everything is going to be okay," Jane reassured her.

Lila smiled and nodded, only half believing her.

CHAPTER FORTY-FIVE

"No way!" Conway exclaimed in disbelief from his desk chair. "He did not suggest The 800!"

"Yes, he did," smiled Rebecca.

"You lucky dog, you," Conway replied. "Maybe you should really pursue him," he winked.

"Maybe not," James chimed in. "You know, since he's a criminal and all."

"Or maybe cause' you're jealous," Conway teased.

James rolled his eyes and changed the subject.

"Okay, so you're meeting him there for dinner at 6:30, right?

Rebecca nodded.

"Why isn't he picking you up like a real gentleman?" Conway asked.

"He doesn't have a car," she answered.

Ignoring Conway, James continued his train of thought, "And after dinner, you'll invite him to your place, and Conway and I will be waiting?"

"Yes," confirmed Rebecca. "Do you think he's really going to confess to anything?"

"I don't know," James replied. "But it's our only hope. I'm hoping we can convince him that the only possible way to keep him safe is if he joins us. Without him, we have no way of proving Alexa's motives and we'd have to go after them both... but with him, we can solely go after Alexa and work to keep him safe."

"It's as good a plan as any," Conway commented.

"We still have a couple of hours," Rebecca said as she reached into her purse. "But I don't want to forget to give you my spare key." She handed the key ring to James. "The black fob will get you into the building and the key will open my apartment. I'm on the fourth floor, apartment 482."

"Thanks," he replied, putting the keys in his pocket.

The office door slammed shut, startling the three of them.

"What have you all been up to?" Shouted Hillsteg angrily.

"What do you mean?" James asked.

"The three of you just up and leave last week at the same time with no explanation. Word on the street is your investigating a closed case... again," he said looking only at James.

"My dad had surgery," answered James.

"I had the flu," added Rebecca.

"I was on vacation," defended Conway.

Hillsteg's nostrils flared and he shook his head.

"If I find out that you three really are investigating that stupid Mines case, you're all fired," he threatened. Hillsteg stormed out of the room and slammed the door.

"He's such a pleasant man," Conway said sarcastically.

"I can't lose my job," Rebecca nervously admitted. She looked down at her hands and fidgeted with her fingers. "I've worked so hard to get here. I can't lose it."

"It's okay," James said as he placed his hand on Rebecca's thigh. "If anyone loses their job it will only be me. I dragged you both into this and I won't pull you down. Plus, I'm sure Hillsteg will change his mind when we solve the biggest case of the year. Are you kidding me?" James jokingly asked himself. "That man would live for his face on the front page of the paper, claiming he solved the case."

Rebecca laughed, "You're so right."

"He's the worst," Conway added. "How many donuts do you think he's had already today?"

"Oh, an easy half dozen," James chuckled.

The three laughed at the thought, and for a moment, felt the stress of the evening ahead lifted off of their shoulders.

CHAPTER FORTY-SIX

Rebecca sat at a table set for two, next to a large glass window overlooking the city. Her silver necklace and dangly, fake diamond earrings perfectly complimented her strapless red dress. Her hair was pulled back in a loose bun with a few curls shaping her face.

"Dress to impress and never show up early," her mother's words ran through her mind.

"Well, at least I did one thing right," she laughed to herself.

She took a deep breath and prepared for the evening.

"Just think about it like a true second date," she thought. "He doesn't suspect a thing, so just be yourself and Conway and James will help you take care of the rest later."

In the middle of her thoughts, she looked up and saw Daniel stepping out of the elevator. He was very well dressed in a tan suit with a white shirt, navy tie, silver tie clip and brown leather shoes.

He approached the hostess stand and the young lady gestured back toward Rebecca.

Rebecca shyly waved as Daniel began to make his way to the table.

"Good evening, Elizabeth," Daniel said. He reached out, grabbed her hand and kissed it gently.

"Hello, Daniel," she replied.

"Have you been waiting long?" He asked.

"No," Rebecca replied, "I was early."

"I apologize," he replied. "My father taught me to never leave a girl waiting."

"It's quite alright. My mother taught me to never show up early," she laughed.

A young, Italian man with black hair and brown eyes approached the table. He was wearing a white shirt with a black vest, black slacks and an emerald green bowtie.

"Good evening and welcome to The 800," he said. "My name is Leo and I'll be taking care of you tonight. Our special this evening is a six-ounce ribeye, paired with a cold-water lobster tail and your choice of a side item from the list at the bottom of your menu," he said motioning toward Rebecca's menu on the table. "Could I get you started with something to drink? Our choice bottle tonight is a Baco Noir from Leelanau Peninsula and in my opinion, it is truly delizioso," he said as he kissed his hand.

"Do you like red wine?" Daniel asked.

"Yes."

Daniel looked at Leo.

"We'll do a bottle of the Baco Noir, please," he requested.

"Of course. I'll be right back with that," Leo said as he left the table.

"Did you have a good day at work?" Daniel asked.

"I didn't work today," Rebecca replied. She didn't want to dig herself too deep into a lie. "I typically have Tuesday's off."

"Oh, that's nice," Daniel replied. "So, what did you do with your day?"

"I just ran a few errands and did some stuff around the house, nothing much," she said. "And you?"

"The usual," Daniel said. "Hung out by the beach and wasted my life away," he half-heartedly laughed.

"Well... I guess there are much worse places you could be," Rebecca countered.

"That's very true."

Leo came back to the table with the bottle of wine.

"Your 2018 Baco Noir," he said as he showed them the bottle. He opened the wine, moved Daniel's glass closer to the edge of the table and poured a small amount. "Please let me know if it's alright."

Daniel swirled the wine in the glass softly to release the aromas and brought it up to his nose to smell. He took a small sip.

"It's perfect," he confirmed.

"Wonderful," Leo replied as he moved Rebecca's glass and filled it halfway. He then filled Daniel's to match. "I'll give you both some time to look over the menu and enjoy the wine."

"Thank you," said Rebecca.

Leo walked away and Daniel lifted his glass.

"Cheers to an unforgettable second date," he declared.

"Oh, it's sure to be unforgettable…" Rebecca thought as she raised her glass.

"Cheers," she smiled as they clinked glasses.

CHAPTER

FORTY-SEVEN

"What time do you think they'll be back?" Conway asked. "It's been like two and a half hours."

"Probably any minute now," replied James. "Nice dinners like that can be very long."

"That's true... do we even have a plan? I mean, I know you said we're just laying out everything for him but is that really going to work?"

"The plan is to have basically no plan," James said. "It seems like that's worked well for us so far."

"So, does it bother you?" Conway asked.

"Does what bother me?" James questioned.

"Does it bother you that Rebecca is on a date with another guy right now?"

James squinted and stared defensively at Conway.

"Why would that bother me?" He asked.

"Oh, come on, Wilde. Do you really think I haven't noticed? The whole station has noticed," he replied. "You're head over heels for her."

"I don't know what you're talking about," denied James. "And even if I did... it's not something I could act on."

"Sure, you could," Conway replied.

"How?"

"You just need–" Conway stopped at the sound of keys

rattling in the hall.

"So, this is my little place," Rebecca said, as she fumbled her keys. "I probably should have warned you sooner… but I do live with roommates."

"Roommates?" James whispered to Conway.

"Sounds good to me," Conway whispered back.

The door slowly opened, and Rebecca walked in first.

"Hi, guys," she greeted James and Conway. "This is my friend, Daniel," she said gesturing toward him as he walked into the small apartment.

The front door opened into the living room where Daniel and Conway were seated on the brown, faux leather couch. The couch faced a small television with a wooden coffee table in between. The open concept led to a kitchen on the left with a counter that overlooked the living room. The light, tan carpet was once nice but was now fading and the appliances were old. Although it was outdated, Rebecca's warm décor made it feel like a welcoming home.

"Hello," Daniel said as he offered a small wave.

"Hi," said James.

"Hey," added Conway.

"I'm sorry," Rebecca said again. "I probably should have told you we would have company," she looked at Daniel.

"It's alright," Daniel replied. "I don't mind at all." His words sounded sincere but the look on his face alluded to his disappointment.

Attempting to balance the awkward date and approaching investigation, Rebecca suggested, "Would you guys want to play cards?"

"Where would we play?" Conway asked. "You don't even have a dining room table."

"That's a good point," James agreed. "*We* are working on getting one because we thought Rebecca was going to bring one and she didn't."

"Wait," Daniel said skeptically to Rebecca. "I thought you said you lived in a one-bedroom?"

"Uh," Rebecca replied. "Did I?"

"Yes," said Daniel. "At dinner you told me you lived in a small, one-bedroom apartment. How can three of you live in a one-bedroom?" He questioned.

"We can't," Conway replied.

James and Rebecca shot him a look.

"Well," Conway continued. "It has to happen sometime."

"What has to happen?" Daniel asked.

Rebecca locked the door behind and pulled out one of the stools from the kitchen bar.

"Have a seat," Rebecca said. "Can I get you something to drink?"

"I think I'm alright," Daniel skeptically replied.

Rebecca pulled out another stool and took a seat next to Daniel.

"I have to be honest with you," she paused. "I'm not Elizabeth."

"What's going on here?" Daniel defensively stood up.

"We're here to help," Rebecca assured him. "I'm Officer Rebecca Good, that's Officer James Wilde and Officer Luke Conway," she said as she motioned toward them.

"What?" Daniel shouted. "I didn't do anything! I'm innocent." He bolted for the door.

Conway and James dashed after him and each grabbed an arm.

"If you leave, you're done for," James threatened. "If you stay, we can work to protect you."

"We can help you," Rebecca added.

"Why should I trust you?" Daniel asked angrily.

"Because," Rebecca explained. "If we wanted to go after

you, I would have had enough information after last night, but we want to help you. That's why we're including you. If you have information on Alexa, then we can use it to protect you," she pleaded.

Daniel was quiet for a few moments.

He took a deep, hesitant breath and reluctantly agreed, "I guess I have nothing to lose."

James and Conway released their grip and watched carefully as Daniel took his seat.

"Actually," said James. "Why don't we switch seats? You take the couch," he instructed Daniel.

Daniel begrudgingly stood up and made his way to the couch where James had been sitting.

"It's warm," he commented.

"You'll get used to it," James replied, now confident they were in control of the situation. He pulled out his phone and set it on the coffee table where everyone could see. He started the voice recording. "We're going to need you to be completely transparent and honest."

Daniel gave a head nod.

"When was your first communication with Alexa Monarch?" James asked.

"Well... I grew up with her around," Daniel said. "Like I told Elizabeth... I mean Rebecca, my family runs her island, so I've virtually known her my entire life. The first time she reached out to me about this task was October 2020."

"How did she approach it?" James inquired.

"She was staying on the island for the weekend and one night, after dinner, she asked to speak with me in her office," he paused. "She flirted with me... she made me feel like the only man in the world, touching my shoulders and my hair. She told me she needed my help, but I had to promise to keep it our little secret. My brother had told me she'd made a move on him once before and I was sure that was what she was doing. I didn't want to, but I reluctantly agreed and told her I'd do whatever she needed. After all, without her, I didn't have a family or a job… which she so delicately liked to remind me."

"So, what happened?" Conway asked.

"I agreed to do whatever she needed, which I assumed would be… well, pleasurable tasks, I guess, to keep it polite but the moment I agreed, a switch flipped. She moved swiftly and began showing me blueprints and documents outlining her plans and how I would execute them. I didn't know what to say. I tried to back out. I told her I thought it was too much for me to handle and that she should ask someone else. She told me she'd claim I'd assaulted her if I didn't comply and that it would be reason to fire my entire family. She'd have footage to show me going into the office with her, then it would be my word against hers…" Daniel explained.

"That's terrible," Rebecca commented.

"I really didn't have a choice and I had no one to confide in, so I agreed to help her," he admitted. "In the months following, she sent me packages with all of the instructions and materials I needed to build the bomb. I don't know where she got her information from, but she told me to use the instructions and burn them as I went along. I complied and by Christmas, I had successfully placed a live bomb in a pair of green Brays identical to Kyle's. The only thing I had to do after that was swap them out," he paused. "The Mines' were set to vacation the following week and Alexa assured me that Kyle would bring his shoes. She also promised me that she'd protect me and would never let the crime be traced back to me. I assume she paid off all of the cops who were even remotely involved. When you have the kind of money she does, you can do whatever you want," Daniel said.

"Good thing she didn't pay us," James grinned.

Daniel let out a sympathetic laugh and continued.

"I was walking through the house on their second to last day of vacation when I saw the Brays sitting by the door. The family had taken the boat out on the water for the afternoon, so I knew I had some time to work with. I quickly went to grab the replica shoes from my room and swapped them out at the door. The replicas looked identical. The bomb was hidden in the sole of the shoe and it was nearly impossible to tell, especially, if you weren't looking for it. I hid the originals in my room and after the family left, I burned them. Two days later, I received a call from Alexa informing me that Riley had been arrested… instead of Kyle. She overnighted me a check for one million dollars to get me started and told me to get off the island and never come back… she couldn't risk me outing her and she threatened again to claim assault if I didn't abide by her rules. I made up the thing about falling in love to tell my parents and left the island. I haven't run out of money yet, but Alexa says she'll keep paying me as long as I keep quiet."

"If Alexa will pay you as long as you keep quiet, why would you share this information with some random girl you met in a bar on a Monday night?" Conway suspiciously questioned.

"I don't know," he replied defeated. "Something seemed different about Rebecca… and I was really drunk and I'm tired of hiding and I want my life to go back to the way it was and I hate that Alexa ruined it, so I figured I had nothing to lose," he paused. "Let's just say I also didn't anticipate you being a cop," he added, looking at Rebecca.

She guiltily smiled back.

"At least I'm a cop who wants to help you."

"So, do you have any sort of proof? Anything to help us point to Alexa?" James inquired.

Daniel searched his mind for any evidence he could think of.

"She was really good at not putting things in writing. Everything she sent me was cryptic and hard to decipher. She also always gave me specific instructions to dispose of it immediately," he explained.

"I'll give it to her... she's smart," Rebecca said.

"Wait!" Daniel exclaimed. "There might be something." He continued, "Now that I think about it, she sent me her final instructions a day or two before the Mines arrived. I didn't burn them because I wanted to double check and make sure I did everything correctly... so much for that. After Riley's arrest, everything happened so fast and she sent me away. I think the instructions are still in my room on the island."

"Really?" James shouted. "Do you think they'd still be there?"

"I would assume," Daniel replied. "My dad still thinks I'm coming home any day now. I'm sure he hasn't touched my room to make sure it's ready for me when I return."

"Well, that's great!" Conway declared. "When can you go get it?"

Daniel busted out in laughter.

"You think I can just go back to the island and casually grab the documents?" He asked in disbelief.

"Come on, Conway," Rebecca said annoyed. "We're going to have to be more creative than that. "I'm sure Alexa is watching him like a hawk. Do you think you could ask your mom, James?"

"I don't know," James replied. "At this point, I'm pretty confused why Alexa let me on the island in the first place. I doubt she would do it again."

"But what if your mom went for you?" Rebecca suggested.

James' stomach dropped.

"I'm starting to worry that my mom might have known about this. I don't feel comfortable asking her..."

"Is there anyone you trust on the island that you could call?" Rebecca asked Daniel.

"I don't really know," Daniel replied. "I guess maybe, my brother, but Alexa keeps things very tight. I'm not even sure he'd be able to send it."

"Surely, he could take a picture of it," James replied. "He could take a picture and send it to me. A picture would at least allow us to figure out if what you have will hold any value. If it will, we can worry about physically getting the document later."

Daniel took a deep breath and with fear in his eyes he replied, "I guess if that's our only option…"

"We'll protect you," James promised. "If you can get us the documents… If you can get us anything worthwhile… we'll leave you alone. Heck… we won't bother you again until you need to testify in court, if you can get us this information."

CHAPTER

FORTY-EIGHT

Kyle, Jane and Lila sat quietly in the living room, each lost in their own train of thought.

Kyle broke the silence.

"So, you're really telling me that Riley is going to show up out of nowhere tonight? Like live and in person?"

"Uh huh," Lila replied.

"What time do you think he'll come?" Kyle asked.

"I think any second now," Lila said.

Kyle tapped his foot anxiously.

"Are you excited?" Jane asked.

"I don't know, Mom," Kyle got defensive. "I really don't know how to feel right now. My supposed to be mother-in-law tried to kill me, or at least imprison me, or something… and she messed up and put my brother in prison instead and now he apparently teleports… and has a chance to clear his name… and I learned all of this in the last five hours so I don't know how to feel. But, yes," he threw up his hands. "If I have to answer, I'm excited to see my brother."

"Sorry, I asked," Jane replied.

They heard a thud come from the back of the house.

"Riley?" Lila hesitantly called.

"Honey, I'm home," Riley sang as he walked into the kitchen.

Lila jumped up and greeted him with a hug and kiss. She stood next to him as Riley and Kyle made uncomfortable eye contact.

Unsure of what they'd told him, Riley waited for Kyle to make the first move. Kyle stood to his feet and smiled at Riley.

"I would never have bet that you would go to prison before me," he grinned.

Riley laughed and opened his arms to invite Kyle in. They took a few steps toward each other and embraced.

"Missed you, bro," Riley said.

"I've missed you, too," Kyle replied patting him on the back.

"So," Riley started as he walked to the living room and made himself comfortable on the couch. He had always been naturally calm in the most intense moments.

"What have we been talking about?" He asked.

Lila rolled her eyes; Riley's nonchalant manner drove her crazy in times like this.

"We've been waiting on you so that we can call James," she said. "He's texted me a few updates and it sounds like Daniel is being cooperative... which is great for us."

"Well, then, what are we waiting for?" Riley asked. "Dial him up."

Lila nodded and grabbed the laptop that had been sitting next to her. She typed in her password and opened up the video chat.

"Come sit by us on the couch, Kyle," she instructed.

The four of them sat comfortably on the large sofa and Lila set her laptop on the coffee table to ensure they were all in the frame. She clicked on James' contact and turned the volume all the way up as it began to ring.

"Wait!" Jane shouted. "Does Daniel know Riley will be here?"

"I assumed they were going to tell him," Lila said. "But I guess I don't know for sure."

The chat continued to ring.

"Maybe, it's better if he's out of frame," Jane suggested. "Just in case."

The video chat started to connect, and Riley awkwardly threw himself off the back of the couch. He crawled to the side of the coffee table so that he could still see the screen.

"Hello!" James excitedly greeted. "Riley must have made it back successfully," he said as he looked for him on the screen. "Wait, where is he?"

"Guess we're in the clear," Lila laughed as she motioned for Riley to come back to the spot, he'd been sitting in next to her.

"Hi, James," he said. "We weren't sure if Daniel knew I was going to be here or not."

"He doesn't," Conway, who was seated to the left of James on the screen, said.

Sensing their confusion, Rebecca explained, "He's already gone. We kind of hammered him earlier and ended up getting the information we needed. We didn't want to press our luck and add another unnecessary layer with Riley tonight."

"Good thinking," Jane complimented.

"What did you find out?" Lila asked.

James pulled his phone out of his pocket and clicked a few times on the screen. He turned his phone toward the camera for the four of them to see. They stared intently, trying to make sense of the photograph. The picture displayed a white piece of paper with the black words that looked like they came from an old typewriter in the center:

December 27, 2020 – January 3, 2021
Enact second to last day.

"What's that supposed to prove?" Kyle asked doubtfully. "Anyone could have printed that out."

"I know," James replied. "And originally, we were bummed with the picture as well," he paused. "But look at what's under the paper."

They studied the photo again, looking at the hand holding the white paper off the ground and noticed an envelope behind it on the floor.

"The envelope?" Lila questioned. "It doesn't look like there is a return address," she commented.

"There's not," James replied. "However, there is a tracking number and that has the potential to take us places. If we can find out where the stamp was purchased, most likely, we'll be able to identify the credit card holder."

"What if she used cash?" Kyle questioned.

"Then, we start over," James replied honestly. "But, for now, it's a lead and we'll follow it as far as it allows us."

"Where did you get the photo?" Jane asked.

"Daniel reached out to his brother, Matthew," Rebecca explained. "He remembered he'd left the instructions under his bed and he called him to see if he could find them. He didn't share much information with him... he just told him he wanted to come home and he'd need the picture to help him get there."

"Where's Daniel now?" Riley inquired.

"He went back to the Perennial," answered Conway.

"And you just trusted him to do that?" Lila was surprised.

"Yes," said James. "Mostly, for two reasons. The first being he seemed more than willing to cooperate all night... I don't believe he wants to live the life he's living at all anymore and he sees a potential out, so he's willing to comply. The second being he really has no other choice because we sort of..." he paused. "We might have threatened him a little bit."

"I thought you weren't going to go with the blackmail

tactic?" Jane questioned.

"Well, we're this far in researching a case we're not supposed to be reaching, so I figured we might as well play all of the cards we can," James defended.

"Fair enough," Lila replied. "So, what happens next?"

"We can start researching the tracking number tomorrow and see if we can trace it back to her. Unfortunately, even if we're successful, it still doesn't give us much evidence. We will need Daniel's testimony, and our proof she sent the letter, to give us even a sliver of a chance," James replied.

"Then, what?" Lila asked. "I mean who do we take this to and where do we go? How can we reopen the case and pin her as a suspect?"

"All very good questions, Lila," said James. "I think if we can successfully trace the letter to her, it might be best for us all to take a trip out to Los Angeles."

Lila was annoyed, "Alright, keep us posted. Do you have anything else for us?"

"Not at the moment," James replied.

"Okay, please let us know as soon as you get any information," she pleaded. "Have a good night," she waved.

"You too," the officers simultaneously responded.

Lila hung up the call and exclaimed, "Ugh! They seriously have no idea what they're doing! I swear they've never solved a case before."

"They're trying their best," Riley tried to calm Lila down.

"Their best? They're trying their best?" Lila stood up with anger. "I need 'their best,'" she motioned with air quotes, "to get my husband out of prison and I'm not feeling any hope with the three of them running the show."

"Oh my gosh," Kyle whispered to himself.

"What?" Riley asked, thankful for the interruption.

"I just remembered a conversation I once had with

Keagan," he replied.

They waited for him to go on, but he didn't.

"Annnd?" Riley prompted.

"Well, it might not be anything," he started. "It's just that I remember when Keagan and I were dating, like super early on… probably still high school… she told me that her mom always used the same ridiculous and embarrassing password. It was years ago but I'm just thinking if we could get into her email account, maybe, we could find some information."

Lila jumped and clapped her hands, "That's genius, Kyle!" She exclaimed, "It's worth a shot at least!" She sat back down and grabbed her laptop. "What's her email?" She asked.

Kyle was already searching on his phone.

"Let me double check," he said, scrolling. "Okay, it's almonarch@indfilms.com."

"Okay," she said as she typed furiously, whispering the email slowly out loud to herself. "And what's the password?"

"Keageyboppergirl#1," Kyle replied with a smile. "k-e-a-g-e-y-b-o-p-p-e-r girl, number sign, one," Kyle explained.

Lila carefully typed in the password and hit enter as she nervously closed her eyes.

"Ugh," the others groaned together.

Lila opened her eyes.

"Maybe, I typed it in wrong," she suggested.

She slowly began to type the password in again, talking to herself.

"Wait!" Kyle shouted, "Are you typing a capital K? There's probably a capital at the beginning," he said.

"I didn't do that the first time," Lila replied. "I will try it."

She meticulously retyped the password. She took a deep breath in and clicked enter once more.

"Oh my," Jane said.

"No way!" Riley exclaimed.

"I can't believe it!" Lila added.

"Thanks, Keagan," Kyle smiled looking up.

CHAPTER FORTY-NINE

Debbie stretched her arms up as she relaxed on the lounge chair by the pool.

"I never want to leave California," she yawned.

"I don't think you ever should," Alexa replied as she sipped her cucumber-mint water.

"I mean, what's really waiting for me back in Florida?" She asked hypothetically. "A son who might soon hate me and a husband who … well, I don't even know what he does," she rolled her eyes. "What has my life come to?"

"Your son will never hate you… because there's nothing he will ever find out," Alexa bluntly replied. "Even if they had the help of Riley Mines himself," she joked. "They still couldn't solve the case. Anyone who knows anything at all has been well taken care of and compensated to keep their mouth shut."

"Why did you let him go to the island?" Debbie asked.

"I thought he needed a vacation," Alexa replied.

"You knew he was going to look for evidence," claimed Debbie.

"Whaaat? I didn't know," she smiled.

"Why would you let him openly search for evidence like that?" Debbie questioned; she was getting worked up.

"Everything is fine," Alexa persuaded.

"No," Debbie said. "Everything is not fine. What if they find out? What happens then?"

"You've always been such a worrier," Alexa replied.

"Nothing is going to happen. Don't I always get us out of trouble?"

"This is a little bigger than underage drinking or cheating in college, Al. Don't you think?" Debbie argued.

"What's the worst-case scenario?" Alexa asked.

"We go to prison," Debbie stated matter-of-factly.

"Look at this place," Alexa said gesturing toward the pool and enormous home behind them. "This is money and power and everything one needs to avoid punishment. We don't go to prison," she explained. "*We* claim we're mentally unstable and end up at some five-star mental rehabilitation clinic for a number of years instead. You're telling me that doesn't sound kind of fun and nice to you?"

"I guess it doesn't sound terrible," Debbie admitted.

"Exactly," Alexa replied. "And that's our worst-case scenario. So, quit ruining my chi because we only have three more days together and I want to spend them relaxing with my best friend… not worrying."

With a deep breath, Debbie closed her eyes and tried to relax.

A few minutes later, her phone began to vibrate.

"Who's that?" Alexa asked.

"It's Kevin," she replied. "I haven't talked to him since I left… I should probably grab it."

She stood up and walked into the large living room of the house, shutting the glass doors behind her.

"Hello," she answered the phone.

"Hi," the familiar voice greeted on the other end.

"Hi, James," she replied. "How are you?"

"I'm well," he responded. "And how's Cali?"

"Lovely," Debbie said.

"Mom, you seem tense," James lightheartedly commented. "Are you tense?"

"I'm alright," replied Debbie. Her white cover up flowed as she paced back and forth in the living room.

"I could help you, Mom," James said, his voice now growing serious.

"Help me with what?" She asked.

"I know," James replied. "You think I don't, and you think I'm incapable, but I know, and I want to help you. You say the word and I'll help."

"I don't know what you're talking about," Debbie said coldly.

"It will be the biggest case I ever solve, Mom," James stated. "I'm giving you the option right now to pick which side you'd like to be on."

Debbie's chest tightened and she sat down on the edge of the uninviting white, leather sofa. She opened her mouth to respond but no words came out.

"I know you're hard on me and I know you've made mistakes but I want you to know that right now…" he paused, "Right now, I'll forgive all of them and if you say the word, I'll protect you. I'll need your honesty and your help, but I want to protect you," James pleaded.

Debbie nervously looked at her hands and played with her fingernails.

After a long pause, she took a deep breath and replied, "I'll take the help."

James' stomach dropped. He'd had a feeling his mom had been involved with the case but hearing her admit it impacted him more than he'd expected. He knew he could only do so much to protect her.

He finally responded, "I need everything you have," James explained. "Anything and everything you could give to me to potentially help solve the case."

There was silence on the other end of the line.

"Can you do that for me?" James asked.

Debbie set the phone down in her lap and rubbed her fingers across her eyebrows and over to her temples. She began to massage the sides of her face.

"Mom, are you still there?" She heard the quiet voice coming from her phone.

She picked the phone up from her lap.

"Yes," she replied. "I'm here."

"Can you do that for me?" James asked again.

"I can do that," Debbie agreed.

"I need it as soon as possible," James insisted. "We're running out of time."

"Okay," said Debbie. She spoke softly, "I will see what I can gather from my phone and send it to you soon."

"Thank you, Mom," James replied.

Debbie hung up the phone.

"I was right," James said with widened eyes. He was sitting at his desk in the office and Conway and Rebecca had been listening intently to the entire conversation. "I can't believe it," James said. "I've always known my mom to be cold but an accomplice in a criminal case… I never would have guessed."

"That's crazy," Rebecca replied. "Do you think she'll really send you stuff?

"I hope so," said James, "If she doesn't, I don't know what to do."

"You don't know what to do?" Conway chimed in. "You don't know what to do?" He asked again angrily. "We have the case. We've risked everything for this and it's all coming together. What you do, is you present the facts of the case, no matter what they are."

"It's okay, Conway," Rebecca interrupted, trying to calm him down. "We don't have to worry about that yet."

"He's right," James said rubbing his chin. "We have to use

everything we gather, and we can only try to protect those who help us. If she doesn't comply, then she'll have to learn her lesson the hard way." He paused, "She said she'd send us what she has soon. We'll give her until the end of the day."

Conway and Rebecca agreed.

CHAPTER FIFTY

"I feel like I shouldn't have come," Riley said. "This seems like a wasted trip."

"What makes you say that?" Lila asked. "Things are moving along as fast as they can. Everything is looking up."

"Yes," Riley agreed. "But it's all stuff you could have done without me. I didn't get much sleep before I came and now, I've been up like seventeen hours and I'm so tired, but I don't want to go back yet because I don't really have any answers."

"Riley! We got into her email and we found a few things we think we can use. What more do you want?" Lila asked.

"No, don't get me wrong... that's amazing! It's just that you could have done it without me," he claimed. "At this point, I'm not really sure what my trips here are helping. I don't know what the next step is, and I don't know how I'm getting out of prison. I have one trip left and then what? I just wait until the day someone comes into my prison cell and tells me I'm free? That's a lot to wait on and hope for."

"Isn't that what you were doing before?" Lila asked harshly.

"Well, sort of," answered Riley. "But before I didn't have anything to hope for. I felt helpless. Now, I know so much of what actually happened, but I don't know what to do about it. I have this overwhelming sense of unobtainable hope."

"It's not unobtainable," Lila replied. "We're so close and I'm sure the officers have uncovered something today. They're supposed to call in like an hour. What can we do to keep you awake?" Lila asked, reaching for Riley's hand.

"Hmm," he smiled. "I could probably think of a few activities. How long until mom and Kyle are home with the kids?"

"Well, the movie started at three and it's about four o'clock now, so I think that gives us a very safe thirty minutes to work with," she grinned.

"I like the way you think, Lila Mines," Riley said as he picked her up. She wrapped her legs lightly around him and hugged her arms around his neck.

They stared into each other's eyes; their noses almost touching.

Lila smiled, "I've missed you, Riley Mines."

"I've missed you, too," he replied as his lips met hers.

CHAPTER FIFTY-ONE

The only light filling James' small living room was the beam of sun coming in from the west window. Rebecca sat on the floor, surrounded by a barrage of papers, while Conway paced the room and James sat focused on the couch, staring at his computer.

"I think confrontation is our only option at this point," Conway broke the silence.

"I agree," Rebecca quickly added.

"We don't have enough evidence to fully prove anything yet… but we do have enough to make the accusation. If we go to LA and give Alexa an ultimatum, maybe we can get somewhere."

"You seriously think three random cops showing up at her front door will make her admit to being the mastermind behind a huge crime?" James asked rhetorically.

"I don't see another option we have," Conway said. "Maybe, if your mom wasn't being such a bi –"

James leapt off the couch and grabbed Conway's shirt with both hands.

"Don't you ever talk that way about my mother," he shouted.

Rebecca jumped up and tried to pry them apart.

"Stop it!" She yelled. "Both of you, stop it!"

James let go and Conway straightened his shirt while keeping eye contact.

"There's nothing else James can do, Conway," Rebecca pleaded. "It's not his fault his mom isn't being cooperative, and we are still giving her a couple of hours. Maybe, she'll come through."

James shot Conway a cocky look, seeing as Rebecca had taken his side.

"And as for you," she turned to James. "Since when is resulting in physical violence the best option? Don't overreact like that when we're here trying our best to help you," she reprimanded.

Conway shot James the same smirk back.

"We can't turn on each other now. We're so close," said Rebecca. "Imagine if we solve this... our careers will be made," she paused. "But it will be pretty hard to celebrate our success if you guys kill each other before it happens." Rebecca looked back and forth at them with a piercing stare. "Do you understand?" She demanded an answer.

"Yes," they replied.

"Good," she said with pursed lips and an I'm-right-you're-wrong nod.

James' phone buzzed.

"It's from my mom," he said looking at the screen.

"Right on cue," Rebecca grinned.

"What is it?" Conway asked.

"She said, 'Sorry, it took me so long to respond. I had to get a few more drinks in Alexa before she'd really start talking' and there's a video."

"A video?" Rebecca exclaimed. "Play it!"

The three of them stood closely together around James' phone as he played the video.

It appeared as though Debbie had placed the camera in her lap to discretely capture the conversation. Alexa sat across from her on a couch outdoors with palm trees in the background. She held an iced, pink-colored drink dramatically in her right hand with her head tilted back.

"I talked to James this morning," Debbie said.

"Oh, yeah?" Alexa responded.

"Yeah, he called about his nonsense again," replied Debbie.

"Of course, he did! How is he not over that ridiculousness yet?" Alexa asked.

"I don't know. I still don't think he has a clue what he's doing," replied Debbie.

"Gee, thanks, Mom," James groaned.

"Shh," Rebecca and Conway demanded.

"Of course, he doesn't," Alexa replied. "I'm still not even concerned in the slightest but if I had known he was going to be so interested in this case... I would have paid him off, too."

"I'm sure he wouldn't have taken the bribe anyway," Debbie shrugged. "He's too into the law to participate in any foul play."

"Well, still," Alexa paused. "I'll be sure to keep him in mind next time around."

"You're not seriously thinking about trying, again are you?" Debbie questioned.

"Of course, not," Alexa said gesturing with her hand. "At least... not in the same way."

"Alexa! You're lucky to have gotten away with everything you already have... you can't seriously want to try again?"

Alexa's rolled her eyes and moved her head dramatically, "Oh?" She questioned. "I seriously can't want to try again?" Her body language was now exaggerated in every way. "Because last I recall, Kyle killed my daughter and suffered no consequences!"

"He didn't really kill her," said Debbie. "He lost his best friend, too."

"Whose side are you on?" Alexa raised her voice. "That boy ruined my life and I vow to ruin his!" She stood up and began to pace back and forth in front of the couch, "Hell, I'll ruin their whole family's lives if I have to. And in that case, I've already taken care of Riley. What are the odds? The same shoes? Really? I think they all need to go," she was ranting now.

"Let it out," Debbie encouraged. "It's okay to be angry."

"Oh, I know it's okay to be angry!" Alexa shouted. "I've been angry for two years now. My only daughter. My only child," Alexa cried. "He took her away." She fell back down on the couch.

The video shook for a second, turned black and came to an end while James, Rebecca and Conway stared in awe.

They stood in silence for a few seconds.

"Wow," was all James could get out.

"She's still scheming?" Questioned Rebecca.

"I guess so," Conway replied.

"She essentially just admitted to the crime," James said.

"And maybe, to future ones," Rebecca added.

"Okay, Mrs. Wilde. I see you," Conway said. "Sorry, for doubting."

"So, what do we do next?" Rebecca asked.

"I think we take it to Hillsteg," James said. "We'll talk to the Mines' tonight and then compile everything we have to present our case. There's no way he'll be able to deny our findings."

"And what if he does?" Rebecca questioned.

"Then, we'll go to California and arrest her ourselves," James declared.

"Under what authority?" Rebecca worried.

"I'm not that concerned," James replied. "Like we've said before, Hillsteg wants power and attention, he can gain both from this case and we did all of the legwork, I'm confident he'll be on board."

"He's right," Conway agreed.

Rebecca hesitantly bit her lit and nodded.

"Are we ready to call the Mines'?" James asked.

"Yeah," they answered.

The three of them sat down close together to fit on the small couch in James' living room. James grabbed his laptop and started the video chat with Lila.

The call connected and the Mines' family was sitting around the dining room table.

"Hello," they waived.

"We've got big news," James jumped right in.

"So, do we," Lila replied.

"You go first," James insisted.

"We were able to log into Alex's email account, thanks to Kyle guessing the password, and we found some email exchanges between Alexa and Daniel. They're all very cryptic and honestly, we don't understand them, but they could be beneficial if we paired them with something else, or if Daniel deciphered them?" Lila explained.

"Well, that's great and I'd normally say we shouldn't hack emails for information but at this point, with this case, I'll use anything," James replied. "We have a video to show you. My mom sent it to me of a conversation she had with Alexa earlier today," he paused. I made my mom the same promise I made Daniel."

James turned his phone toward the computer camera and tried to focus it for them to see.

"Oh my gosh," Kyle said when the video finished playing. He had chills across his body. "Isn't that the case?" He asked. "Doesn't that prove everything?"

"In a way," James replied. "We still have to piece together all of the evidence and take it to our chief of police, Hillsteg but I don't see how what we have won't be evidence enough."

"I can't believe it," Riley said, feeling his small sense of hope grow.

"Have you spoken with Daniel today? Did he see that video?" Jane asked.

"No, we haven't," Rebecca answered. "We received it only a few minutes before our call with you. It's a good idea to loop him in though, we'll contact him after we get off with you."

"I think the next step in our course of action is simply for the three of us to gather everything we have tonight, and we'll plan to take it to Hillsteg tomorrow. Of course, we'll keep you updated on everything and we'll try to move as fast as possible. We obviously don't want to leave Riley in prison a day longer than has to be," James explained.

"When should I come back?" Riley asked.

"That's a tough question," James replied. "How tired are you?" He asked half joking.

"Well, I'm not sure I could make it until tomorrow afternoon," Riley chuckled. "But, of course, I'm willing to try."

"It's not like you'll be able to help much if you're here, but I hate the fact that you'll be completely out of the loop if you go back," said James. "And, right now, we don't have a solid timeline of how things will unfold."

"I guess you could go back now and plan to come back in twenty-four hours again?" Rebecca suggested.

"But what if we haven't accomplished anything or we're all in California and he wastes a trip," replied Conway. "James is right. There are too many variables."

"That's true… but with only one trip left, we need to be careful," James agreed, looking at Riley. "I don't want to mess it up and leave you in prison with no idea what's happening." He continued, "I hope we will have a better sense of a timeline after meeting with Hillsteg tomorrow. I think Rebecca's option might be best because I don't really foresee us hopping on a flight tomorrow night to California." He looked at his watch. "It's about 6:15 now so if you go to sleep, you could be back around 6:30 tomorrow night, right?"

"Theoretically," Riley replied. "Depending on how long it takes me to fall asleep… and assuming I get a silica gel right away."

"Okay," James said. "There are no guarantees, but I think it's safe to guess we could at least see a rough timeline by tomorr—"

Lila interrupted, "What if we plan for him to come back early Friday morning instead? It seems like it would be better for you guys to have all of tomorrow to focus on Hillsteg and him to have a full day and not have to stay up through the night?"

James nodded, "I hadn't thought of that possibility. That makes perfect sense! Plus, that way he can try to stay up as long as possible with you guys tonight and have plenty of time to fall asleep and make it back on Friday."

Everyone nodded in agreeance with the newest plan.

"Okay, well I think we're good for now," James said. "Please send me the email log-in information and we will take a look at that and get stuff put together for tomorrow. Y'all enjoy the rest of your night and don't worry too much. You're in good hands."

"Thank you," Lila replied.

"Thanks, guys," said Kyle.

"See you Friday," Rebecca waved to Riley.

"See ya," Riley said as he hung up the call.

"That video is huge," Kyle said. "I mean… that's basically the case. She admitted to it and it's on tape."

"I know," Lila replied. "But crazier things have happened in court rooms, so I'm not ready to get my hopes up yet. I hope it's good timing with you coming back on Friday morning," she said to Riley.

"It's great," Riley agreed. "I think it will be much easier to come back during the daytime. It's hard to stay up alone through the night."

"I think it's a great plan," Jane agreed. "Hopefully, we can get you out of prison in no time." She stood up from the table and went to hug Riley. "I need my boy back home."

CHAPTER FIFTY-TWO

Hillsteg walked into the back office where the large, glass windows were poorly covered with strips of sporadically taped paper in an effort to keep the conversation private.

Rebecca and Conway's desks were pushed together in the center of the room and displayed numerous pictures and sheets of paper associated with the Mines case.

"What in the name of Sam Hill is going on in here?" Hillsteg shouted as he made his way to the table.

James and Conway were standing by the desks and Rebecca shut the door behind Hillsteg.

"Sir," James started. "Please hear us out."

"You three were working on this case after I explicitly ordered you not to!" He accused.

"Well, we were working on it before," James explained. "And then, yes, we continued —"

Hillsteg's nostrils flared and he shouted, "You're all fired! Get out!" He stormed toward the door.

Rebecca stood in front of the door, blocking it with her arms held out.

"Hillsteg, please," she begged. "We have something you'll want to see. It could be huge for the station."

Hillsteg could live without James and Conway but he'd always had a soft spot for Rebecca.

"I don't know, Rebecca," he said, lowering his voice. "How will it make me look if I threatened to fire you and I don't follow through on my word?"

"But... how much worse will it look for you when we continue with the case and tell everyone we had to go against our chief's orders to solve the biggest case of the year?" Rebecca countered.

Hillsteg tightened his jaw and looked at Rebecca with disapproving eyes.

"You're that confident, huh?" He questioned.

"Yes," Rebecca replied. "We are."

There was a long pause as Hillsteg stared at Rebecca, then back at James and Conway.

"You have three minutes," he finally said.

Rebecca rushed to the table to join them.

"Okay," James said. "This stuff is all great and good supporting evidence for the case but what you really need to see is this."

He picked his phone up off the table and pulled up the video. He made sure the sound was turned up all the way and handed it to Hillsteg.

"Is that Alexa Monarch?" Hillsteg asked as he started the video.

"Shh," Rebecca said. "Yes, it is, but listen."

Hillsteg watched the video in awe. When it finished playing, he looked up at the three officers in disbelief.

"Is this for real?" He asked.

"As real as it gets," James replied.

"How did you get this?" Hillsteg questioned.

"My mom is really good friends with Alexa," James explained. "She took that video yesterday while she was out in California visiting her."

"So, you're telling me that the famous movie star, Alexa Monarch, is responsible for the Mines airport bomb?" Hillsteg said, trying to wrap his mind around the new information.

"Yes," said James. "We're one-hundred percent confident that she was the mastermind behind the case. We're fully prepared to walk you through all of the evidence we've found."

"Well, what are you waiting for then? I said three minutes. Get to it," Hillsteg demanded.

James started at the left side of the table and worked his way across, describing each piece to Hillsteg.

He gestured to the first picture.

"The first picture here I took when I went to the island the Mines family had been visiting the week before Riley was arrested. Alexa Monarch purchased the island a little over twenty-five years ago. I found this pair of Brays, identical to the pair Riley wore in the airport, randomly sitting in the massive treehouse at the back of the island. We've since learned that these are actually Riley's brother Kyle's shoes. For years, the two have had matching pairs as a tribute to their dad who died in 2009," James continued. "Evidently, Kyle's fiancé, Keagan Monarch, who is Alexa's daughter, died in January of 2020. This specific pair of green Brays were Keagan's favorites, so Kyle claims he brought them on the island to leave ceremoniously for her. The two grew up playing together in the treehouse and he wanted to have a moment of closure when he went back to the island for the first time without her."

James paused and looked up to ensure Hillsteg was still listening intently.

"Which brings us to our next piece of evidence," he motioned toward the next picture. "This is Benjie Mendoza," he said. "Since Alexa purchased the island, the Mendoza family has been running it. However, Benjie only started working on the island last year, shortly after the incident. We found out that he went to the island to fill the place of his cousin, Daniel Mendoza, who according to his parents, fled to the mainland to pursue the love of his life. Although, after speaking with

Daniel about the situation," James gestured toward the next photo which pictured Rebecca and Daniel sitting together at the bar in the Perennial Hotel. "We learned that he'd instead been blackmailed and paid to leave the island. Thanks to Rebecca's flirting skills," James winked at Rebecca. "We were able to have a candid conversation with Daniel and learn more about the series of events connected with the case. He explained to us that last October, Alexa had been visiting the island and she cornered him in her office. He didn't think it was totally unusual because he'd heard of her doing this with his brother and others. She was known for requesting 'special favors'" he motioned. "She outlined her plans and explained she'd pay Daniel with a sum of money larger than he could ever imagine if he carried them out for her. Daniel didn't want to agree but she threatened to claim that he'd assaulted her and fire his family if he didn't. He knew it would be her word against his and not complying would ruin his entire family's lives, so he agreed to work with Alexa. She sent him confidential packages with all of the information and materials he needed to build and plant the bomb. The messages were cryptic," James pointed to the photograph of the only package still in existence. "And Daniel was instructed to burn each one after he'd finished the task. This is the only one still around because Alexa kicked him off of the island before he'd gotten a chance to dispose of it."

"Wait, why didn't the whole Mendoza family get fired?" Hillsteg interrupted.

"Hang on," James replied. "I'm getting there." He continued, "It's important to note that, like I mentioned earlier, Riley's brother, Kyle, was engaged to Alexa's daughter, Keagan. The two were planning to be married on December 31, 2020 but in January 2020, Kyle was driving Keagan home after one of Alexa's movie premiers and they were hit by a drunk driver. Kyle didn't do anything wrong, but Keagan's side was hit, and she died on impact. Rumor has it that many people, apparently including Alexa, felt it was Kyle's fault Keagan was dead. The old, 'he wasn't good enough for her and I never liked him anyway,' kind of attitude from a sophisticated and snobby Los Angeles crowd."

Hillsteg appeared to be getting lost in all of the details.

"Still following?" James asked.

"I think so," Hillsteg answered. "Lot of pieces."

"I know," replied James. "So, getting back to your question. The Mendoza family was not fired because the task was not successfully executed, and Alexa couldn't risk information getting out. You see, Daniel messed up. Neither Alexa nor Daniel had accounted for the fact that there could be two pairs of identical shoes. After all, they weren't a very popular brand and Kyle was the only person she knew who wore them. On the second to last day of their vacation, the Mines family was out on the boat for the afternoon and Daniel saw the green Brays by the front door, he knew it was his opportunity. He quickly went to swap out the pair of replica shoes he'd built with the bomb and figured his job was done. He expected Kyle to either pack or wear the shoes and get caught at the airport."

Hillsteg's mouth dropped.

James continued, "But, as you know, that wasn't the case and evidently, Riley came back and decided to wear *his* pair of Brays to the airport, while Kyle's were left behind, sitting in the treehouse."

"So, she was after Kyle?" Hillsteg confirmed.

The officers nodded.

"And Riley was accidentally made the focus of this entire case?" He questioned.

The officers nodded again.

"What's Daniel doing?" Hillsteg asked.

"She paid him to go away," Conway answered, wanting desperately to be a part of the conversation. "She didn't want to risk the rest of his family finding out, so she paid him a lot of money to stay away and threatened him with the same threat to claim assault and destroy his family if he went back."

"We assume she paid everyone else off as well," Rebecca added. "If you look at the details of the filed case, Riley was never questioned and there was never a court date or any formal investigation at all. One day, he's in the airport with a shoe bomb and virtually the next, he's housed in the world's most inescapable prison."

"Money yields immense power," Hillsteg commented, shaking his head.

After a few moments of silence, Hillsteg sighed.

"Congratulations," he said. "I was wrong. It looks like you've most likely solved your first big case."

The officers smiled and took big sighs of relief. They waited patiently, knowing Hillsteg was not finished with his comments.

"But this is where the work really begins," he said. "It should be fairly easy to get Riley out of prison, but it will be much harder to get Alexa in. It all depends on how safe we want to play it."

Conway was amped up.

"We can throw safe out the window!" He shouted.

"And we might have to," Hillsteg agreed. "Because, according to that video, Alexa could be planning more felonies and we can't have the threat of a criminal looming out there for long." He paused, "If I hadn't listened to you guys… what was going to be next on your agenda?" He inquired.

They looked back and forth at each other.

"Probably fly to California and accuse Alexa in person,"

James answered hesitantly.

Hillsteg nodded slowly, processing the idea.

"Normally, I would say that's insane," he paused. "But, after everything you've shown me, I think insane is our best option. Book the last flight out tomorrow for the four of us," he instructed. "Tomorrow is National Hot Pastrami Sandwich Day and my favorite deli is offering a buy one, get one deal. I can't miss it." He walked toward the door and grabbed the handle. He turned back to the officers before he exited.

"Good work," he complimented. And with that, he left and shut the door.

Rebecca and Conway began to jump and clap with excitement.

"We did it!" Rebecca shouted.

"I can't believe he didn't fire us," Conway said.

James wasn't ready to celebrate.

"We still have to execute," he explained. "We can have all of the evidence in the world, but we have to use it successfully."

Disappointed by his lack of excitement, Rebecca and Conway switched back into planning mode.

"I will look to book the flights," said Rebecca.

"This should work well with Riley," Conway added. "We will be able to tell him we're moving forward and that Hillsteg is on board. How long do you think it will take for us to get him out of prison?"

"I don't think long," James replied. "We can prove him innocent now. It's more so a matter of proving Alexa guilty."

CHAPTER
FIFTY-THREE

"Riley should be here any minute!" Lila announced as she scurried around the house, helping Jane and Kyle to get everything ready. "He said he'd aim for 9 a.m. and it's 8:55."

"Good," Jane replied, "I want to see him before we leave."

"We don't need to head to the airport until noon, so we have plenty of time," Kyle said.

"Uncle Kyle!" Chandler called from the top of the stairs, "Will you please come play dress up with me before you go?"

"He can't, Chan," Lila replied. "Eliza's mom will be here in a few minutes to take you girls to the children's museum. Will you please put your shoes on?"

"Can Uncle Kyle help me?" She begged.

"That's up to him," shrugged Lila.

"Pleaaaase, Uncle Kyle," Chandler pleaded.

"Of course, Chan, Chan," he said as he hoped up the stairs to help her.

"That girl is obsessed with him," Lila laughed.

"It's so sweet," Jane replied. She paused, "Almost sweet enough to make you want to move to L.A."

Jane had been pressuring Lila to move to L.A. since the day they'd met. The persuading had greatly increased over the last year with Riley's absence.

"For now, I'm just focused on getting my family back

together," Lila replied. "I'll worry about the next step of our lives after this horrible chapter ends."

There was a knock at the door.

"Coming," Lila called. "She's here, Chan! Are you ready?"

Chandler came running down the stairs with Kyle walking behind her.

"Yes, Mom!"

Lila opened the door.

"Hi, Susan," she greeted. Susan was a tall woman with brown, shoulder length hair and a thin frame. She was perfectly put together from her head to her toes and held her purse in a way that made every woman feel inferior. "Thanks for taking the girls to the museum today."

"Of course," Susan replied. "It should be a good time."

"Make sure you say goodbye to grandma and Uncle Kyle, Chan," Lila instructed. "They won't be here when you get back."

Chandler's lower lip puckered up and her eyes began to well.

"Do they have to go?" She cried.

"We'll see you very soon," Jane comforted her as she leaned down for a hug. "I love you, sweetheart."

Kyle bent down for the next hug.

"I promise we'll see you again before you know it," he assured her.

Chandler nodded and wiped her hand across her sad, wet face. She turned around to see her smiling friend, Eliza. Eliza and Chandler could have been sisters with their matching blonde hair and big eyes.

Lila squatted down to eye level with Chandler.

"Please be good and have fun today, Chan. If Mrs. Taylor reports back that you're on your best behavior today, I might just have a surprise for you when you get home."

Chandler's eyes lit up.

"Really?" She asked excitedly.

"Be on your best behavior and you'll see," Lila hugged Chandler tight.

Chandler ran out the door, grabbing Eliza's hand.

"Thanks, again," Lila said.

"Of course," Susan replied. "We'll be back around 3 p.m."

"Prefect," Lila said as she shut the door. She took a deep breath. "I'm glad they're gone," she said. "I was worried Riley would show up right when she got here and that would have been quite a nightmare to explain…"

"Well, she probably wouldn't have recognized him anyway," Jane replied. "Remember how Riley told us only people who want to help him can recognize him?"

"Oh yeah…" said Lila. "I guess you're right."

"Wait, what?" Kyle asked.

"Riley explained to us that when he travels with the gel, only people who are on his side will be able to recognize him. For instance, if you had been against Riley and you thought he really was guilty, you wouldn't have been able to recognize him, even though he's your brother. Or at least that's how I understood it?" Jane looked at Lila for confirmation.

"Yes," Lila nodded. "Apparently, it's a fail-safe with silica gel to help protect the users. I don't fully understand it but when we went to get ice cream with him in Miami, no one looked twice and his face had been plastered all over the news, so I believe him."

"Wow," Kyle responded. "That's crazy."

"This is all crazy," Lila concurred.

"Okay, Riley should be here soon and I'm getting anxious. Anyone interested in making some hot chocolate to pass the time?" Jane suggested.

"You know I can't turn down a cup of mom's famous hot

chocolate," Kyle replied.

"Sounds good to me," Lila agreed.

"Wonderful," Jane clapped as she turned to walk to the kitchen. Lila and Kyle followed. They were all anxious about the days ahead. They felt the possibility of success at their fingertips, but the lingering possibility of failure was all too real.

Jane found some chocolate in the cabinet and set it out on the counter and then got out the cutting board. She carefully began to chop the bittersweet chocolate into small pieces.

"You put my hot chocolate making skills to shame," Lila joked. "The powdered stuff just isn't the same."

Jane smiled as she continued to prepare the hot chocolate. She pulled out a saucepan, placed it on the stove and poured in milk and sugar.

"Unfortunately, you never had Warren's," Jane replied. "He put everyone's to shame."

"That's true," added Kyle. "Dad's hot chocolate was out of this world."

"He left me the recipe and mine is close… but there was something truly special about his," said Jane.

Lila smiled. She'd always wished she'd had the opportunity to meet Warren.

"I wish I could have tried it," she replied.

Jane added the chopped chocolate and a dash of vanilla to the saucepan and stirred with gentle hands.

"What time is it?" she asked.

"9:15," Kyle replied.

"Anyone else anxious or is that just me?" She asked. "I feel like he should be here by now."

"Anxious in what way?" Kyle asked.

"I don't know," Jane answered as she stared down, whisking the hot chocolate. "Like what if he went to Miami by mistake," she replied. "What if he traveled somewhere else this time?"

"He went to Miami because we were there," stated Lila. "He came here last time."

"Yes, but he didn't really know we were there," Jane responded. "He said the gel must have taken him where it knew he needed to be. What if that happened again?"

"I think you're getting a little worked up, Mom," Kyle calmly replied. "He said he'd aim for 9 a.m. and it's barely past. Let's not get worried yet."

Jane nodded.

"You're right. I'm probably just overreacting." She opened a cabinet and pulled out three mugs. Then, went to the refrigerator and got out the whipped cream.

"Let's just enjoy this delicious hot chocolate and flip on the television for a bit to kill some time," Lila suggested as Jane poured the hot chocolate.

"That's a good idea," Kyle agreed. "We'll watch a show and if he's not here by," he paused to think. "Let's say 10 a.m. Then, we can start to worry."

Jane topped off each cup with a generous helping of whipped cream and then squirted an extra dollop in her mouth.

With a little bit of whipped cream still on her lips, Jane smiled and passed the cups to Lila and Kyle.

"I can get on board with that," she agreed.

CHAPTER FIFTY-FOUR

"Gooood morning, sunshine," Aus greeted as he entered Riley's cell.

Riley opened his eyes and began to stiffly stretch in bed.

"What time is it?" He asked.

"It's 8:30," he replied. "You said you wanted to go back around 9 a.m., didn't you?"

"It's 8:30 already?" Riley was shocked. "I haven't slept that soundly in months." He sat up. "Maybe, it's because things really are looking up."

Aus broke his eye contact with Riley and looked down at the ground.

"Maybe, so," he mumbled.

Sensing his lack of enthusiasm, Riley asked, "Do you not think things are looking up?"

Aus looked back up at Riley.

"Err no... I just, uh... I'm just going to miss you," he said.

"Ahh, don't worry, Aus! We can keep in touch and maybe, if you're lucky," he winked. "I could offer you a job and get you out of this dump," Riley suggested.

"That would be lovely," Aus replied. He reached into his pocket and pulled out a small, green packet.

"What is that?" Riley asked.

"Silica gel," Answered Aus.

"Why is it green?" Riley questioned.

"Uh, it's a different color when it's your final trip," Aus

said, unsure of himself.

"Oh," Riley replied. "That's interesting."

"Yeah," Aus replied. "The strange never seems to end with the silica gel world," he rolled his eyes. Aus reached out his arm to hand Riley the silica gel packet.

"It still works the same?" Riley clarified.

Aus nodded.

"You don't have much to say this morning..." Riley commented.

Aus shrugged.

"Just not feeling it today, I guess."

"Well, do you have anything else to say before I go?" Riley inquired. "Normally, you're full of wisdom."

"Uh, not today," Aus replied.

Riley raised his eyebrows at Aus.

"Okay," he said rather confused. "I guess, I'm going to go now."

Aus nodded.

Riley stood at the center of the cell, gripped the green packet in his right hand and closed his eyes.

"One, two, three, four, five," he counted.

Riley opened his eyes in the center of an unfamiliar room. He slowly turned around, trying to take everything in.

In the circular room, the walls were covered with dark stones and the floor was smooth cement. Around the perimeter of the room were large, golden chairs with red velvet padding. Above each chair was a golden plate with a name engraved.

Riley walked toward the chair straight ahead of him and read the name to himself.

"Miles Beckham," he whispered.

He began to walk around the room, reading each name.

"Hansel Westley, Maclan Andrews, Chance Briggs, Colton

Sterling, Micah Bryant." He stopped when he came to the last chair.

"Duke Wilkinson." His heart was pounding. "Could it be?" He thought.

As if on cue to answer his question, he heard a gravelly voice come from behind him.

"Welcome, Riley," the man greeted in a condescending tone. "We're so pleased to have you here today."

The man held out his arms and suddenly, each chair became occupied.

Overwhelmed, Riley slowly turned to look at each new face in the room. An eruption of coughing and heavy breathing came from behind him. He quickly turned, thankful to see a familiar face.

"Aus?" Riley asked, "What's going on?"

Duke moved swiftly in between Riley and Aus.

"Your final trip has been revoked," he declared.

"What? Why?" Riley exclaimed.

"You have already taken five trips, Mr. Mines," Duke explained. "We can't go around awarding everyone an infinite number of trips and not enforcing our own rules now, can we?"

"I've only taken four trips!" Riley argued.

"Well," he spoke in a matter of fact tone. "That is sort of true. However, before your travel was approved, a certain someone," he motioned with his head toward Aus in a disapproving manner. "Supplied you with an unauthorized silica gel packet and due to foul play in your later travels, we're going to have to count that first trip in your total. Thus, you have taken all five of your supplied trips."

"What? Foul play? I don't know what you're talking about!" Riley was angry.

"Did you or did you not travel to Miami?" Duke

questioned.

"I did but–" Riley answered.

Duke interrupted, "Did you or did you not take the poem from your prison cell and leave it in your home?"

"I did but –" Riley answered again.

Duke continued before Riley could finish.

"And did you or did you not take five trips using silica gel as your mode of transportation?"

"I did but –" Riley tried to answer.

Duke cut him off again.

"Well, then, it's settled. You've committed too many violations and we won't stand for it. You're done." He declared.

"Don't do this to him!" Aus shouted. "I told you! None of it was his fault!"

Duke turned and slapped Aus across the face.

"Quiet!" He demanded.

Riley gasped.

"We've already given you your chance to fix things, but it seems you can't handle even the slightest task," he stared at Aus. "So, we're taking things into our own hands now. Send him home," he motioned to Sterling.

Sterling quickly stood up and walked to Aus. He gripped his hands tightly and after a few seconds, Aus disappeared, leaving a puddle of water behind.

Sterling sat back down, and the room was silent.

"Sorry about that Ri," Duke said, breaking the silence. His voice and demeanor shifted drastically. "Can I call you Ri?" He asked sweetly.

"Sure," Riley replied, squinting his eyes in confusion. He was overwhelmed by the fourteen eyes staring intently at him.

"Well, Ri," Duke started slowly. "You see, we had to," he paused. "Well, we had to create a scene, if you will." He motioned his hands dramatically. "We needed to get Aus out of the picture."

Riley didn't reply.

"As I am sure you know by now, we're the Desiccant Keepers. And I apologize for not formally introducing us all," he spoke in an impossible to discern tone teetering on sarcasm and seriousness.

Riley nodded.

"And in this world," he corrected. "Sorry, in *our* world... things are more complicated than common Contenders can ever know."

Riley stared blankly back.

Duke continued, "So, for Aus' safety, and the safety of all Contenders really... he can't know what happens next."

Riley's heart beat faster. He could hardly breathe, and his stomach felt like a million butterflies had just taken flight.

"Sterling," Duke shouted. "Up!" He snapped his fingers and pointed his thumb up signaling him to get out of his chair. Although Sterling was not the youngest or newest board member, he was the one picked on most often.

Duke waved his arm, gesturing for Riley to go sit in the now unoccupied seat.

"You see, Ri," Duke started as he placed his hand on Riley's back and guided him to the seat. "There's something special about you."

"What do you mean?" Riley asked as he sat down.

"The way you're able to travel is something of a phenomenon," Duke explained. "It took many of us and our ancestors' months to achieve the art of traveling to a land other than home," he paused. "And to successfully bring something with you through the gel wall is simply unheard of."

Riley raised his eyebrows at Duke.

"Okay?" He asked. "And?"

"You're gifted, Ri," Duke continued. "And we want to protect you."

Unamused, Riley replied, "I don't need your protection. All I want is to get out of prison and be home with my family. This is not a world I want to be a part of. I never asked for any of this."

"I know," Duke understandingly replied. "We aren't asking you to be a part of anything." He lightened his tone and spoke in a songlike manor, "Not a part but a piece and our fears can all cease."

"What?" Riley asked, frustrated. "Can you please shoot straight with me? Stop with all of the riddles. What is going on here?"

Duke loosened his tie and rolled up his sleeves.

"You're right," he laughed in a way that held all authority in the room. "Sometimes, I just get so carried away." He paused, "A power like yours is quite desirable, Riley and one that can't go ignored. While *we* have no desire to capitalize on this power," he spoke firmly. "With our role being to limit silica gel power use and all. However, others out there don't feel the same way…"

Riley waited for Duke to continue.

"The threat of Z is too real in the world today and with your abilities, it's almost a given he'll try to recruit you," he said.

"Me?" Riley was shocked. "How will he even know about me?"

"We don't know," Duke replied. "We don't know how he works or where his true motives lie. The Keepers haven't been able to gather much information over the years, but we do know that he has a history of going after the most skillful Contenders."

"I don't understand," Riley countered. "All I did was take

one of your packets and hold it and travel like the poem instructed. I didn't mean to cause any commotion."

"We know," Micah Bryant said as he stood up from his chair across the room. He walked toward Riley. "We're not blaming you and we're not recruiting you. Sorry... Duke can get a little too dramatic and fail to reach the point," he shot Duke a look out of the corner of his eye. "We brought you here today simply to educate you. We want you to understand that there's a strong possibility Z will go after you," he paused. "And we want your promise that when he does, you will let us know." His green eyes were like daggers staring into Riley's.

"Is that all?" Riley asked, confused by the commotion.

"Yes," Bryant answered.

"Then, sure," Riley agreed. "Can I go see my family now?" He asked impatiently.

"Of course, not!" Duke exclaimed. "Have you not heard anything we've been saying? You're a threat! Your travels are over. We have to do everything we can to prevent Z from finding you."

"Are you serious?" Riley asked angrily. "Then, I'm not helping you! I need to get back to my family!"

Duke moved quickly toward Riley and gripped his neck.

"I don't think you're fully comprehending the weight of the situation, Riley," he hissed. "You have two options here. You either agree, quietly return to Nadirehs and let us know if you hear or see anything suspicious that could be tied to Z," he released his grip on Riley's throat and reached into his pocket. He pulled out a pocketknife and flicked out the blade. He grabbed a tuft of Riley's hair and pulled his head back against the chair. He placed the blade softly on Riley's neck. "Or you simply don't return at all."

Trembling with fear and lit with anger, Riley replied, "Aus will know. My family will find out," he said through gritted teeth.

Duke slightly increased pressure on the blade.

"Ahh, if only that were the case," Duke spoke in a false empathetic tone. "You see, when a Contender dies, his travels die with him. We would simply return your cold, dead body to your prison cell and Aus would happen upon you, having no recollection of your time together. Surely, word would travel fast back to your family, and they'd mourn the loss of their beloved husband, father, son, brother and friend. And to top it all off... you'd die a guilty man."

"That can't be true," Riley could hardly breathe out the words.

"Would you like to test it out?" Duke taunted.

Riley winced and tried to pull his head back away from the knife.

"No," he finally gasped.

Duke released Riley's hair and pulled the knife off his throat.

"Thank you for your cooperation," Duke grinned.

"So, what happens next?" Riley impatiently inquired.

Bryant interjected, "What happens next is you're going to quietly return to Nadirehs and refrain from sharing any details of this encounter with Aus," he stated. "Then, you're going to hope and pray your family will be able to get you out of prison without your help. And in a perfect world, after that, you'll return home and your life will go back to normal, never hearing from Z or us again."

"What do I tell Au –"

Riley was interrupted by Duke's fist nailing him in the face.

"Tell him that we taught you a lesson about disrespecting our rules," he declared.

Riley softly touched his eye. He removed his hand and looked down to find it red with blood.

"Here," Bryant said as he pulled out a green packet of silica gel from his pocket and walked it to Riley. "If you ever hear from Z and need to let us know, this will allow you to travel back to us," he handed Riley the packet.

"I thought green packets were used for last trips?" Riley questioned.

"No," Bryant answered. "They're used exclusively for travel to headquarters."

"Oh," Riley replied as he touched his already swelling eye again.

"Do you have any other questions?" Bryant kindly asked.

"I have about a billion other questions but none I feel like asking," Riley answered.

"Alright," Bryant said. "Well, in that case... Sterling!" He summoned. "Send him back to Nadirehs."

Sterling quickly moved from the place he'd been standing across the room to his chair occupied by Riley. He grabbed his hands and in a matter of seconds, Riley disappeared, leaving a small puddle of water behind him.

"I feel like that went better than expected," Briggs announced.

"It was alright," Duke commented.

"I think we can trust him... in fact, I kind of like him," Bryant smiled.

"Let's just hope he keeps quiet and doesn't confide in my idiot nephew," Maclan commented.

CHAPTER FIFTY-FIVE

Lila paced the living room in a panic.

"It's 11:45 now," she said. "He's not coming. You're not going to get to see him before you leave, and I have no idea what to do. Surely, he would have called if he had showed up somewhere else."

"I'm sure he would have," Kyle commented. "I'm sure he couldn't leave the prison for some reason and he's probably even more upset than we are."

"There has to be a reasonable explanation," said Jane. "He wouldn't stand us up unless it was something obscure."

Frustrated, Lila groaned and replied, "I guess you're right. I just want him home for good and we're so close!"

"We'll get him home, Lila," Kyle comforted. "In less than twenty-four hours, we should be at Alexa's with the officers and hopefully, getting answers. I don't think it should take long to get Riley out of prison, once we have enough evidence gathered that he's innocent. I mean... it's America! He's supposed to be innocent until proven guilty. He just never had a fair trial! All we need is enough evidence to get him out and give him a case."

"Which we already have," added Jane.

Lila took a deep breath and tried to calm down.

"You're right," she agreed. "We just need to get him out."

"And we will," Jane assured her. "The officers aren't supposed to land until around 10 p.m. tonight. I'm assuming they will just wait until tomorrow morning to go to Alexa's. We will follow their lead and obviously, we'll keep you posted every step of the way."

Lila nodded.

"I hate to leave you alone right now," Kyle admitted. "Do you want to come with us? I'm sure we could buy tickets for you and the kids at the airport."

"That's ridiculous. You guys need to leave in like ten minutes and Chandler is out with her friend and Warren is napping and what if Riley ends up coming later and no one is home? I really want to go with you, but I know I need to stay here…" she rambled.

"It's okay. I know you want to go but you're right, it's too much," Jane agreed. "The kids need a stable environment right now and if Riley does come home, someone needs to be here. I am confident we can handle everything, and I know it will be hard to be here alone waiting for updates, but I think that's what needs to happen. And then, hopefully soon, the whole family can come out to California for a nice vacation… just like things used to be."

"That sounds like a dream," Lila replied. "I hope it's not too long until that can be a reality."

"I don't think it will be," Kyle said. "I really have a good feeling about this."

Lila's face changed from anxious to kindly concerned. She looked intently at Kyle.

"I'm sorry… I haven't really asked you until now," she started. "I guess I've been so focused on getting Riley out of prison," she paused. "But how are you doing with all of this?"

"Do you mean the part where originally I was accused of sending my only brother to jail or the part where my dead fiancé's mother tried to kill me?" Kyle asked sarcastically, trying to avoid any real feelings per usual.

"Kyle, really," Lila replied. She always had a way of getting him to share. "Are you okay? How do you feel about confronting Alexa?"

Kyle sighed.

"It's pretty weird," he finally admitted. "I guess, I'm…" he paused. "Lila, I don't have anything to say."

"Are you sure? I just want to make sure you're okay," she said. "There's obviously a lot going on right now and you're kind of at the center of it." She looked at Kyle, offering him one more chance to be serious.

"Okay," he finally sighed defensively. "You caught me. It all sucks," he began to rant. "I can't believe my should-have-been mother-in-law tried to plant a bomb in my shoe. That's insane! And I feel torn because I want to hate her but then I think about the disappointment Keagan would feel if she knew I hated her mom, but also, wouldn't Keagan hate her mom for trying to set me up? I don't know. It's a lot to feel and I don't want to feel any of it. At this point, I just want Riley out of jail, and I don't want to worry about anything else." Kyle looked down at the ground.

"I'm sorry, Kyle," Lila said. "You shouldn't have to think about any of this. You shouldn't have to deal with any of this from her family and it does suck. You're right. I just want you to know that you have a right to feel these emotions. You have a right to be angry."

"I don't like to be angry," Kyle replied.

"I know," Lila said. "It's okay. Hopefully, all of this will work itself out quickly and you can go back to feeling no emotions and burying them deep, deep down inside. But right now, I think it's important to feel the burning emotions because without those, we might not get Riley out of prison. We need Alexa to know that you're against her. Based on everything we know; she assumes you know nothing about anything and are still on her side."

"She brings up a good point," Jane agreed. "I know conflict isn't your thing but we're really going to need you to be strong over the next couple of days." She paused, "For your brother."

"And for Keagan," Lila added.

Kyle nodded.

"You're both right." He breathed in heavily and let out a slow breath. "I have to let myself be angry with her. She tried to ruin my life. I want my life back. I want my brother back… I want Keagan back." His eyes began to well.

Lila moved toward Kyle and offered a hug.

"I know, Kyle," she said. "I'm sorry… It's not fair. None of it is fair."

"Remember the quote I used to read you about life?" Jane smiled.

Kyle nodded.

"It's been a while. Do you still remember it?"

"Of course," Kyle replied. "Life is like a puzzle. We start out with very little and we gather pieces along the way. We grow and we start to see a picture form but then we lose a piece. We keep going and a new picture begins to form, and another piece is lost. We persevere and we lose another piece. We're always trying to finish the puzzle, but we don't have a picture on the box to follow. It's the journey of figuring out the picture that we must learn to enjoy because if a completed puzzle is what we're after, then we'll never be satisfied."

"I've never heard that before," Lila said. "It's lovely."

"It was Warren's favorite quote," Jane replied. "You're just in the midst of losing a lot of pieces, Kyle. A new picture will surely start to form soon."

CHAPTER FIFTY-SIX

Rebecca walked into the sunlit kitchen to find Jane seated at the large, white table, sipping on a cup of coffee and tapping her fingers anxiously.

"Good morning," she said.

"Good morning," Jane replied. "How did you sleep?"

"Marvelously," Rebecca answered. "The bed was so comfortable. Your home is just immaculate," she complimented.

"Thank you," Jane responded. "It's nice to have some company to fill it. It can get pretty lonely with only Kyle and me."

"I'm sure… you're an early riser," Rebecca observed.

"It's easy to get up early when you don't really go to bed," Jane sighed.

"Couldn't sleep?" Rebecca asked as she moved to sit down at the table next to her.

"Not a wink," Jane answered. "It's already 9 a.m. in New York and Lila still hasn't heard anything from Riley. I'm worried about him. I'm worried about her. I'm probably the most worried about Kyle. I'm just worried about everything."

"That's understandable," said Rebecca.

"I mean," Jane started. "Today, I have to go to my friend of thirty plus years home. The friend whose daughter I watched grow up and whose daughter was supposed to marry my son. The friend who was there for me when the kids graduated, when Riley got married, when Warren died. All of the big things. She was there for me through everything. I now have to go to her home and watch as she's accused of planting a bomb in my son's shoe. What even is that?" She was crying now. "What has my life come to? I can't trust anyone."

Rebecca didn't know what to say.

"I'm sorry," was all she could muster.

The two sat silently as tears continued to run down Jane's cheeks.

"You don't have to come with us today, if you think it will be too much for you," offered Rebecca.

"I think I want to," Jane replied. "I know it will be a lot but I'm angry. I want to see everything play out and… and," she trailed off.

"And what?" Asked Rebecca.

Jane gathered all of the courage she had left to say, "And I want to see her get what she deserves. I hate to be that way, but she tried to ruin Kyle's life and in turn, she ruined my whole family's lives. She can't get away with this."

"You're right," Rebecca said as she placed her hand on Jane's shoulder. "And she won't. That's why we're here."

Jane nodded and took another drink of her coffee.

Slightly changing the subject, Rebecca inquired, "So, what do you think happened to Riley?"

"I'm not sure," Jane said. "I assume he wasn't able to get a silica gel packet and couldn't make a trip. It sounds like a very complex world and I don't really understand much of it. All I know is that if he could be here, he would be. I am mostly upset because I didn't get to see him, and I feel so bad for Lila. She has a lot on her plate."

"Yes, she does," agreed Rebecca. "Well, hopefully, he doesn't have to travel anymore after today anyway. He can just be home for good."

Jane's eyes lit up.

"You think that could happen as soon as today?" She questioned.

"I wouldn't doubt it," Rebecca replied confidently. "If we get anything solid at all that sheds light on Riley's innocence, we can get him out. I know Nadirehs has strict rules about when inmates can go in and out, but I think with a case as idiosyncratic as this, they'd have to make an exception."

"I had no idea something could happen that quickly," Jane smiled. "That would be amazing!"

"Good morning," Hillsteg greeted as he walked into the kitchen.

"Good morning," Jane replied.

"I was not expecting you to be the next one up," Rebecca admitted.

"And why's that?" Hillsteg questioned.

"I don't know," Rebecca shrugged. "You just don't strike me like a morning person."

"Rebecca, have you seen how many donuts I eat in a typical day?" Hillsteg patted his gut. "I need all the morning hours I can get."

Rebecca shook her head and laughed.

"I don't have donuts, but I do have coffee and cardamom bread," Jane offered.

"I'd love a cup of coffee," requested Rebecca.

"Both for me, please," said Hillsteg.

"You got it," Jane said as she stood up from the table and began to move around the kitchen.

Hillsteg made his way to sit down across from Rebecca.

"This place is unbelievable," he whispered.

"I know," Rebecca responded. "I think this table alone is bigger than my bedroom at home."

"How big of a piece would you like, Mr. Hillsteg?" Jane

called.

"Oh, you can make it a pretty hefty helping," Hillsteg replied. "And call me Walter," he smiled.

"Walter," Rebecca thought. "I did not know that was his first name. Really... Walter?"

A few minutes later, Jane returned to the table with two cappuccinos and two large slices of warm cardamom bread.

"Wow, a cappuccino," said Rebecca. "This is fancy!"

"I'm sorry," Jane replied. "I can get you a cup of regular if you'd like. I just figured a cappuccino was nicer, but I should have asked and," she stood up from the table and hurried toward the kitchen.

"Jane, no! This is lovely. It's perfect," Rebecca said. "I was just pleasantly surprised is all."

Jane took a deep breath.

"Sorry, I'm a little on edge."

"It's quite alright, Ms. Mines. Thank you very much for breakfast," Hillsteg said. He took his first bite of the cardamom bread and exclaimed. "Mm, this is delicious! What is in this?"

"Thank you," Jane grinned. "Family recipe."

The three of them sat silently for a while. Each was lost in their own thoughts.

Hillsteg eventually broke the silence.

"The plan is to head over around 8 a.m. still, correct?"

"Yes," Jane replied.

"And Alexa just thinks Kyle is coming over for breakfast?" He clarified.

"Yup," she answered. "They get together every so often, so it's nothing out of the ordinary. I'm sure she doesn't suspect a thing."

"And James' mom is still in town, isn't she?" Rebecca questioned.

"Yes," Hillsteg confirmed. "Her flight isn't until this

evening... I think James told her we were coming this morning."

"Ahh, I don't know," Rebecca replied. "He was really going back and forth yesterday trying to decide if he should give her a heads up or not."

"Oh," Hillsteg said. "I don't really care either way. I'm just excited for some good old-fashioned confrontation," he rubbed his hands together anxiously. "Let's convene around 7:30 in the living room and we'll make sure we're all on the same page."

"Good with me," Rebecca replied.

"Sounds like a plan," added Jane.

CHAPTER

FIFTY-SEVEN

Riley opened his eyes to the hanging blue light and sat up quickly. Unsurprisingly, he met the gaze of Aus seated in his usual chair in the corner.

"Are you okay? Did they hurt you? What did they say? Do you get your trip back? Are you in trouble? Do you have to go back?" Aus rambled.

Riley rubbed his already bruising eye and tried to get his bearings.

He closed his eyes tight and yawned, "That's a lot of questions."

"Then, surely you can answer one," Aus retorted.

Riley cleared his throat.

"They just disciplined me for not respecting their rules. It wasn't that bad."

"Disrespecting their rules?" Aus exclaimed. "You didn't disrespect anything! None of it was your fault!" He was now pacing the cell.

"Aus, it's fine," said Riley. "Honestly, it was one disciplinary punch in the face and a stern lecture. I'm fine. I'm not one for confrontation."

Aus grunted.

"I hate how much power they have. I'm sorry, Riley. I feel like I really let you down."

"Aus, it's fine!" Riley was becoming impatient with Aus' inability to move on. "I promise, I'm good. I have full faith that my family will get me out."

"Wait... did they really revoke your last trip?" Aus was angry. "I really thought they'd discipline you and give it back. This is ridiculous!" He threw up his arms.

Riley stood up from the bed and put his hands on Aus' chest.

"It's okay. Please calm down. I am fine. I don't need the trip. I think I'd be useless on it anyway. Last I heard, it sounded like my family had everything they needed together."

Aus was fuming as he continued to pace back and forth.

"I'm going back," he declared. "I'm going back and I'm going to fight them until they give you back the trip you so rightfully deserve."

"No, you're not," Riley argued. "Everything is fine."

Aus stopped mid stride and stared back at Riley. He squinted his eyes.

"There's something you're not telling me," he accused.

Riley pursed his lips and slowly shook his head no.

"Yes, there is. What is it? Did they threaten you?"

"No," Riley replied. He'd never been good at lying.

"Riley," Aus looked intently into his blue eyes. "You can tell me."

"I really can't, Aus," Riley replied. "I wish I could."

"You can," Aus pleaded.

"It would be the end for us if I did," Riley replied. "I can assure you everything is okay and it's going to be okay but right now, if I tell you, they'll kill us both."

A shiver ran down Aus' spine as he processed the harsh truth.

"I understand," he finally said.

"Everything will be okay," Riley reassured him. "Have

faith."

"If you say so," Aus mumbled.

"My family is going to get me out of here and then I'm going to get you out of here."

"Sounds like a dream to me," Aus replied.

CHAPTER

FIFTY-EIGHT

Conway walked into the living room and took a seat on the edge of the large white sectional. He fell into the soft white sofa like it were a cloud and sighed "ahh."

Hillsteg shot him a look. "Well, now that we're all here," he looked down at his watch to see the time was 7:35. "And comfortable," he coughed. "We can go over the plan altogether. I know most of us have heard it but from different sources and I want to make sure I get everyone straight, right here and right now because we have one shot to get this right."

There were nods all around the room and everyone was locked in.

"Kyle, you will drive yourself over to the Monarch residence and begin breakfast as usual. As you've outlined for me, usual means Alexa's staff will prepare and serve something for you while you sit out on the terrace," Hillsteg looked to Kyle for approval.

Kyle replied, "That's correct."

"We believe Mrs. Wilde will also be joining Alexa and Kyle but we don't have confirmation on that. We have a small camera we're going to pin on Kyle's tie so that we'll be able to see and hear everything going on inside. The five of us will be staked out a couple of blocks away," said Hillsteg.

"Do we get a cool van? I've always wanted to be in a cool

stakeout van," Conway commented.

"No," Hillsteg responded and rolled his eyes. "I've arranged for us to use a police car from the local station. We'll need you and the girls to squeeze in the back."

Conway disappointedly looked down.

"Moving on," declared Hillsteg. "When Kyle feels comfortable making the accusation, he'll do it and that will be our cue to head to Alexa's. As we know, she has loads of security but that doesn't matter because we're police officers and we have a warrant."

"You got a warrant?" Exclaimed James.

"Of course," Hillsteg replied as if he should have known. "I called in a couple of favors and got things turned around quickly.

"Wow," James excitedly rubbed his hands together. "We're really doing it. This could really happen."

"Of course, it could happen," Hillsteg sternly replied. "You think I'd fly us all out to California for a flop of a case? I don't think so. This is the real deal." His speech turned motivational, "This is the turning point in our careers and the turning point in the Mines' lives. If we pull this off, we'll have solved the case of the century. The case everyone believed to be closed. The case where the celebrity is caught, and the glove does fit!"

James leaned in as Hillsteg spoke with a gaze of determination, Conway nervously rubbed his cheeks processing what was at stake and Rebecca shook her right leg in anticipation.

Hillsteg sensed the officer's enthusiasm contrasting the Mines' anxious energy. He turned to face them. "Please don't think we're too concerned about ourselves," he begged. "Our job as officers is to serve you and protect you. We're here for you. We're working for you. And we want things to go back to normal for you."

Jane quietly replied, "Thank you."

Kyle couldn't form words as the knots tied in his stomach.

"Are we ready?" Asked Hillsteg.

Sensing Kyle's apprehension, they all waited for him to make the first move.

He was staring down at the ground, leaned over with his arms resting on his thighs.

After a few moments of slow breathing, Kyle looked up at the faces staring back at him and said, "Let's do it."

CHAPTER FIFTY-NINE

Hillsteg and James sat in the front of the police car while Conway, Jane and Rebecca squeezed in the back, behind the glass. They found an empty church parking lot a half-mile away from Alexa's home to park and wait.

They'd placed a small camera in a button on Kyle's shirt and intended to watch his meeting with Alexa.

"We're up and rolling," James said as he placed the laptop on top of the dashboard.

They watched the screen as Kyle drove up the cobblestone driveway and parked by the large, circular fountain outside the entrance. He turned off the ignition and took a deep breath. He looked at himself in the rear-view mirror.

"You can do this," he said. "For Riley…" He bit his lip. "And for Keagan."

"That was sweet," Jane commented.

"It really was," Rebecca smiled.

Kyle got out of the car and approached the house. Before he reached the door, it swung open.

"Kyle," Alexa kindly greeted him. "How have you been?" She asked out of obligation.

"Mrs. Monarch," he opened his arms for a hug. "I've been well. And yourself?"

"Splendid, darling," she replied accepting his hug. "You remember Debbie, right?" She asked, gesturing to Debbie who'd been standing a few feet behind her.

"Of course," Kyle replied as he reached for her hand. "Lovely to see you again."

"You too," she winked.

"Ugh, that's it…" Kyle thought to himself. "I forgot to ask James if Debbie knew. How did I forget to ask? Surely, she knows. That was a blatant wink, right? I am an idiot. I can't believe I forgot…"

"Did anyone else see my mom wink or was that just me?" James asked.

"No," Conway replied. "I thought the same thing!"

"Wait, does she know?" Asked Rebecca.

"Yeah," James casually replied.

"Are you kidding me?" Rebecca shouted.

James' eyes got wide as he turned around to face Rebecca in the car.

"We didn't tell Kyle that!"

"Yes, we did," James replied.

"No, we didn't," Conway confirmed.

"Shhhh," Hillsteg quieted the car. "James, you're an idiot. We didn't tell him. In fact, you didn't tell anyone but there's nothing we can do now, so just shut up and listen, so we know what's going on."

The car was tense with all eyes fixed on the screen once again.

"You can probably let go of her hand now," Alexa suggested, interrupting Kyle's wandering thoughts.

Kyle chuckled and let go.

"Sorry, I was distracted by the chandelier. Is that new?"

Alexa rolled her eyes.

"No, Kyle. That came with the house. It's literally been here for twenty years."

"Whoops," Kyle shrugged. "Guess I just need to be more observant."

"Well, like my father always said, we often have a tendency to ignore the obvious for fear of the harsh reality it could bring," Debbie said.

"She knows," Kyle thought. "She definitely knows."

"That's an odd thing to say about a chandelier," Alexa squinted her eyes at Debbie.

"I know," she sighed. "Maybe, I'm drunk on mimosas already," she laughed.

"I wouldn't be surprised," Alexa said. "I'm famished. Let's head outside."

The three of them walked through the winding mansion, past the parlor and out onto the terrace. The large garden table was set for three with fruits and breads already on display.

"Looks delicious," Kyle commented as he took a seat on the far side across from Alexa.

"Yes, it does," agreed Debbie.

"So, Kyle, how have you been?" Alexa asked. "Did I hear correctly that you were recently in New York?"

"I've been alright," he replied. "And yes, I actually got back yesterday."

"Did you?" Responded Alexa. "How was it? How is Lila? How are the kids?"

"Oh," Kyle started. "She's okay. Pretty tough when your other half is in prison and you're raising two children under five alone, but she gets along."

"I can imagine it's terribly difficult," Alexa sighed unempathetically.

"How tragic," added Debbie.

Kyle felt uneasy moving toward the topic of Riley so quickly.

"How long are you in town for?" Kyle asked Debbie to change the subject.

"I've been here since last Friday and I leave this evening," she replied.

"Not long enough," Alexa chimed in. "I keep telling her she needs to move out here, but she won't do it. I mean, what's not to love about L.A.?" Alexa asked rhetorically.

"Well, for starters, there's the traffic, the crime, the parking, the earthquakes, the cost of living," said Kyle. "Not to mention those attention seeking celebrities," he teased Alexa.

"I hear they're lovely," she replied. "Those are all things Debbie would hardly need to worry about anyway. She has plenty of money to live comfortably and we'd basically never have to leave our homes to go out in the traffic. If we did, we wouldn't have to drive ourselves and we wouldn't need to worry about parking. Besides the few strange stalkers I've had over the years, crime essentially doesn't apply to this neighborhood. And earthquakes, well what are you going to do?" Alexa paused, "I believe that counters every point you made," she grinned. "For our kind, L.A. and all its glory is served on a silver platter."

"Our kind?" Kyle raised his eyebrows.

"Yes, darling," Alexa replied. "Anyone who said money couldn't buy happiness simply didn't have enough. We're untouchable." She said as she sipped her mimosa.

Kyle's eyes widened and the blind optimism he'd viewed Alexa with over the years quickly faded.

"Wow," he gasped, shaking his head. "I really didn't see it before but," he hesitated, building the strength to light the match of what he knew could be a devasting fire. "Keagan was right about you."

"Oh, wow," Conway commented. "Is he really about to do this?"

"Surely not," James replied. "That seems pretty qui –"

Jane interrupted, "Let's go. Let's head to the house now."

"Really?" Asked Hillsteg. "You think he's going to accuse her already?"

"Go!" Jane demanded. "I'm telling you. If he gets fired up, there's no stopping him. I think he's about to blow and we need to be there."

The car erupted with shouts of demands for Hillsteg to drive.

"Hurry!"

"We gotta go!"

"This is it!"

"Come on!"

Hillsteg put the car in drive, turned on the sirens and lights, and took off down the road as the others continued to watch the screen.

Alexa stared blankly back at Kyle as she slowly lowered her drink to the table. The tension was thick enough to cut with a knife. Debbie sank down slightly in her chair, now wishing she was far away from the action.

"What did you say?" Alexa replied earnestly.

"I said," Kyle started, now feeling confident. "Keagan was right about you."

"Right about what?" Alexa demanded.

"Right about your no good, self-obsessed attitude toward life," he stated.

"Oh, is that so?" Alexa questioned. "Is that what Keagan said about me?"

"Yeah," Kyle replied. "She also said you were certifiably insane, but I don't have to quote everything," he smirked.

Alexa rolled her eyes unphased by Kyle's comments.

"You think you're so cute, don't you? Trying to taint my perfect memories of my daughter." She sighed, "The only thing that taints my daughter's perfect life is you."

"Hmm," Kyle hummed arrogantly. "That's weird."

"What's weird?" Alexa asked annoyed.

"Nothing," Kyle replied.

Alexa looked to Debbie for backup.

"Someone's in a mood today," she said as she picked up her mimosa once again.

"Well, you'd probably be in a mood too if you found out your should-have-been-mother-in-law tried to plant a bomb in your shoe but mistakenly sent your brother to prison instead," Kyle bluntly stated.

Alexa dropped her crystal champagne glass and it shattered as it hit the concrete.

"Oh, shit," Conway said. "You weren't kidding." He looked at Jane whose face was frozen with fear.

Hillsteg pulled up to the grand, gated entrance and rolled down the window.

"Police," he declared as he flashed his badge to the guard.

The guard nodded and opened the gate.

"Don't be ridiculous," Alexa flipped her hair and nervously chuckled.

Kyle stared back at Alexa with a piercing gaze.

"Don't be ridiculous?" Kyle asked as he stood up from the table and threw down his napkin. "*You're* telling *me* to not be ridiculous? This is too much." He stormed away from the table and headed inside.

"Don't walk away from me!" Alexa called as she got up to follow him.

Debbie stood up quietly and made her way around the side of the house.

"I can walk away if I want," Kyle declared. "In fact, I don't know why I didn't walk away years ago. We don't have a connection without Keagan. Without Keagan, I'm just a lonely twenty-eight-year-old man hanging out with some fifty-something-year-old mom. It's weird and it doesn't make any sense," he yelled as he continued through the house to the foyer.

"Stop," Alexa shouted. "What has gotten into you?" She questioned calmly, trying to diffuse the situation. "You can't just come over and make brash and absurd accusations and expect me to sit and take it quietly."

"Oh, I can't?" Kyle replied. "But you can?"

"What do you mean?" Alexa innocently replied.

"I can't accuse you of planting a bomb in my shoe without you taking offense, but you can tell everyone in town that I killed your daughter and sent my own brother to prison and I'm just supposed to sit idly by?" Kyle questioned; his face stone cold. "Again, I'll say it…"

"Don't you dare say that again!" Alexa shrilly screamed as she darted across the foyer toward Kyle.

She reached up her hand to hit Kyle, but he grabbed it before she reached his face.

He gripped her arm tight and through gritted teeth said, "Keagan was right about you."

Alexa screamed and began to cry hysterically.

"Let go! Leave!" She demanded.

Kyle gripped her arm tighter. His eyes were blood shot with rage.

"How could you? As if losing the love of my life wasn't already bad enough. How could you try to kill me?"

"I didn't try to kill you," Alexa firmly replied as she tried to break free from Kyle's grip.

"I know what you did," Kyle exasperatedly replied.

Alexa breathed heavily, stuck in Kyle's grip.

"You killed my daughter," she cried. "My only daughter."

Kyle released his grip and shook his head.

"I don't even know how you can think that," he replied. "We were hit by a drunk driver. There was nothing I could have done."

"Bullshit," Alexa replied. "You made her wild and you ruined everything. If you had just gone to the party like I'd asked things never would have been this way," she shook her head.

Kyle took a deep breath. He'd never heard how Alexa truly felt about the night of Keagan's death.

"And don't flatter yourself," Alexa added. "I didn't try to kill you. That would have been too tranquil. I wanted you to slowly decay in prison. I wanted you there for the rest of your life."

"That really is just too bad," Kyle sarcastically replied. "I'm sorry about foiling your oh-so-perfect, radically-disturbed plans."

"Oh, I'm not too concerned," Alexa confidently countered. "I'm certain I'll get my way eventually. I don't care how long it takes. I'll ruin you... just like you ruined me."

"I guess we'll just have to see about that," Kyle mumbled as he turned and opened the door.

The officers, Jane and Debbie stood at the bottom of the entry steps intensely staring up at the two of them.

Kyle continued, "Considering they heard every word."

"Police," Hillsteg announced as he flashed his badge. "You're under arrest for the framing of Mr. Riley Mines and for possession of illegal, explosive materials."

"You can't prove anything!" Alexa shouted.

"We have all of the evidence we need," responded James.

"Debbie!" Alexa called. "What are you doing out there? You're acting crazy!"

"Oh, darling, I hardly think I'm the one who's been acting crazy," Debbie replied.

As James and Conway began to walk up the steps toward Alexa, she began to slowly back away from the door.

Kyle reached to grab her but barely missed as she took off running. Kyle started to run.

"We've got this," James shouted at Kyle. "Don't chase her."

James and Conway sprinted through the house and out to the back onto the terrace. Alexa pulled the tablecloth off the table and sent the glassware flying, giving her a little extra time. She continued to run out onto the grass that led to the immaculate garden grounds.

James and Conway maneuvered around the broken glass and sprinted down the steps to the garden.

Alexa reached the gravel path that marked the beginning of the garden with pools and fountains symmetrically forming the landscape. She continued to sprint, looking back every so often to check on her pursuers.

The rest of the group had made their way to the elevated pool deck and watched as the chase unfolded across the garden grounds below.

Alexa was fit and had always been a good runner. She turned back for a quick glance and realized she'd widened the gap.

"You'll never catch me," she called. As she turned back into a full sprint, she lost grip with the loose stones beneath her feet and began to stumble. She tried hard to catch her balance, but lost control and tripped into a fountain, splashing water everywhere. She sporadically tried to get up, but James and Conway were already at the edge.

She flailed her arms attempting to avoid their grip with black mascara running down her face. They each grabbed an arm and James handcuffed her hands behind her back.

She squirmed as they walked back through the gardens, around the house and to the police car.

The rest of the group joined James, Conway and Alexa out

front.

"It sure is a shame 'your kind' isn't immune from the law," Kyle commented with air quotes.

"This isn't the end," Alexa taunted.

"Oh, I think it is," James said as he placed his hand on Alexa's head and lowered her into the backseat of the car.

They all started clapping as James shut the door.

"I can't believe we actually did it," Hillsteg whispered to Rebecca.

"Good job, Kyle," Jane complimented. "I'm so proud of you."

"Thanks, Mom," Kyle replied as he pulled her in for a hug.

Debbie hesitantly walked toward James.

"I'm so sorry, Son," she apologized.

"It's okay, Mom," James replied. "We'll get everything figured out."

"Alright," Hillsteg declared. "Conway and I will take Alexa downtown and the rest of you can follow in Kyle's car. James, please alert the press. I'm sure they'll want to be there when we arrive," he smirked. "I'll make a few calls and see what we need to do about getting Riley out ASAP."

CHAPTER SIXTY

Hillsteg was beaming with pride as he pulled up to the police station surrounded by local press with Kyle pulling in behind him. There were dozens of reporters lining the sidewalk with microphones ready to absorb any and all information.

Hillsteg opened the door to the back seat and grabbed the, still soaking wet, arm of Alexa Monarch.

The crowd roared with questions and statements all beckoning the attention of Alexa.

"Mrs. Monarch."

"Over here!"

"What did you do?"

Hillsteg led Alexa through the crowd as Conway met the rest of the group as they got out of Kyle's car.

"I'll be back to answer questions momentarily," Hillsteg informed the crowd. "In the meantime, you can speak with my assistant chief of police, Mr. Wilde." He winked at James before turning into the building.

"Assistant chief?" James smiled at Rebecca. "Did he just promote me?"

"I think he did," she grabbed his face and pulled him in for a kiss.

"Get a roooom," Conway rolled his eyes.

"I've wanted to do that for a long time," Rebecca whispered.

"Me too," James agreed.

"Mr. Wilde," a reporter called.

"Mr. Wilde, what happened?" Another reporter shouted.

James made his way up the steps of the courthouse and began to answer questions.

"Is it true that Mrs. Monarch was the mastermind behind the airport bomb in the shoe of Riley Mines?" A reporter asked.

"At this point in time, we are unable to share specific details on Mrs. Monarch's case," James stated.

"Do you intend to put Mrs. Monarch on trial?" Another reported shouted from the crowd.

"Yes, that is our intent," James answered.

"Will Riley Mines be released?" A reporter called.

"We are working on release plans as we speak. While we can't confirm Mrs. Monarch's guilt at this time, we are able to confirm Mr. Mines' innocence," James replied.

James heard the door open behind him and Hillsteg walked out.

Hillsteg reached out his hand and shook James'.

"Congratulations on a job well done," he proudly said.

"Thank you," James replied. "I'll let you handle things from here."

Hillsteg nodded and James turned to weave through the crowd to join the others at the back.

"Good morning," Hillsteg greeted the crowd. "At this time, we do not have many details to share but I can indeed confirm that Alexa Monarch has been arrested and will be tried for the framing of Mr. Riley Mines. We are currently working to release Mr. Mines from Nadirehs Island prison for wrongful incarceration and we are hoping to have him home by tomorrow. I will be taking no further questions. Thank you," stated Hillsteg as he left the steps and made his way through the press back to the rest of the group.

"We'll meet you back at the Mines' house," Hillsteg said to James as he gestured for everyone to load back into the cars.

"Sounds good," James replied.

"We need to call Lila," Kyle said to Jane as they got into the car. "She's probably freaking out right now having not heard anything from us."

"That's a good idea," replied Jane. "Should we wait until we know when Riley will be released to fill her in?"

"Probably not," James chimed in. "Considering the arrest of Alexa Monarch has probably gone viral already."

"I agree. I'd give her a call right now," Rebecca added, smiling lovingly at James in the driver's seat.

"You're right!" Agreed Jane. "We have to call her now."

"I'm already on it," Kyle said as he put his ringing phone on speaker.

"Kyle!" Lila exclaimed when she picked up the phone. "Is it true?"

"It is," Kyle replied. "I'm sorry we didn't call you sooner, we just got in the car and it's been a little crazy," he tried to laugh lightheartedly, feeling guilty Lila had been left out of the loop.

"I don't care! That's amazing!" Lila shouted. "That's the most wonderful news in the world."

"We're headed back to Mom's house now and I'm sure we'll reconvene and talk about plans," Kyle explained. "We'll keep you posted. For now, you just sit tight and relax in knowing Riley will be home soon."

"Thank you, Kyle," Lila said, her beaming smile audible through the phone.

"Of course," he replied.

CHAPTER SIXTY-ONE

Riley was standing at his cell window, meditating over all that the last few weeks had brought him. He'd spent the three days staring desperately toward the shoreline, his heart aching for an update.

He couldn't travel home. He couldn't confide in Aus. He couldn't sleep. He couldn't eat. He felt equal parts hopeless and optimistic at the same time.

The stomping footsteps of a man nearly out of breath interrupted his daydreaming.

"RILEY!" Aus called, running down the hall. "RILEY! THEY DID IT!" He shouted.

"What?" Riley whispered to himself as he turned to see Aus frantically flipping through his keys to unlock the cell.

"They did it, Riley! Alexa has been arrested and you are free! They did it!" Aus exclaimed.

Riley stood speechless staring back at Aus. He could feel the weight of the world lift off his body, but his mind wasn't processing as quickly.

"What?" He asked again.

Aus finally got the cell door open and hurried to the center of the room. He gripped Riley's arms and stared intensely into his bright blue eyes.

"You're an innocent man," he explained. "You're free. They're taking you off of the island right now."

Riley fell to his knees. He couldn't believe it had actually worked.

After a few moments, he looked back up at Aus, his cheeks warm and flushed.

"Thank you," he said. "I can't think of anything else to say right now besides thank you."

Aus reached out his hand and helped him up. Riley pulled him in for a hug and squeezed tight.

"Thank you," he said again patting him on the back.

"I think your wife will be upset if you spend another second in here flirting with the prison guard, when you could be on your way home," Aus teased.

Riley shook his head.

"You're probably right about that," he smiled.

"Come on," Aus waved. "They sent a special boat just for you. I'll take you to the dock."

Aus walked out of the cell and Riley followed close behind.

"This is crazy," Riley commented as they weaved through the white-bricked halls of the prison.

"It really is," agreed Aus. "This is the only time in my twenty-four years here that I've seen a boat make a special pickup. Prisoners only come and go on the first of the month. It's the seventeenth," Aus was giddy. "The seventeenth!" He said throwing his hands up, "This is awesome!"

They quickly walked in silence the rest of the way outside and made their way down the rocky path, leading to the small dock with a black, police speed boat waiting.

They stopped at the edge of the dock, neither wanting to say goodbye.

Riley turned to face Aus.

"Thank you," he said again. "I will get you out of here," he insisted. "It will be the first thing I do."

Aus smiled.

"I'll be okay. It's been twenty-four years… what's a few

more?" He laughed. "You need to focus on your family."

"Oh, no…" Riley smiled. "Oh, no… Aus, this is about to sound so cheesy."

"Don't do it," Aus shook his head. "Don't you dare," he teased.

"You're part of my family now," Riley smiled. "I need to take care of you, too."

"Ahh, you did it anyway," Aus laughed. "Thank you, Riley." He reached out his hand, grabbed Riley's and pulled him in for a hug. "We'll be in touch."

Riley let go, smiled and turned to walk down the wooden dock. He greeted the officer who'd been waiting for him and carefully stepped onto the boat.

Riley sat comfortably in the back of the boat and waved to Aus as they backed out of the dock and took off toward the shore.

Aus grinned and waved goodbye, his eyes welling with tears of joy.

CHAPTER SIXTY-TWO

One month later.

Chandler sat on Lila's lap, sipping a vanilla milkshake.

"Grandma makes the best milkshakes," Chandler announced.

"She does make pretty great milkshakes," Lila agreed. "Although, I'm not sure why you're drinking one when it's snowing outside. That makes me cold," she laughed.

Riley was sitting across the living room holding Warren in his arms.

"You're crazy, Chan," he agreed. "I'd be freezing."

"I'm not crazy, Daddy" she replied. "It's delicious."

"Whatever you say," Riley teased.

"I don't think you're crazy, Chan," Kyle said as he walked into the living room carrying a chocolate milkshake. "Grandma does make the best milkshakes."

"Only for my favorites," Jane said as she followed Kyle into the living room.

"You probably could have let your mother sit down before you suggested milkshakes," Lila lectured Kyle.

Jane sat down on the couch.

"Oh, I don't mind at all. I'm just happy to finally be here and have all of us together," she said. "This is so lovely."

"It's pretty wonderful," Lila agreed. "I'm so glad you guys could come visit."

"Us too," Jane replied. "Sorry, we didn't come sooner. We wanted to give you guys a chance to settle down a bit and not bombard you."

"I appreciate that," said Lila. "It's been good to get back into a rhythm."

"I'm sure," agreed Jane.

"I talked to Hillsteg last night," Riley announced, changing the subject. "It sounds like everything is rolling right along but most likely, it will still be months before the official trial."

"Yeah," Kyle added. "I talked to James earlier this week and he said they've been speaking with Daniel and Debbie a lot. Those two have loads of information and I guess the case is basically painting itself."

"That's so good to hear," Lila replied.

The front door opened, letting in a rush of cold air.

"Uncle Aus!" Chandler shouted as she ran to greet him at the door.

"Hi, Chandler," Aus said as they started doing their secret handshake with a series of claps and high fives.

"The kid's known him for like a week and I swear they're best friends already," Riley laughed quietly to Kyle.

Jane stood up and made her way to the door.

"It's a pleasure to finally meet you, Aus. I'm Jane," she reached out her arms and invited him in for a hug.

"Nice to meet you," Aus replied. "I've heard so many great things."

Aus took a few steps into the living room and Kyle met him part way. He reached out his hand and gave a firm shake.

"You must be Kyle," he said.

Kyle nodded.

"Nice to meet you," he replied.

"You as well," responded Aus.

"How was your day at the station?" Riley asked.

"It was good," Aus replied. "Nothing too special. Just another causal day of living out my dream as an officer for the NYPD. It's fine, I'm fine," he smiled.

"They're lucky to have you," Lila said.

"And don't worry, I spoke with my realtor today and it sounds like he has a couple of places for me to look at this weekend. I'll be out of your hair in no time," said Aus.

"Nooo," pouted Chandler. "You can't go."

"You're not a bother at all, Aus," Lila urged. "Stay as long as you'd like. If it weren't for you, we wouldn't even have our Riley back."

Aus smiled.

Riley stood up with Warren in one arm and his drink in the other.

"I want to make a toast," he declared, raising his glass slightly. "I haven't gotten the chance to officially say thank you to everyone in person. I am so blessed to have this family," he winked at Aus. "A family who would literally do anything for me and a family I can always count on," he paused. "The past year was the worst year of my life, but it taught me more than I could ever have imagined. I know this chapter is not quite over and there will still be many hurdles, but I don't want to spend too much time fixating on those because right now," he paused again. "I'm the happiest man in the world. I am forever grateful for all of you. Thank you and I love you. Cheers!"

"Cheers" they collectively replied.

Lila stood up and walked across the room to kiss Riley.

"I love you, too" she whispered as she sat on his lap.

They sat for a few moments, taking in the pure joy of a united family.

"Brr," Riley broke the silence. "I really don't know how you two are eating ice cream right now," he said to Chandler and Kyle. "I'm freezing."

"Me too," Lila agreed.

"I'm going to grab a sweatshirt," Riley replied. "Want me to grab you one?"

"Yes, please."

Riley headed up the staircase and into the master bedroom. He was making his way in front of the bed, toward the closet, when he noticed something out of the corner of his eye.

He walked over to his pillow and examined the small, black gift box tied neatly with a silver bow. He carefully unwrapped it to find a packet of silica gel and a note that read:

Well done, Riley Mines. I look forward to working with you.
— Z

Made in the USA
Monee, IL
27 April 2021